Readers' comments . . .

Big House Dreams is a classic in the purest sense: it transcends barriers of time, space, culture, and custom to involve the reader in the very personal journey of three female members of the Jenkins family. I found a bit of myself in Emma, in Sara, and in Sheila, for theirs is a universal quest for fulfillment, sharing, and belonging. *Big House Dreams* follows the Jenkins women in their journey toward the dream of "having a big house filled with love someday."

      Lisa McNaughton
      Daughter, mother, student, teacher, and friend

Through the customs and mores of the Deep South, *Big House Dreams* artfully weaves a story of the ever-changing roles of mothers and daughters – the joy, the angst, the pride, and the challenges faced by the Jenkins women. This tale of the human condition – the need to receive and bestow love, the consequences of accepting or rejecting care or advice, and the desire to demonstrate independence – draws the reader into experiencing the joy and pain of being a woman. The experiences of Emma, Sara Mae, and Sheila are those shared by girls and women who survive and even blossom and grow stronger in spite of economic, social, and sometimes unspeakable obstacles in life. Via these unassuming Southern women, Judith DeChesere-Boyle has given a powerful understanding of how life's path is not set for a woman, but is dynamic and altered continually as she opens and closes relationships, accepts or rejects opportunities, and in fact, defines herself.

      Rebecca Drake
      Educator

Big House Dreams takes the reader on a journey through the lives of the Jenkins women. From the first generation to the last, one will find oneself on a journey with these women who are relatable in different ways. All the women show strength throughout their stories dealing with friendship and family. Through this life journey we learn who real friends are and how family relationships can be tested. This book is based in the South and focused around women but also demonstrates there are good men as well. A great read that takes the reader through four generations.

      Hilda Castillo-Abate
      Bilingual Educator

Big House Dreams

A Novel

by

Judith L. DeChesere-Boyle

This book is a work of fiction. Names, characters, places, and incidents either are products of the author's imagination or are used fictitiously. Any resemblance to actual events or locales or persons, living or dead, is entirely coincidental.

Copyright © 2012 Judith L. DeChesere-Boyle

All rights reserved.

ISBN: 1480177695

ISBN 13: 9781480177697

Big House Dreams is dedicated with love to my mother, Nola Jean Baird DeChesere. She was my mother and she also was my friend.

Many people affectionately called her "Honey", including me.

She was an absolute Earth angel.

Acknowledgements

My deep appreciation goes to my husband, Rick Boyle, who never stopped believing in me and to my son, Alex Stevenson, who in his own inimitable way admonished, "Quit talking about it, and just write it." I wish to acknowledge my son, Justin Stevenson, and his wife, Amy, who also supported my efforts. Finally, I give my sincere thanks to my friends, who have given me support and encouragement – Hilda Castillo-Abate, Rebecca Drake, Corinna Gneri, Lisa McNaughton, Heather Smith, Susan Thompson, and Deb Titus.

When we walk to the edge
of all the light we have
and take the step into the
darkness of the unknown,
we must believe that
one of two things will happen....
There will be something
solid for us to stand on
or we will be taught to fly.

PATRICK OVERTON

Part One

Chapter One

Mama died on the first day of summer which was appropriate because she hated the heat and humidity that fell over Tennessee like a damp blanket in June, July, and beyond. In the midst of summer, she'd shuffle around in a limp cotton dress and raggedy duster ranting in her misery, taking everyone in her path along with her. Mercifully her life ended with the spring she loved just behind her. The bright sunshiny days and brisk winds of April had always filled her with energy and eagerness to clean the house from top to bottom or to plant her summer garden, digging with delight in soil that was just warming to the season. The freesias, daffodils, violas, and pansies gave her permission to stop for a brief rest as she studied them, marveling at the intricate beauty she knew God had created. "Just look at that little face," she'd say as she gently lifted the blossom toward her for better scrutiny. "Look, Sara Mae. Look how sweet." She'd ooh and ah, feeling blessed to be alive, savoring the beauty of every new leaf, the mew of spring lambs, and the incessant chatter of nesting birds staking out their territory. Spring had filled Mama to the brim with happiness, even when the context of her life sought to forbid it. Spring had always intensified her hope, for new beginnings were stirring all around her. Spring spoke to change, to nurturing, to creativity, and to gratitude. It was her season. She had been born in late May and died in June just after her forty-ninth birthday.

Why Emma Jenkins's life was cut so short was a mystery to the community of Cam's Corner. She hadn't been sick a day in her life. She'd been a sober woman, not one to smile often, and although she was generally soft-spoken, she had been known to have her say when need be. She had been quietly self-sufficient, relying on her garden and her skills as a seamstress to provide. Her neighbors perceived her as pious and proper, volunteering her time and offering charity as she saw fit. She owned a little plot of land and a modest house, had a few friends, her church, a husband of sorts, and a daughter.

"But, Mama, I don't want t' wear them ol' black stockings." Sara looked at her mother with defiance.

"Ya' will wear them stockings. Ya'll catch a death a' cold without 'em. An' don't sass me, young lady." Mama was not an obese woman, but she was fat around the hips and stomach, with sagging breasts and a face that had aged before its time. While not wrinkled, her sour skin was creviced and etched with furrows that reflected reams of pain and hard work. She already smelled old.

"Mama! I'm the only one. I don't want t' be the only one." Sara tried once more.

"Git the brush! Ya' mind me or git the brush!" Mama would not be deterred. She would have her way.

"Okay, I'll put 'em on." Knowing that she did not want the brush but certainly would not wear those black stockings to school, Sara tugged them up on legs skinny and pasty white. She fastened them with wide, elastic bands, rolling the thick cotton material around the bands, over and over to alleviate the annoying pressure that was sure to come as they constricted into her thin skin. She recalled times in the past when ugly, horrid holes had worked their way into old and shabby stockings leaving her white skin exposed and conspicuous. She'd had to use black pigmented polish then, wiping it into the opening on her pale skin to obscure the tear. It was a hideous embarrassment for her, one that stung and angered much below the surface.

"I hate ya'," she thought to herself, as she stared at the back of Mama's full figure, and then, immediately tried to retract the thought. Doing so was not easy though. She tried once more, "Mama, when are ya' goin' t' let me be like the other girls? They don't got t' wear these ol' things."

"Yer goin' t' act like a good Christian girl, Miss Sara, and ya' won't be embarrassin' me by not coverin' up. An' I don't want t' hear another word. Ya' hear me?" Mama was clear the argument was over. Sara was sure it wasn't.

Sara cast another angry glance at her mother before turning away. She hoped her mother did not see in her dark brown eyes the intense defiance that engulfed and smothered her, crushing her spirit like a hot-weighted stone. She would win the game of wills though. She would rally her determination and prepare herself for the next confrontation. Mama had a will that was as solid as steel, but Sara had learned from her and was, in fact, simply a smaller version of the powerful woman who was now shoving Sara's patched and slightly soiled sweater toward her.

"Put on yer sweater, now. It's cold out," Mama said.

Sara did not respond. She simply grabbed the sweater and threw it haphazardly over her shoulder.

"I said don't sass me, Sara Mae." Mama's voice rose as she again showed Sara her strength.

"I didn't say nothin'," Sara retorted hatefully.

"Ya' didn't have t', Sara Mae Jenkins! Now ya' better come home t'day in a better frame a' mind. I'm not goin' t' put up with no more sass." Mama had the last word, at least for the moment.

Sara slid her thin arms into the scratchy sleeves of the sweater and hopped down the wooden porch steps barely missing the scruffy stray mongrel pup that recently had found its way to their farmhouse that was situated in a boggy meadow a mile from town. The dog looked up at Sara with watery eyes amid a sad but friendly face of brownish-red, tight, curly fur. He seemed a bit wary of her and slipped quickly under the wooden porch for safety. The cold morning fog still gathered and swirled on the tops of dew-covered, scraggly grass and weeds that covered the yard in front of the house. Sara shivered inside the thin sweater and was momentarily happy for the warmth those ugly cotton stockings provided; yet at the same time, she couldn't wait to reach the high school in town where she would, as always, slip quickly into the girls' room and slide the stockings from her legs, hiding them behind the commode in the last of three stalls. She would bide her time.

Emma Jenkins would do the same, although for Emma time was becoming an enemy, creeping behind her like a caustic cloud that tormented her with loneliness, angst, and anxiety. Alone now in the empty kitchen she glanced at her face, almost foreign to her, in the tiny scratched mirror that hung crookedly on string that had been tacked next to the wooden front door frame. Seldom did she allow vanity to draw her to this place and looking now at her reflection she caught her breath, and stared. She touched her cheeks with hands that were rough against soft skin that was beginning to lose its elasticity. Deep lines had formed beneath her cheeks and ran perpendicularly to her thin lips that were dry and chapped. Angry circles of puffy skin beneath her grey eyes caught her stare and she remembered the dreams, the reoccurring nightmares, that frightened her time and again, making her cry out in the night and steal her sleep. The "No, no!" she had grunted into the darkness just hours before this very moment had been a cry, a whimper, and then a low guttural groan that had awakened her, and she recalled now the vision of a child, floating helplessly in a creek, an unsullied Ophelia, trapped amid twigs and vines that twisted about her threatening to take her toward the muddy creek bank where slithering snakes and snapping crawdads abounded in the shallows, or it would pull her farther downstream toward rolling rapids that gently, but definitely would batter and bruise her. The dream was as dark as its midnight setting, the only light being that offered by a waning moon that lingered on the young girl's face. Yet Emma could not make out the details. Was it Sara Mae? The mere thought that it could be gripped her gut and she winced visibly.

Emma's gaze left the mirror then and she watched, through a broken pane of glass, the thin figure of her daughter who stood alone in the fog at the gate by the road. As she turned away the line of broken glass seemed to cut the image of Sara Mae in two, one half holding her clearly in sight and the other half blurring her figure into an alarming aura. The dichotomous form caused Emma's heart to pound erratically for a long moment and as she clutched her hands together at her breast, she turned again to the mirror. She glimpsed her face for a split second and then turned the mirror's face to the wall. She could not bear to look at herself again.

"Vanity's a sin," she said out loud. "I reckon Sara Mae's goin' t' have t' learn that lesson real soon, jist like I did. If she don't, there'll be hell t' pay."

Sara waited at the front gate that was one hundred yards from the house for Addie Gilbert's daddy's pickup. This was her ride to school on the days Addie could go. If the old brown Ford pickup didn't round the bend soon, Sara knew she'd have to walk, and quickly too, the mile into town. The cold morning air gathered around her like a moist mantle. Fortunately today the ride arrived, rumbling around the corner and coming to a sharp stop right where Sara stood.

"Mornin', Mr. Gilbert. Mornin', Addie," Sara said as she scrunched into the front seat, pushing Addie closer to her father whose big, hairy hands gripped the steering wheel with firm control. He drove that truck like he drove Addie and her mother, with fierce command.

"Mornin', Sara," Mr. Gilbert offered. "How's yer mama?"

"Oh she's the same as always," she replied with two meanings to her response. To Sara, Mama was a source of power to which she constantly had to surrender, but she knew that to George Gilbert, Mama was Emma Jenkins, the Sunday school teacher whose reputation for goodness and piety was well-known in the small Tennessee town.

"Well, I reckon that's good then," Mr. Gilbert replied, "and yer lookin' real nice there too, Miss Sara."

"Um. Well, thank ya'," Sara mumbled, feeling uncomfortable with the compliment from her friend's father. In fact, without thinking, she quickly latched her hand through Addie's arm and pulled her closer. Addie glanced furtively at Sara, and flexed her arm quickly, letting her friend know that she recognized her discomfort.

The mile to school mercifully was covered quickly and in silence except for the grinding of gears, the rumble of the engine, and the crunch of gravel under the tires. The truck bounced over and into potholes that were a prominent fixture on the rural road. A strange stench of unwashed clothing, perspiration, and gasoline filtered into the cab of the truck, making Sara feel slightly nauseous. While she was thankful for the ride to school, she couldn't wait to reach the red brick high school that she attended with three hundred other adolescents from around Maury County.

When Mr. Gilbert braked at the corner, Sara threw open the door and stumbled out onto the broken concrete sidewalk with Addie right behind. Addie and Sara both threw a, "Bye!" over their shoulders at the same moment, not turning to look at their driver. Mr. Gilbert said nothing, but as the door slammed, Sara could hear a long, loud hiss of gas expelled into the cab. No wonder the truck always reeked.

The girls tore up the steps and into the school where they shivered in the dampness of the drafty lobby. Sara said, "I got t' go in there," pointing to the girls' room that was situated in a dingy corner.

"Yeah, go," Addie replied. She knew Sara's plan to stash her stockings before speaking to anyone and certainly before going to class. Addie was a patient friend who at times secretly wished Sara would stop making this issue so paramount in importance. If only Addie's problems were this simple.

Sara had met Addie at the annual Bethel Baptist Church bazaar seven years prior when both girls were just eight. They had eyed each other cautiously at first. To Addie, Sara had seemed self-important and Sara saw Addie as arrogant, but the fact is they were both a bit shy, Sara just naturally so, and Addie because she was new to the community. She was reticent about making friends because her early years had been steeped in turmoil as her mother and father moved every year, sometimes more often. Friends were not a commodity easily grasped, and if Addie did make an acquaintance, the relationship was short-lived because of her family's wandering lifestyle. And she was poor. Her father was never able to hold a job for long, and her mother was incredibly introverted, having been for years so belittled and manhandled by her father that she seldom left the house. Her mother had evolved into a mouse-like woman, afraid of her husband, afraid of storms, afraid of her shadow. She scurried silently from one unimportant task to another keeping herself busy and out of the fray which always was created when Mr. Gilbert lost a job, or spent his pathetic paycheck on liquor, leaving the family in need of simply the basics - food and shelter.

When the family finally stumbled upon Cam's Corner, Mr. Gilbert auspiciously acquired a steady job working at the local Ford dealership as a janitor, and they constructed some semblance of security in the tiny town. No one asked their history; no one pried; no one encroached on the fragile family circle. After years of meandering around the South, they stayed, and they stayed longer, until seven years had passed. The stability of a place to call home gave way to a blossoming Addie who stifled her apprehensiveness around others and became a funny, outgoing youngster at school. At home, however, she remained quiet and pensive, secretly protecting her hidden personality as she watched her mother grow thin and old before her time.

Addie had lived along side her mother in terror at times when Mr. Gilbert's anger had boiled over; he raged and was enraged at miniscule mishaps. A dropped coffee cup, a missing button, or a slice of burned toast was enough to earn Margaret Gilbert, a full-face slap that would knock her against the sideboard, bruising her ribs or hips. Addie had watched in horror as her father clutched at her mother's neck, squeezing tighter and tighter until her face was ruby. George Gilbert's face would contort like an alien monster and spittle would spurt from his lips into his wife's terrified eyes. He was big and strong with arms that rippled with muscle and that bulged with his fury. And then, he would stop. He would push Margaret into the bedroom, panting heartily from the effort of his anger. Addie would listen to her mother whimpering like a forlorn and forgotten pup; she would hear her father's mumbling duplicitous apologies. An admission of guilt was never forthcoming, but often he would ask for forgiveness, swearing that, "This ain't goin' t' happen no more, Margie. No more."

The sobbing would subside in time, as would the murmurs of remorse until silence reigned. Addie would crawl into her bed shaking and shivering, holding the stuffed rabbit she had had since infancy next to her heart. And then she would hear new sounds: a soft voice, a shuffle of feet, the movement of bodies, and then the slow, rhythmic squeak of the mattress. She had learned what was happening as she grew older and was shaken by the acquiescence of her mother and the arrogance of her father. This cyclical display of her parents' conduct confused and embarrassed her. She promised herself she would not live a life like this one. She promised over and over.

Chapter Two

Sara slid her stockings from her legs and threw them in a tight bunch behind the commode. She felt free and strong. She had won this battle. Her mother would never know; she was becoming a stupid old woman anyway.

"Addie, we got t' go." Sara slipped in beside her best friend, remembering for a brief second the moment they had met. They had sized each other up, stared each other down, and walked directly toward each other.

"I ain't goin' t' like her," Sara had thought to herself. And Addie had felt likewise.

"She thinks she's Mis'Aster!"

Mama had intervened just then, though, as Sara and Addie were introduced and then pushed together behind a cardboard table covered with gaudy flowered oilcloth. Scattered over the table were handmade macaroni angels and pinecone Christmas trees. "Ya'll sell this here an' put what money ya' git in this here cigar box. Ya' hear? These here sell fer a nickel, an' them pinecone trees is a dime."

And before they knew it, Addie and Sara were chatting and giggling as though they had known each other forever.

They became friends at that bazaar and had remained constant companions from that moment.

"Addie, we got shorthand. Let's go." Sara pulled Addie toward her and the two marched down the freshly waxed hallway to their favorite class. Learning to write words in little squiggles was intriguing to Sara; she loved the element of secrecy it provided. Mama could never read her notes to Addie, messages that spoke of fear, friendship, and dreams of the future. She loved the little spiral notebooks where she wrote pages and pages practicing to perfection. She loved the peaceful monotony of the task and puffed up pleasantly when Mrs. Monroe complimented her work.

Addie felt the same. Someday she would find a good job as a secretary and she would please her boss with her persistent, perfect efforts. As the pages of scribbles and scrawls fell away, she felt comfort in knowing that this skill would lead her to a better life, one she would control, not the one in which she existed presently, dominated, confused, and often fearful. She dreamed of graduation day, of moving from Cam's Corner, of a future far away. Thinking of this now made her face flush and her lips curved into a small smile, noticed only by Sara.

"What are ya' doin', Addie? Daydreamin' again? Where are ya' – Nashville, Louisville, Tallahassee? Where's that little mind takin' ya'?" Sara often teased her friend this way because it frequently led to laughter and a common creation of years yet to come. Both girls wanted more than their tiny town and constipated community offered them.

When class ended they moved in unison to English. This was not Sara's favorite class, but she loved to look at the handsome Wallace Wilson who sat three seats away in the row of desks next to hers. Wallace was a dreamboat and Sara often envisioned them walking hand in hand on a beach somewhere, anywhere. She had never been to a beach, but the idea sounded romantic. She had to settle for a movie star smile that made her heart stop, her neck bloom pink, and her hands quiver in her lap. She felt like a fragile porcelain plate ready to shatter when he said, "How ya' doin', Sara? Goin' t' my football game t'night? We're goin' t' win this one fer sure."

"Oh, I reckon I will be, Wallace. It's goin' t' be real cold t'night, but I'll be watchin' ya' from the bleachers. An' I know yer goin' t' win."

"Why ya' always callin' me Wallace? I'm Wally, Sara. Call me like ever'one else does."

Sara's cheeks grew hot with his scolding and simultaneously with distinct delight. He had noticed her!

"Okay, Wally. I'll be cert'in to." And with that, class began with a poem read by Mrs. Gibson. It was a poem by Emily Dickinson about love and loss. The poem bored her. She only liked poems by e. e. cummings because he broke the rules. He could write with no punctuation, no capital letters, and no rhyme. He did what he wanted and got away with it. If she had a choice, she would be just like him. Breaking rules, she'd learned, gave her instant satisfaction, although her experience with doing so was limited. Mama kept her life restricted and constrained, but that would change some day. Sara's hand silently slid down to her bare calf and she swallowed a smile enjoying her self-approval.

Mrs. Gibson droned on and on. Sara sat rigidly, facing forward, feigning attention, but reveling in her thoughts of Wally. Addie, on the other hand, was rapt, as the teacher continued reading, reciting, and waving her arms in animation and delight as she lost herself in her obsession, her love of literature. Addie shared this passion and when the theme to compare love and loss was assigned, Addie was instantly scribbling in her best cursive on tissue thin composition paper. Her head was cast downward over the paper, her thin fingers firmly clutching the ink pen. Her wispy blond hair hung down past her cheeks and neck, touching the top of the desk delicately. She stopped writing briefly, and flipped her head around to glance at Sara. Her face was pale, but very pretty, with deep dimples that were revealed when she smiled, and with eyes as blue as an azure wave. She was lovely, and exquisitely beautiful at times such as this, when she lost herself in creativity, as imagination and inspiration guided her beyond her often pathetic place in life.

Sara looked at her blank paper. "Write in cursive in blue or black ink, only," Mrs. Gibson had said. Sara stared at the empty space and finally filled in the first line – "I dream of having a big house filled with love someday."

After a horrible hour of equations and proofs, Sara and Addie sat numbly eying the clock at the front of the room. Algebra made Sara rage inside. She didn't know why; she only knew she hated being confused. Addie seemed to understand a bit more, but she shared Sara's sentiments about mathematics.

"I swear t' goodness I don't know why we have t' know this. I ain't goin' t' use it never!" Sara whispered, garnering as she did a stern scowl from Mr. Hardin.

Mercifully the class ended and the two girls scurried out the door into the cold hallway. Amid a herd of other students, they shuffled into the cafeteria which was saturated with myriad obscure odors – perfume, perspiration, fried fish, steamed spinach, and spoiling milk. Sara picked at her plate, settling finally on a chunk of carrot cake covered with crème cheese. Addie, on the other hand, politely but completely consumed the entire meal, including the carrot cake. She had been hungry many times in her life; she would not discount victuals freely given.

The cafeteria was abuzz with adolescent chatter. *"That there game's goin' t' be somethin'." "I bet Wally's goin' t' wallop 'em!" "Cam's Corner's goin' t' kick 'em real good!" "Ya goin', Ronnie Lyn?" "I'm goin', I reckon." "I don't know what t' wear t' keep warm. It's goin' t' be freezin' out t'night." "Bring a blanket." "Bring a hot brick." "Bring a boy t' smooch with."* Laughter. *"Goin' t' the dance, too?" "Don't have nobody t' go with." "Go with me." "We'll I swannee, I thought ya'd never say nothin' 'bout that." "Well, I jist did." "Ya' goin'?" "I sure reckon I will."* Friday. One more class to go: elocution.

While Addie wandered off for her bookkeeping class, Sara headed straight toward the theater. It was a small affair, but offered a warm, inviting atmosphere. Sara loved being here. The smell of dust and mold invaded her senses; the heavy, faded purple curtains hung limply onto the apron of the stage. The rows of mahogany seats were scratched and wiggled and squeaked when students plopped into them. They were old. The place was old. Yet Sara felt invigorated there. She quickly found herself lost in imaginings of actors performing brilliant dialogues, stirring soliloquies, and inspiring speeches. She fantasized about a future of fame but knew deep inside it was only a pipe dream. Still she would often lose herself in her reveries, only to be wrenched into reality by her rigid, exact speech teacher.

"Sara Mae Jenkins, you are first today. Have you practiced?"

"Yes 'um."

"Yes, what, Sara Mae?"

"Yes, Mam. I've been practicin'."

"Sara Mae! Yes, Mam. I have been practicing. Don't forget your endings."

"Yes 'um."

"Oh, my, Sara Mae. Proceed. You practiced the poem *Moo Cow Moo* by Edmund Vance Cooke."

Sara skipped up the steps to the stage and turned to face her audience, a group of lanky, freckle-faced, pimply, eager actors whose turn was yet to come. The *Moo Cow Moo* was a short little speech, but one Sara had practiced over and over, even in front of Mama, and Mama had approved, giving only suggestions as to how to stand or what hand gesture to make. Sara looked up searching for a pleasant face on which to light and concentrate. None was discernible. Her body began to fail her; her stomach rumbled hungrily, her throat was dry, and her underarms were suddenly moist. She patted the front of her corduroy skirt and tossed her long, brunette hair behind her shoulders. Her dark eyes glistened, but she steadied herself and began.

My papa held me up to the Moo Cow Moo so close I could almost touch. Sara stood straight, tall, and serious. *And I fed him a couple of times or so, and I wasn't a fraidy-cat, much. But if my Papa goes in the house, and my mamma she goes in too, I keep still like a little mouse for the Moo Cow Moo might moo.* Again, Sara's voice mimicked innocence. *The Moo Cow's tail is a piece of rope all ravelled down where it grows.* She turned sideways here and swished her hand back and forth behind her emulating where the tail would be. *And it's just like feeling a piece of soap, all over the Moo Cow's nose.* Sara's hand moved to her face and in a circular motion she pretended to give herself a superfluous scrubbing. *And the Moo Cow Moo has lots of fun just switching his tail about, but if he opens his mouth, why then I run, for that's where the Moo comes out.* She set her stance and stared at her audience wide-eyed. *The Moo Cow Moo has deers on his head and his eyes stick out of their place.* Her hands moved to her head to form antlers. *And the nose of the Moo Cow Moo is spread all over the Moo Cow's face.* She scrunched her nose and formed her mouth into an explicit pout. *And his feet are nothing but fingernails, and his mamma don't keep them cut.* Sara twisted her features into a snarling look of disgust. *And he gives folks milk in water pails, when you don't keep his handles shut. But if you or I pull his handles, why the Moo Cow Moo says it hurts.* Again, with eyes wide, Sara duplicated the ache she imagined. *But the hired man sits down close by and squirts, and squirts, and squirts.* Sara simulated the action and then bowed to the polite applause of her classmates.

She smiled relief. It was over. Sitting afterward, Sara could not help replaying every line and movement over and over in her mind. She was so intent on her self-review that she could not focus on any other performer. Her analysis moved to anxiety. As was her nature, she examined why she made such ordinary events so important. It had been a trivial and plain performance. The simplicity of it strangely annoyed her, and she was suddenly sad. Her emotions imploded and tears welled into her eyes. With blurry vision, she tucked her head and let her long, brunette hair conceal this unwarranted sensation. Her mundane life smothered her. It was so uninteresting and common. She wanted so much more and yearned for a change that would lend excitement to her existence. Little did she know that change would indeed occur and quickly too.

Chapter Three

A cold Arctic chill dipped down into the Tennessee hills as a small group huddled on wooden bleachers to watch the Cam's Corner High School football game, the last one of a mediocre season. Sara's mother had allowed her to attend the event and the dance following it for one reason. Mama was in attendance as well, chaperoning the dance with a few of the other ladies from the Cam's Corner Women's Circle. It was a rare event for Sara to be allowed to venture from her house after dark. Mama always told her it wasn't ladylike. So, this evening was special for Sara. Securely wrapped in woolen coat, scarf, gloves, and the hated black stockings, she watched Wally deftly throw the football to his players on a field that was frozen solid in places and mired in sticky mud in others. Above the voices of the students and parents who surrounded her, she could distinctly hear the crunch of cleats upon the packed dirt as players plodded up and down the field. Sara's cheeks and face were numb from the cold. She was sure her nose was bright red; it even hurt to the touch when she dabbed it with a stiff handkerchief. She longed for the game to end, and mercifully it did with a dash into the end zone by Wally himself. They had won. Sara jumped up and down excitedly amid the noisy accolades of the fans, careful to hide from Mama her inner joy of watching Wally victoriously salute the meager crowd as though he had attained the state championship. Her heart pounded deep in her chest; she felt flushed but frozen at the same time. She hoped this night would be perfect.

Sara wandered into the school cafeteria looking for Addie who had not attended the game as planned. Sara had searched the stands for Addie during the game. She would have been wearing her bright red ear muffs and handmade scarf of yellow yarn, her first completed knitting project. Addie adored bright colors and wore them well; they accentuated her golden hair and made her blue eyes as dazzling as a crystalline gemstone.

"Mama, I kain't find Addie," Sara slid up next to her mother. She didn't want to be seen near Mama, but she needed to voice her apprehension and concern about her friend.

"I ain't seen her neither," Mama responded dismissively. "Maybe her daddy wouldn't let her. Ya' know how he can git."

"But he said she could go," Sara whined. "She don't usually git t' go out, but this time he said yes 'cause yer here."

"I ain't in that man's head, Sara Mae," Mama replied. "Like I say, nice as he can seem, he likes t' keep his women put."

"That's easy t' say, Mama!" Sara thought, not uttering the words out loud, but bristling inside. Her own father, who had married Mama twenty years before, seldom was home, spending most of his days sitting on the courthouse stairs with his cronies, chewing tobacco, and just watching. Mama called him "a good fer nothin'" but she'd married him and, as she often said, "I ain't 'bout t' do nothin' t' change what's what. Fer some reason God's given me this here place an' I'm acceptin'." Sara didn't see her papa much, but occasionally he would crawl home for Mama's "good cookin'" and a good night's sleep in a clean bed. Mama and Papa didn't look at each other much, and never touched. When he did enter the house it was as though a cool wind had drifted in behind him. It settled on Mama and she was strangely silent for a spell. She would busy herself with her embroidery, crocheting, and darning. She was an adept seamstress and used her skill to keep food on the table. The house had been Mama's daddy's so the plot of land was secure in her name alone. Papa had never asked for it and Mama hadn't offered. Sara knew that was a good thing or her existence would have been equivalent to Addie's.

Sara glanced around the lunch room once more. The stench of stale food lingered in the cafeteria even though it had been transformed for the evening into a dance floor. The ladies from the Cam's Corner Women's Circle had helped a teacher or two hang purple and gold crepe paper around the windows and from corner to corner across the room. The twisted strands began to hang limply in the warm air as couples circled the room. Balloons fell to the floor and bobbled around feet that moved awkwardly to a slow scratchy song played on the record player in the corner. It was uncomfortably humid and hot in the room, a stark comparison to the frigid football field.

Sara stood alone. She felt a bit forlorn as she wished for Addie's companionship. Where was she? Sara feigned a small smile as she watched others move to the music that now was faster, jazz-like. Maybe if she acted as if she were having fun, she would. Mama always told her to create her own bliss, but she didn't feel happy. She was worried and her anxiety welled up inside like an overflowing fountain.

And then, he was there. Wally had wandered her way and stood awkwardly beside her. She perceived his rare self-consciousness but then looked across at Mama whose gaze had followed him.

"Howdy, Sara," he muttered. "Did ya' like my game?"

"Oh yeah, Wally. It was jist swell." Sara face flushed and her hands were moist. "Ya' played real fine!"

"Did ya' want t' dance or somethin'?" Wally asked. "I ain't much of a dancer. Better at football," he grinned. "But I'm willin' t' try."

"Okay, Wally." Sara slid her arm into Wally's and they eased into the crowd of dancers. Sara was conscious of Wally's hand on her back. Her small hand was lost in his large, rough one, a hand that worked hard on his father's farm when not tossing a football. She felt momentarily content, hidden by others from her mama's watchful eyes. Wally was right. He wasn't much of a dancer, and his big boots squashed her feet a time or two, but she hardly noticed. Wally was a dreamboat and she bubbled inside with delight. He had selected her.

When the dance ended they sauntered to the punch bowl. Sara sipped the sweet strawberry concoction while Wally quickly inhaled three cups. "Ah, that's good stuff," he said.

"My mama made it," Sara said, and then wished she hadn't.

"Yer mama's here?" he asked.

"Yeah. Over next t' the door. She's watchin' us. She don't like t' worry herself 'bout where I'm at."

"Well, she's a good mama, then," Wally said, surprising Sara with his reply. In truth, Sara detested her presence. She resented her mama more and more each day and wasn't really sure why she took exception to her mothering. Mama wasn't a bad woman, really, and Sara knew she loved her "more than tongue could tell". It was a sentiment Sara had heard repeatedly over the years.

"Have ya' seen Addie?" Sara suddenly blurted.

"No, I ain't seen her t'night. She's usually yer sidekick," Wally said. "I ain't really never seen the two a' ya' apart at school an' such."

"She's my best friend, my very best friend." Sara mused, "But she didn't come t' the game like she said she would an' she ain't here now. I'm a little worried 'bout her. She ain't got the best home life ya' know."

"I don't know much 'bout that, but I seen her daddy a time or two 'round town. He's a big son of a gun. Wonder if he ever played football?" Wally's words landed where they always did.

"Well, I ain't never seen him smile. He drives us t' school most days, but don't say much on the ride. Jist 'How's yer mama?' or 'Yer lookin' good.'"

"Well, he's right 'bout that," Wally stammered. "Want t' dance again?"

Wally grabbed her hand in his and they started for the center of the room amid the throng of noisy students who were trying to do a jitterbug. Sara and Wally found themselves caught up in the chaotic movements unsure really of when to twist, kick, or jump. They just flailed their arms and kicked a few times for good measure. Suddenly, in a quick instant, the music stopped, interrupting as it did the frenetic frenzy.

Sara looked around and was astonished to see her papa, sullen and serious, leaning against the door. He looked as he usually did, with deep furrows in his cheeks above a week-old stubble of grey and brown. He wore his familiar stained red plaid jacket, and a brown hat with flaps that hung loosely over his ears. He was looking soberly into the stricken face of Mama. Sara and Wally were at their sides in an instant and in the moments that followed, Sara understood the gravity of Papa's news. She didn't understand, however, that her view of the world would forever be changed. The innocence of the evening quickly turned into a gruesome reality that she had never fathomed possible.

The Gilbert house smoldered at midnight under an eerily bright sky. The full moon cast a light on the scene and millions of stars, beacons of doom, speckled the smoky black sky. Sara stood weakly between her papa and Wally. She shivered in the icy cold watching as the lone sheriff went about the task of cordoning off a scene that would forever be etched in Sara's visual memory.

The humble dwelling that had housed the Gilbert family still stood in part, but the side section of the house that had been the living and bedrooms had collapsed into a mass of timber and smoking furniture. Sara could see glowing embers within the mound of rubble and the smell of charred wood filled the air. The bulk of the fire had been extinguished, and the one engine, three-man fire department continued to dowse the ruins.

A crowd had gathered by the road, eager onlookers who fed on the excitement and a few faithful friends who watched carefully for signs of movement and life. The latter were to be disappointed. The men at the house skirted the debris searching the standing section, aided only by flashlights and the headlights of the fire engine. Slowly they moved through the portion of the house that had been Addie's mother's kitchen, her place of solace and calm, a place where she created a semblance of warmth and hominess for her daughter, a refuge from the wrath of George Gilbert.

From her distant vantage point Sara watched the men plod into the wreckage, stepping carefully over things she could not see. She heard their mumbled voices. She watched their heads bob from left to right as they rummaged around and then they stopped. They knelt. Their voices were silent. And then they were yelling.

"Sheriff! We got somethin'. Oh, God. We got somethin'! Sheriff!"

Margaret Gilbert's limp body was dragged a bit and then carefully collected and placed on a makeshift gurney on the ground beside the fire truck. Her hair was thrown back above her head in a stiff tangled, bloody mass. Her dark eyes were wide open and her face revealed a distorted, sickly grin, showing places where teeth had been. Deep purple bruises lined her eyes and her nose had swollen to the size of a plump plum. She was covered in ash and dirt with one arm clearly broken, a white bone sticking through the pallid skin. Her legs were bare and straight, jutting out directly from the cotton skirt that still covered her privates. Margaret Gilbert was dead. She already was beginning to stiffen.

"Git back! Git back!" Orders were yelled by those in charge.

Sara couldn't move. She was frozen with cold, with shock, with rage, with fear. Margaret Gilbert had endured years of violence and neglect but the community at large recognized her as a warm, sweet woman whose timid smile stole hearts. Sara looked at the still body and suddenly shuddered in grief. Tears streamed down her face and she gasped for air, gulping in the miserable cold that was sucked into her chest. What had happened? Where was George Gilbert? Where was Addie? Maybe her father had helped her run from the fire. Maybe she was safe in town somewhere. Maybe she didn't know what had happened. Maybe she did. Sara's mind launched her into hysteria. Both Papa and Wally had to support her as she flailed at nothing, and screeched like a banshee at the night sky. It was over then. She collapsed into the arms of the man and boy, unconsciousness taking her from her terror.

She awoke to a grey morning. Clouds had stolen the clear sky and lay in deep, thick layers. Rain would come soon. Sara searched her memory for images of the night before. She saw the blackness, the glowing embers, the sunken roof, the still form of Margaret Gilbert. Lingering in her nose was the smell of burnt wood, of blood, of frozen turf. She recalled the distant din of nosey onlookers, of the crunch of boots, of shouts and cries, of Wally's gasp at the sight of the dead woman. Where was he? Where was Papa? Where was Mama? Where was Addie?

"Mama!" Her scream shattered the silence of the morning.

"Here, Sara. Here. I'm right here!" Mama shrugged off a thin quilt and pushed herself out of the overstuffed chair that sat next to Sara's bed. She had spent the night there, watching, waiting, and finally succumbing to a sporadic sleep. "I'm here, Sara Mae. I ain't goin' nowhere."

"Don't leave me, Mama."

"I ain't goin' t' leave ya', Sara Mae. I ain't goin' t' leave ya'."

⁂

When the rain finally came, it inundated Cam's Corner as if to wash away the memory of the fire and the corpse that had been pulled from it. Yet it had the counter effect. The rain seemed to create a flood of mishaps that tumbled one over the other crushing the otherwise quiet community and devastating and forever changing lives.

At dawn the search for the remaining Gilberts had begun. It took only a short time for a party of searchers to find the body of George Gilbert, hunched into an unbendable arc at one of the side doors of the high school. The gun was still in his grip, and it lay flat underneath his chin where a clean bullet hole could be detected. Not so clean was the rest of the scene. Head blown nearly away at the top, Mr. Gilbert slumped by the warped wooden door which was matted with dried blood and pieces of bone and brain. An eerie tuft of hair played in the wind at the threshold. The torso of the body was strangely shielded from the pelting rain, but the legs and feet were immersed in a putrid puddle that swirled in circles with the curious current created by the storm. Reports of the bizarre scene rapidly traveled through the town, and it was hastily photographed by a newspaper reporter who later vomited violently into the gushing gutter.

Among those in the search party had been Sara's father who recognized his rare duty to his wife and daughter. He would have to tell them about the finding. He would also have to tell them that Addie was still missing.

Chapter Four

Robert Jenkins somehow clutched his weak courage and slogged the mile to his wife's house in the storm. He needed the time to think about what to say. Deeper than the news of the death of George Gilbert was a sudden realization of his empty life; it might as well have been him lying in that doorway. He felt equally dead inside. He knew he was a disappointment to his family. He was a failure to himself. His existence was an empty pot. He had nothing to give; time had taken his productivity and stolen his dreams. He was nothing. He knew it. Yet he summoned the audacity to do what he had to do. He knew he had the guts to report the morning's events; beyond that, he was completely uncertain.

When he knocked on the front door of Emma Jenkins' home, Robert was soaked. He was soaked and shaking with cold. Emma took one look at him, shut the door, and then opened it again.

"What on Earth?" she questioned.

"Need t' talk t' ya', Emma. Real important."

Instinctively, Emma realized it was. "Wait," she said, and closed the door again. In minutes she returned with blankets and motioned for Robert to enter. "Come in. Jist inside now. Ya' strip off now an' git them wet clothes int' this here basket."

Wrapped in blankets and sipping a steaming cup of coffee, Robert reported the news to Emma and Sara. Sobbing began again. Sara had never encountered significant loss before and while she had not cared for Mr. Gilbert she mourned for her friend, Addie. What would Addie do now? Where would she go? Who would take care of her? Where was she?

Myriad questions swirled about the room as both Emma and Sara searched for answers.

"We ain't found Addie, yet. She ain't been found. Nobody ain't seen her nowhere."

But Robert was wrong.

At that moment, trudging along Turtle Creek, two men, one old, one young, discovered the girl. She had been stripped naked and lay partially submerged in a muddy bog adjacent to the creek. She looked strangely serene from a distance as though she had sought this resting place herself. On closer inspection, however, the men cringed at what they saw. A rope was taut around her thin neck; her eyes were wide and her matted yellow hair stuck to her colorless cheeks. The mouth was opened ever so slightly and the lips were bluish purple. A trickle of dried blood had oozed and dried on her chin. Addie's thin legs were slightly parted and a bit askew. A trace of color indicated bruises on her thighs. Rigor mortis already had gripped her. She was gone.

"Aw, Jesus. This ain't right. This ain't right." One man said, sliding off his jacket and placing it over the girl. The younger man uttered a grotesque groan. He gently hefted the corpse and carried it quietly then up the creek bank to the road. His chest shuddered abruptly and unexpectedly as he clutched the girl's body. Tears dropped heavily onto the sopping jacket that shrouded her. The men tenderly placed the tiny girl in the trunk of the car and closed it firmly. They looked at each other, one with eyes hollow and hardened; the other with eyes laden with tears.

One of the men was the sheriff. The other was young Wally.

⁂

In the days following, the community of Cam's Corner drew into itself. The inhabitants waved off reporters from Nashville and Memphis who merged on the little town seeking to suck out the sordid details of what had occurred there. The sheriff made a quick appearance before clicking cameras, stating that this was a case of domestic difficulties taken to the extreme by an unstable man. It was established that George Gilbert had been fired from his job as custodian earlier on that awful Friday and clearly, as he was accustomed, had taken out his anger and frustration on his family. Fingerprints had verified that he had manhandled his wife and had purposefully set fire to his house to cover the evidence. Putting the pieces together, officials assumed that the daughter, Addie, had walked into a horrific scene. One could only imagine.

Addie parted from her friend Sara after their chilly walk from town. Addie's house, which was just more than a shack, was a quarter of a mile beyond Sara's. She bid Sara goodbye and they giggled with momentary excitement as they chatted about where they'd meet for the big game and the dance afterward. Addie's father had given her rare permission to attend and she bubbled inside with anticipation. Such fun usually eluded her, but tonight would be different. She would be free!

As she strode up the path to her front door, anxiety gripped her. How quickly her emotions evolved from anticipation to fear. She saw her father's Ford pickup parked haphazardly in front of the house, tires askew, and the front door ajar. She slowed her pace and listened. The voices she heard where not unfamiliar. "Ya' witch! Yer goin' t' git yers! Ya' jist sit all day, wastin' time. Ya' git over here!" Margaret Gilbert did not answer with words but with a gasp, a yelp, and then silence. She had been pushed to the floor and lay unconscious while George pummeled her mercilessly. His rage was so intense that he could not stop himself. He hit, hit, hit, and then finally he stopped. He gazed through vapid eyes at the purple face below him. He didn't recognize it. It was not real. He stared and then started in alarm as the door behind him swung open.

Addie screamed. And then she was the recipient. One strong backhand slammed her into a vacant wall, and her slight form fell into a lifeless heap on the barren plank floor.

What happened next? Near imperceptible indications drew the attention of the sheriff: a shoe wedged into the door jam, a once bright yellow scarf stiffened with blood, a swash of flattened weeds that ended adjacent to wide tire tracks, and deep ruts where a truck's tires had dug into the soft soil as it hammered away from the place. On the porch were streaks of blood, barely perceptible, but evident in the hazy morning light. The sheriff and a handful of men had soldiered themselves at the scene, ready, even eager, for the next steps.

George Gilbert hefted his daughter onto the passenger's seat. She was heavier than he had anticipated and he sweated profusely with his effort to hold her. He shoved her rump onto the grimy floor board, hastily rounded the front of the truck and swung his tense body into the driver's seat. He drove with no destination in mind, but he intended to drive far, very far. A sputtering of the engine just three miles down the dark, mucky road, however, curtailed his ludicrous plan. The Ford's sudden lack of momentum launched it into a shallow ditch next to the road. George was thrown hard into the steering wheel, and he cursed, "Ya' goddamned son of a bitch. Ya' bastard!" And then he looked at the heap next to him. He snarled odiously, "Yer a bitch too, jist like yer mama!"

George was numb. His rage had morphed into a seething, crazed state. He was vaguely aware of his surroundings, near the woods, close to the creek. In the cold, wet haze he continued to perspire heavily as his dreadful actions intensified. The passenger door of the truck was jammed into the dirt, so he grabbed Addie's thin shoulder with thick, hateful hands and pulled her headfirst out of the truck. Her neck bounced against the edge of the door frame before she was thrown to the ground. And then, the unspeakable. George grabbed a short rope from under the seat and stuffed it into his wide pocket. He was not fully aware as to why and yet the action was deliberate. In a rushed and thoughtless motion, he then ripped every piece of clothing from his young daughter's body; she was exposed and vulnerable as he dragged her, past a broken fence, over barbed wire that lay twisted in the weeds, and down an embankment to the creek. When he had tossed her like a limp doll into the brambles beside the water, a sickly, suffocating lust overcame him. He shoved her legs apart and thrust his erect member into the tight vaginal opening. It was over quickly and he heaved himself, sticky and bloody, from her. Her eyelids flickered ever so slightly and she groaned softly. He did what he needed to do. Around her soft neck he placed the rope, almost gently, and then he tugged, and tightened. The body flinched and bobbled briefly. Fingers curled and grasped the air and then all was still.

One can only imagine.

George Gilbert stumbled away from the child, a child really at fifteen, mindfully stroking his trousers. He was overcome with an unexplainable hunger as he approached the broken Ford. His thick hand clumsily reached under the seat for his salvation. He touched metal, hard and sure. He pulled the gun out and caressed it next to his chest. And then he was gone, sprinting into the darkness, hurrying into the night. When his strained conscience finally returned to him, he knew what to do.

Hardened, but not broken, the sheriff shifted uneasily on his feet in front of the reporters. "It's over folks," he stated. "Go home an' let us git on with it."

For a week following the deaths, Cam's Corner slowed as folks gathered in small groups for comfort, families hurried to restore relationships, and individuals searched for some semblance of understanding. Among those most affected by the events were Sara and Wally, but the way they dealt with their grief and shock was very different. For nearly a week, Sara stayed in her room. She would sob uncontrollably for hours and then suddenly stop, staring at nothing for a time. She refused to speak, except to plead with her mother, "Mama, don't leave me!" and Mama did not. She stayed, she prayed, she stroked her daughter's arms and back, combed her long dark hair, and sponged her clean with warm soapy water. She was intent, and in time, Sara responded to her mother's compassion. On a morning that dawned sunny and very cold, Sara climbed from bed and slipped into the warm kitchen where her mother was silently sipping tea.

"I love ya' Mama," Sara said simply. "Thank ya' fer tryin' t' help me understand, an' I don't, but I'm ready now. I need t' git up an' move, an' git on. I kain't cry no more."

"I love ya' too, Sara Mae, more than tongue can tell."

"I know, Mama. I know." And in moments she added, "I jist feel kind a' empty now, like my heart's been twisted apart. Aside from you, Mama, I don't know if I can love nobody no more. An' I don't understand God neither. Why does he rip folks away from us? Don't he know it hurts? Don't he care?"

Mama's answer was pat. "The Lord works in mysterious ways."

Sara had heard that over and over. Her mama's faith was steady and strong. Sara's was not and she seethed suddenly with the familiar unrestrained resentment that had gripped her for months. She was surprised to find the feeling suddenly so intense. She resented her mama and she resented God. Her faith shattered, she concluded at that moment in the chilly morning, warmed only slightly by hazy sunlight streaming through the window that she would have to protect herself. She resolved that she would not let anyone close to her again; it hurt too much.

When Wally stopped by later that day, she told him as much. He looked stricken, but said in resignation, "Well, it's jist as well. I'm leavin' this place, Sara. I kain't make sense a' what I seen. I don't want t' be 'round folks no more. When ya' kain't trust yer papa, who can ya' trust? My daddy didn't say much 'bout what happened. Jist shook his head. I ain't got no mama at home. She left when I was a little fella an' darned if I know her where 'bouts. Nobody at my house t' talk with an' I ain't sure I want t' talk t' nobody no way. I got t' git away."

"What's ya' goin' do, Wally? Where ya' goin' t' go?" Sara noticed Wally's eyes as she spoke. While always deep-set they looked now like deep pools. Under his eyes the skin was yellowish-purple, a dark indication that sleep had evaded him.

"I got a' uncle up in East Kentucky. Think I'm goin' t' go see if he'll have me 'round. He's kind a' a mountain man. Stays t' hisself. Ain't got no family. I'll git some work, maybe in the mine. Got t' work this memory away. So, I'm goin', Sara. Ya' take care a' yerself." Wally reached for Sara's face and touched it lightly with his fingers, and then he was gone. The touch lingered on Sara's cheek, cold and hot at the same time.

She stared after him and a wistful smile played on her lips. Her dreamboat had sailed away and she was left alone, except for Mama, and for Sara, that wasn't saying much. Despite Mama's diligent care, Sara felt empty. She was filled with her old companion resentment and felt smothered in her own home. She would return to school, bide her time, and go her own way to a destination she could not yet determine. For the next two years, Sara existed in a forlorn state, seldom smiling, lacking companions, concentrating only on her studies. Her papa eventually moved back into the house and began to contribute some. He would never be a stellar husband to Mama, but she seemed to prefer passable to nothing at all. With her mama occupied, Sara spent hours secluded in her room and joined her parents only for meals or a knitting lesson. Time and grit became her friends.

Chapter Five

While time certainly did serve Sara, grit played with her and sometimes eluded her altogether. Two years had passed and Sara had completed high school. She had been a competent student, but finished her stint in school virtually unnoticed and certainly not acknowledged for any substantial accomplishments. She simply endured and finished it. She remained withdrawn and aloof. With her schooling over, for college was out of the question, Sara was lost. Mama didn't have money to send her even to Bishop College one county over, and although her papa had become a more permanent fixture in their home, he looked at education as a luxury for men only.

"Yer goin' t' have t' git yerself some work, now Sara," he told her. "Yer schoolin's done. I reckon yer goin' t' have t' go on down t' the court house an' find out from that there employment lady, Mrs. Crockett, if she can git ya' somethin' t' do."

"Yes Sir, Papa," Sara mumbled to silence him.

"Yer papa's right, Sara Mae," Mama chimed in, "Ya' kain't jist sit."

"I know, Mama. I know."

Sara looked over at her mama whose face had grown saggy with deep lines dividing her fat cheeks from a large and slightly protruding chin. When had she gotten so old? She had never been one to wear powders and rouge. She thought them frivolous. And she had never worn a bra, detesting its restrictive grasp the one time she tried one. "I ain't goin' t' be tied in by this thing," she had stated flatly. "I'll jist keep myself covered up an' like God made me underneath."

Mama took control of herself just like she did everyone around her. Her grey eyes glared more often than they glittered. She was always looking, forever judging others, and denying it. "Judge not that thou be judged," she had recited many times, but she was quick to call another "white trash" or unchristian and while she would have denied it profusely, Sara had heard her mutter "nigger" under her breath when they were driving through Skilletown where most of the poor blacks lived. As though she were being benevolent, Mama would call them "the coloreds" and might take some of her canning to the charity kitchen at Christmas, but otherwise, she would not give any of those people the time of day. She was a pigheaded woman, pious, prideful, and self-righteous. Sometimes Sara understood why her papa had stayed away in town for so long.

Time had weathered her daddy as well. He had never been a "looker" as Mama referred to handsome men, but he was tall and trim. A crop of dusty grey hair flopped over the furrowed forehead and his eyes, which were grey, green, and brown altogether, were usually cast down. He was an insecure man, who hunched his shoulders and looked at people sideways. Sara knew she had never looked him directly in the eyes. He wasn't much for clothes either; even if he had had the money to purchase them, the idea of dressing nicely was not in his scope of consciousness. Clothes were just something to wear. Sara was used to seeing him in dirty corduroy pants, a dusty blue work shirt, and the red plaid jacket that was his mainstay on cool summer mornings or in the dead of winter.

Papa's head now hung over his supper plate. Mama had cooked a supper of crispy fried chicken, creamy mashed potatoes, and gravy filled with giblets and fried flour that had fallen into the liquefied lard in which it was cooked. Mama called the bits of meat and flour "woo woos". Sara didn't know why, but Emma Jenkins swore by her cooking. She would say, "The woo woos make all the difference 'tween plain an' amazin'." Mama was a first-rate cook who could fry up a skillet of potatoes, or whip up a batch of pancakes in a jiffy. Sitting at Mama's table was one place everyone felt comfortable, and where Sara's companion resentment routinely dissolved like melted butter.

Hearing the demands of her parents this evening, however, put a damper on dinner and she slipped out of her chair to her room. She knew Mama would be expecting her to wash the dishes and clean the kitchen until it was spic and span, but right now she wanted to be by herself. She would go help in a bit. Not now. Not now. Bitterness descended on her like a thick murky haze and settled there. A familiar emptiness crept into her, creating a smothering sensation. What had happened to her determination? What had happened to her dreams? She knew. She knew. Her world had proven to be a nasty place and Addie was gone. The memories of the brutal murders and suicide of the Gilbert family had made a home in Sara's mind and pestered her ceaselessly. She thought about her predicament. She wanted to grow up and living with Mama and Papa was maddening. She was treated like a child and was constantly badgered to do chores she detested. *"Ya' need t' do the dustin', Sara, an' clean up that mud off a' the front stoop. It's a sight out there."*

She stared out her bedroom window, willing the unwanted memories to disappear, and for a moment they did, as she watched the sun slide slowly to the horizon. Summer was beginning to show its colors and she relished it, for it was her favorite season. An unexpected alien joy rose inside her. She watched a spring lamb in the lot outside jump friskily into the air, all four hoofs off the ground at the same time. The antics of the little lamb made her smile and she wondered how it would live its life. Hopefully it would be munching eternally on the green grass that lined the fence and would give Papa a pile of wool to sell in town. She hopped childishly, then, two feet in the air mimicking the lamb outside. She flushed at her silliness, but in the moment, grasped a new understanding. An inkling of hope eased into her consciousness and she thought about her future. She could not continue to stay with Mama and Papa forever so she would need to devise a means and time for departure. When and how that would occur, she had no idea; she knew only that she wanted more than anything to manage her own life. Having her parents dictate to her was stifling, and that must end. As she had learned so well from Mama, but recently disregarded, she did have control over something. She had control over herself. She knew she would have to make her own way.

Surprising even herself, Sara found a job quickly. She became a counter girl at the local Ford dealership, the same one that had employed George Gilbert. It seemed somewhat eerie at first to realize she was entering the same door and walking the same corridors that George Gilbert must have walked a few years before, and the first day Sara began her job, she had to suppress unwanted sensations that were conjured by the unrelenting memories that crowded her mind. Not one day passed when she did not think about her best friend, Addie. Addie had had the biggest dreams of all, and Sara pictured her sweet face as she remembered.

"*We're goin' t' do great things, Sara Mae Jenkins! Ya' jist have t' wait an' see! Someday we're goin' t' be free as a bird!*"

It always had amused Sara when Addie used her full name, just as Mama did when she was angry or determined. And Sara sadly accepted finally that indeed Addie was free. Her life had been a pure hell and Sara liked to think of Addie looking down on her from above like a tiny blond angel. She missed her terribly.

"Yer goin' t' be greetin' people, Sara," Albert Mason, the manager of the dealership told her, "so put a smile on that pretty face, an' make people happy t' be here. Yer goin' t' help sell cars!"

The smile was a little timid at first, but miraculously in only a few weeks, it was wide and genuine. Despite her vow to distance herself from others, Sara found that she was happy and pleased to have a job of her own, one that would provide money and independence, something that Sara had never before enjoyed. She resisted the contented feelings at first, clinging to her dispirited comfort zone, but eventually she gave in to them. She began to see how opportune this job was and hoped it would enable her to reach her dreams. Of course, she stubbornly tried to cling to her despair at first, but despite her deliberate effort to do so, she was pulled into a world that offered more stimulation than she had ever known. She liked feeling worldly. Her inexperience, however, led to a false view of herself as sure and sophisticated.

The Ford dealership was a busy place. Young men strutted in, cocky and sure, looking for a needed part or new tires; businessmen would slide up to a shiny new model stroking the fender as if it were a nylon-enveloped thigh; old men sauntered in searching for used spare parts or just a cup of steaming coffee; and young families would appear, fathers looking serious and mothers looking shy and haggard as they dragged misbehaving children behind them. The salesmen were suave and talked a good line. The accounting girls were rough around the edges, as Mama would have said, using vulgar language and making crude remarks to the mechanics and salesmen who squeezed up to their desks to flirt. *"How's yer hammer hangin', Hank?" "Looks like ya' had a little roll in the hay last night, Charlie." "An' how's the new missus, Luke? Keepin' her happy? Ya' ain't goin' t' want her wanderin'." "Speakin' a' wanderin', Charlie's sure got the eye!" "Wouldn't mind a smooch or two with him!" "Well, I'll be damned, Willie. What ya' lookin' at? Them ain't lemons under my sweater." "That old geezer thinks he gits under my skin! I wouldn't give him the time a' day!"* The girls would chatter guiltlessly with the men, rolling their eyes, covering their giggles with red painted fingernails, and smiling coyly. Their flirtatious games became a ritual.

Sara watched all of this safely from her counter at the front. She answered the phone, "Cam's Corner Ford!" with confidence. Her boss complimented her gentle voice and she puffed demurely with the praise. She was also the coffee girl. Anyone who entered the small showroom was offered coffee or tea. *"Sugar an' cream with that, Sir?" "Yes, Mam, would ya' like tea or coffee this mornin'?"* The salesmen quickly grew accustomed to her service, but they weren't always considerate in their demands. *"Git me some coffee, sister." "Sara, bring some coffee on over here."* They commanded rather than requested. Sara noticed this and bristled inside but she said nothing. She wanted to keep her job and thought this was part of it.

"Jist bad manners. I could sure teach 'em a thing or two," Mama spit her words when Sara told her about their demands.

"There sure are some characters down there, Mama." Sara shared what she could, knowing that to say too much would be a mistake. She didn't want Mama changing her mind about her having a job. "Mama can turn on a dime sometimes," Sara thought to herself. "She ain't got t' know ever'thing."

One particular issue Mama didn't know, and wouldn't if Sara had anything to do with it, was a little detail called Charlie. Charlie Marshall. Charlie's wandering eye had settled on young Sara and he had set his mind to having his way with her sooner or later. He was smooth, smart, and resourceful. He sold more Fords than anyone and knew just what to say to get what he wanted. Even when a customer couldn't afford a new car, he would deliver his spiel, tag him on the line, and rustle up a deal. He was used to getting his way and his outgoing personality and dark, handsome features were certainly a help. Men found his conversation engaging and women were pulled in by dark brown eyes and unnerving dimples in an otherwise rugged jaw. Mama definitely would have called him a looker, and Sara couldn't help but notice him as well. The only problem for Sara was that he was old, having just turned thirty. Sara was just eighteen and she knew Mama would have a hissy fit if she knew of the magnetism that had been generated between them, an allure that alerted Sara's caution. When Charlie came around, Sara busied herself with work and avoided his stares. She could feel her body tighten and she would lose her smile so as not to appear to be inviting his overtures. She still held firm in her decision that she would get close to no one. It hurt too much to lose.

Charlie unceasingly flattered Sara with compliments. More than once he told her, "Yer the most beautiful girl 'round, Sara Mae." He had somehow found out her middle name and used it consistently. He intended to use this tidbit of knowledge as a tool to wedge his way into her conscience, if not her heart. To his way of thinking, she would have to think he was pretty special to know more about her than the other fellows who also admired her good looks. "Ya' look real nice, Sara Mae. That red dress becomes ya'. An' thank ya' fer the coffee. I can see ya' take real good care a' me, sugah."

Sara's limited experience with boys, much less men, left her vulnerable to his cunning comments. No one had ever talked to her in this manner and while at first she was taken aback, it didn't take long for her to blush with unwanted pleasure and flip her long brown hair relishing the attention.

"I'd love t' take the most gorgeous doll in town t' dinner an' a movie sometime. How 'bout Saturday, Sara Mae? Will ya' give me a chance t' show ya' a good time, sugah? I promise ya', ya' won't regret it." Charlie smiled and leaned calmly on the counter in front of Sara. "Please say ya'll go," he pleaded boyishly.

Two months of resistance challenged Charlie even more. He became bolder. On an unusually warm fall morning, Charlie wandered nonchalantly to Sara and looked at her with a mock seriousness. He reached brashly over the counter, taking a wisp of Sara's hair in his fingers. "Yer goin' t' break my heart if ya' don't go out with me, Sara Mae," he said. His mouth remained open slightly and he licked his lips teasing her. She jerked back, grabbing his hand impulsively. Just as quickly, he took her hand in both of his and pleaded once again, "Come with me, Sara Mae. Come with me t' a movie."

It was a surprisingly intimate touch that made Sara's neck crawl with heat and perspiration. She couldn't find words.

"Please, Sara Mae?"

"All right then. I reckon I can," Sara found herself replying.

Charlie answered with a confident smile. "After work. We'll leave after work 'bout five." He had finalized the deal. She was going to be his.

***

Charlie was charming and Sara was captivated by his charisma. Her resistance to him was useless. He became a shadow to her, constantly watching and waiting. He made sure everyone knew she was his girl and his jealousy blossomed when she gave too much attention to a customer, male or female. He wanted her solely to satisfy his interests. An uneasy, indefinable feeling toyed with Sara but she ignored it when it reared up inside her; she was enchanted by her first real beau and helpless when he slid up beside her and smiled, or softly touched the small of her back as he escorted her.

"Come on, Sara. Time fer us, now," he would whisper into her ear, or scribble on a note.

Charlie gently pressured Sara into several clandestine dates to movies, or for walks in the county park, but Sara always insisted that she be home early. "Mama an' Papa are expectin' me," she'd say to the irritation of Charlie. And to Mama, she'd lie, "They kept me late t'day, Mama, fer a meetin'" or "t' help with the paperwork."

"When ya' goin' t' tell them 'bout me, Sara Mae?" Charlie persisted.

"I don't know, Charlie. My mama's real protective an' she'd likely have a conniption fit if she found out 'bout ya'."

"Well, she's goin' t' have t' know. Yer my girl, Sara Mae. She's goin' t' have t' know."

To her chagrin, Charlie appeared at the front stoop just a day later with daisies for Sara and violets for Mama. And astutely he hadn't forgotten about Sara's papa either. He had a couple of hand-wrapped cigars in his pocket, suspecting he might need them for a man to man chat.

Supper was on the table when Charlie stomped onto the wooden porch and banged heavily on the screen door that hung crookedly on the frame. Papa was sopping up thick gravy with a homemade biscuit, too busy in his enjoyment of Mama's cooking to move.

"What on Earth?" Mama said. "Who'd be knockin' now? I ain't expectin' company. Git the door, Sara Mae."

When she saw a muted Charlie through the dusty screen, Sara's heart fluttered. She glared at him suddenly angry and anxious. "What are ya' doin' here, Charlie?"

"Came t' meet the folks."

"Ya' kain't do that, Charlie. They're havin' supper now," Sara said opening the screen door slightly, lightly pushing Charlie away as she did. "This ain't a good time."

"Who is it, Sara Mae?" Mama was suddenly standing directly behind Sara. She looked at the man and the girl and knew instantly that she'd been left in the dark about a few things. "I wasn't born yesterday," she thought to herself.

"Well, well," she said. "Better bring this fella in, Sara."

Charlie presented Mama with the bouquet of blue and purple violets that were tied with a light pink satin ribbon, "Got these fer ya', Mrs. Jenkins." He bowed ever so slightly and then handed the white and yellow daisies to Sara. "An' these are fer the young lady." The twinkle in Charlie's eyes did not go unnoticed by either of the women.

Sara knew her mama's best manners were in place at this moment, but she detected a sharp glint of anger angled her way. She'd be in a heap of trouble.

"Sara, introduce us, now," Mama instructed.

"Yes, Mam. This here's Charlie from my work. Charlie Marshall, Mama. Charlie sells cars an' trucks. This here's Charlie Marshall, Papa," she continued, directing her attention to her daddy. "Charlie's 'bout the best salesman that Ford dealer ever seen. They wouldn't know what t' do without him, I reckon. Sells 'bout ever'thing that comes in." Sara realized she was babbling. She stopped and for a moment all was silent. Just stares all around.

"Well, I reckon it's good t' meet ya' Charlie Marshall. Sit yerself down. Have yerself some supper. Git a plate, Sara Mae," Mama directed.

Charlie smiled at Mama then, planning to win her over too. "Well, I thank ya', Mrs. Jenkins. This looks like a mighty fine supper. I don't git this kind a' good home cookin' very often. Looks real fine!"

Sara sat between Mama and Papa afraid to look at either of them directly and she couldn't bring herself to look up at Charlie either, who sat across from her, eating hungrily, and luring in her folks with casual banter. Listening to the conversation was useless though; she was concentrating on trying to calm her nerves. Her heart was beating quickly and she was perspiring much too much; she could feel heat on her cheeks and neck as she wiped her clammy hands on a cloth napkin. "I'm as red a beet!" she thought to herself.

"Serve up the pie, Sara Mae," Mama instructed, looking at Sara's plate as she did. "Ya' ain't ate nothin', Sara. Don't reckon ya'll be wantin' none."

"No, Mam. I ain't real hungry jist now." Sara stood from the table, relieved to break away from the awkward setting.

After stuffing themselves with hefty portions of pecan pie, Charlie and Papa wandered onto the porch to smoke their cigars. Staring into the evening dusk, Papa searched for words, but Charlie adeptly filled in the silence with talk of cars, the quality of Ford trucks, and questions about the small farm.

In the kitchen a strained silence sliced at the mother-daughter bond. Sara was scared and Mama was stung to the core. Finally Mama spoke. "I reckon ya' got a mighty lot t' tell me, young lady."

"Yes 'am, some."

"Well, I ain't goin' t' ask nothin'. Yer goin' t' have t' do the tellin'." Mama turned sharply then and stepped to the door. "'Night, Charlie. Real nice t' meet ya'. 'Night, Robert. I'm real tired. Goin' t' turn in early."

"Be right in after ya'," Robert said, effectively ending the evening exchange with Charlie.

"Thank ya' fer the supper. It was real fine," Charlie added, looking through the door for a sign of Sara. "I'll be on my way now. Real nice t' meet ya', Mr. Jenkins. Hope t' be seein' ya' more."

He sidestepped the mongrel pup that had leaped on the porch seeking shelter, and hopped down the steps. A glance over his shoulder gave him a glimpse of Sara shutting the door and pulling down the sash behind a broken pane of glass. He was going to take her away from this place, and it would be soon.

Chapter Six

Sara's restless sleep lent dreams that took her flying over oceans and swimming in deep pools of water. She sailed on a boat down a narrow canal and she stopped on a sandy shore to cuddle baby squirrels and raccoons that were not afraid of her. She awoke wondering.

"What on Earth? My dreams don't make no sense at all," she thought.

She slipped out of her crumpled covers and stepped onto the cold wooden floor. The air was chilly and she shivered, recalling the evening before. She did not want to face Mama this morning and she did have her job to attend to, so if she was quiet, and hurried, she'd avoid the confrontation and explanations her mama would expect.

In no time she was dressed and ready. Pulling on the cold metal knob gently, she parted the door ever so slightly peering into what she had hoped would be muted morning light in an otherwise dark house. She was instantly aware, however, that the day had already begun for Mama. Yellow light filtered from the kitchen doorway. She would need to pass by there to leave the house, and she wished ridiculously for an escape route. "If wishes were horses . . ." she thought, remembering the saying she'd heard so many times in her youth. Mama always told her not to make frivolous wishes or selfish demands, because God didn't allow for such idle concerns.

"I kain't jist run off," she thought. "Guess I'll jist face the music."

The music, so to speak, was not sweet. Mama was seething. "What on Earth's gotten int' ya', young lady?" Mama's eyes were red rimmed and puffy. Had she been crying? Mama never cried. At least Sara had never seen her.

"Nothin'," Sara mumbled, hanging her head in an imitation of shame. "I ain't done nothin' wrong." And suddenly her old friend resentment came alive. She raised her head in defiance, her lips draw tight, and her chin jutting forward. "Ya' ain't got no right t' judge me, Mama. I ain't done nothin'."

"Then why ya' tryin' t' slip out a' here this mornin'?"

"I wasn't."

"Ya' were. I wasn't born yesterday, Miss Sara Mae!"

"Mama, I ain't a baby no more," Sara said, "an' ya' kain't judge me, 'cause yer imaginin' I'm real bad an' I ain't."

"I ain't imaginin' nothin' a' the kind," Mama spat. "But I know I wouldn't give too hoots fer a fella like that Charlie. He's got rotten written all over him. I seen them kind b'fore."

"Ya' don't know nothin' 'bout him, Mama." Sara wanted to argue.

"He's a smooth talker, an' he's goin' t' have ya' in a heap a' trouble."

"But, he's . . ."

Sara was interrupted.

"I ain't goin' t' tell ya' nothin' more, Sara Mae. If ya' think ya' ain't a baby, then maybe ya' ain't. Maybe I'm jist a' ol' woman whose done lost her sense, but ya' better watch yerself. I do know that much!"

Was this all? Sara stared at her mother's frumpy form and thought hatefully, "How in the world did she get like this? She's old, an' bitter, an' ugly, an' no fun at all. I ain't never goin' t' be like her."

"Go on. Git yerself on out a' here. Yer fancy job's waitin'."

Sara pushed her way out of the front door as she had so many times before, but this time, when she heard the wooden screen door bang shut, it slammed with a curious finality. Sara had been warned; she knew she would be moving on and it was a wary choice that invited both apprehension and guarded excitement.

❦

For days, Sara lived for one thing: Charlie. She loved his attention and he wanted her in the worst way. He was oblivious to the impression he had left on Sara's parents. Of course they had adored him. Didn't everyone? Certainly Sara did.

"Come on, sugah. We're off t' a good time," he'd smile, grabbing her hand and pulling her toward him. She would puff up pleasurably and his interest in her became the talk of the girls in the accounting department. *"That Sara's got herself a handful." "Bet he's got a good thing waitin' fer her!" "She don't know what's comin'." "Real green, that one." "Bet he'll be pokin' 'round anywhere he wants in no time." "That man's more trouble than ya' can shake a stick at." "Lots a' hearts goin' t' be broken real soon." "I hope it ain't goin' t' be hers!" "I reckon it could be." "Yes, Sir, he's sure got the rovin' eye."*

She couldn't resist Charlie, although his inherent behavior kept her on her toes. A time or two she'd seen his eyes resting on a customer's wife's face or body for a bit too long. At those moments, she could feel herself shrinking inside, conscious that a disappearing act would be welcome.

Her outward reaction, however, was a creative imitation of what she believed would keep his interest in her intact. She would don her sweetest smile, cradle a tray of coffee and tea and sidle up next to the couple in Charlie's sale's grasp. She'd look directly at the woman, silently daring her to react to Charlie's stares, and then she'd twist her attention to the gentleman, making sure Charlie saw her taking precise care to serve his coffee "just so". It was a game, she knew, and while she acted the part, inside she was angry and uncertain. She would remember Mama's warning from time to time, but she'd emboldened herself, "I don't care what Mama thinks. I'm makin' my own decisions now."

As she slid into the soft front seat of Charlie's car, feeling his arm slide around her, pulling her closer, a prickle of fear invaded her chest more often than she liked. She was smitten with Charlie, but her uncertainly perched itself like a clipped bird on her shoulders and her conscience nagged at her. She had noticed Mama's demeanor of late. She looked tired and broken. When Sara was around, she would busy herself with household chores just as she had when Papa was away. They seldom spoke except for daily niceties, and Sara found herself almost missing her mother's nagging, but, as Sara had learned as a child, her mother was strong and tough. She had the reserve of an army force and would not be moved by anything if her mind was set. A pretense of civility gripped the household and Sara came and went at will. No questions were asked. No solicitous comments made. As time passed, Sara grew more ill at ease at home and chose to escape to Charlie, where she felt prized and pampered.

Not a day went by when Charlie failed to place a tiny gift of some kind on Sara's counter: a rose, a Hershey bar, a stick of gum, a folded note with scrawling letters telling her she was gorgeous, beautiful, ravishing, and wanted. On one brisk Friday afternoon he brought her a tiny kitten, a fuzzy black, weepy-eyed ball of innocence, nestled in a box, complete with red and silver ribbons. When Sara peeped into the box, and into the violet eyes, she was instantly in love.

Cuddling the kitten into her neck, she said, "Oh, Charlie. It's cute as can be, but I kain't keep it. I got nowhere t' put it."

"It'll be fine at yer place, on the farm."

"Oh no, Charlie. Not at my house. My mama hates cats with a vengeance. She thinks they're revoltin' an' evil. An' a black one! She'd have a conniption if I brung this home."

"Well, I reckon, yer goin' t' have t' bring it t' my place then. An' maybe I can git ya' t' stay too. What ya' goin' t' name it? Kain't let it go home without a name." Charlie softened his invitation.

"Midnight. It's Midnight fer sure."

"That's real nice," Charlie said as he touched the kitten gently. He added then very directly, "Let's go home, Sara."

It was the first time Charlie had suggested that she accompany him to the tiny house he rented not far from downtown. Moreover, his words had the tone of a direct order rather than a request. His eyes bore into hers at that moment and she felt as though he would have to tear her from the place where her feet were riveted. She was not sure she would be able to move from that spot. And then Charlie's hand was on her elbow. He tenderly placed the kitten back into the box and helped Sara slide her arms into her wool coat. In one smooth motion he positioned her scarf deftly around her neck, touching it lightly as he grasped her long hair. He collected the box with the kitten in one hand, and placed his arm around Sara pulling her snuggly toward his chest.

"Let's go, sugah. Let's go home. Me. You. Midnight."

Sara would recall that evening with mixed panic and unexpected pleasure.

At the house Charlie escorted her gently through the front door and into a small, dark living room. He turned on a small lamp which cast a filmy golden light over a divan, an overstuffed arm chair, a slightly worn ottoman, and a small coffee table on which the *Cam's Corner Register* lay unopened. It was a man's room dominated by browns and greens and smelling of cigar smoke. Yet it was cozy and inviting.

Charlie and Sara sat side by side on the divan watching Midnight frolic on the cushions, trying out his tiny, translucent claws on the weathered upholstery. In time he found the *Cam's Corner Register* and contentedly clawed it into shreds. When his job was done, he made a huge kitten-leap onto the arm chair, rolled into a tight ball, and purred himself to sleep. As Sara was watching him, she slipped softly into the crook of Charlie's arm feeling comfortable and at ease.

He sniffed her hair while toying with the long curls that hung below her shoulders. "Ah, ya' sure smell good," he said, and then gently he turned her chin toward him, kissing her, first with quick, eager pecks, and then lingering with a kiss that caused Sara to pull away with a tiny gasp.

"Oh my, Charlie. Ya' sure know what yer doin'. I never had a kiss like that."

"There's more where that comes from, sugah. Lots more," he murmured, beginning to breathe more heavily.

The kisses were long and wet and passionate. Sara felt Charlie's tongue dip into her mouth and she reciprocated hungrily, not fully aware of how she knew what to do. Charlie impetuously slid his arms beneath her sweater and clawed at her bra clasp, releasing it with ease. And then his hands were on her skin, skin that was growing warm and damp. He reached her ample breasts, touching them softly, almost reverently as if they were made of fragile porcelain;

then he pushed her slowly backward, his mouth not leaving hers. His hands began to roam her body, sliding beneath her skirt, along her thighs, until touching the softness that lay between her legs. She was moist there, very moist, and he made the decision for them that she was ready.

"I'm takin' ya' t' my bed, sugah. I want ya' s' bad." He pulled her up toward him and firmly but gently guided her into his bedroom. There he took time to slide her sweater slowly over her head, watching her brown locks cascade heavily onto her neck and shoulders as he dropped the garment to the floor. Her bra fell away and he looked hungrily at her exposed breasts and wide nipples. "Yer s' beautiful, Sara Mae. I'm goin' t' love ya' forever."

Though her hands were shaky, she unfastened her skirt then, pushing it from her hips to the floor. She wore only her panties. Charlie then took care of himself. He hastily unclothed and pushed Sara a bit harshly into the sheets. He was driven by anxiety that could not be deterred. She started to protest, as a nervous panic seized her, but he was on her then, pulling the panties off and tossing them aside. She wanted to tell him to stop, but her voice failed her. She could utter only a groan which he must have interpreted as sheer pleasure. His lips were everywhere – on her cheeks, her neck, her breasts and back to her lips. His kisses lost their softness and he bore down on her, smothering her mouth with his. She could feel his penis, hard and erect upon her abdomen and it took very little time to find its place between her legs. His gentle touch disappeared then and he hungrily lunged upon her, burying his shaft inside her. She squealed as an abrupt, sharp pain enveloped her. Her virginity was gone, and she could feel her body tighten as Charlie moved atop her, shoving in and out until he uttered his own cry. She felt his chest heavy against her and she wanted to shift her body beneath him, but he was there, on top of her still, unmoving now. The kisses had stopped.

Tears had welled in her eyes as finally he rolled away from her sighing heavily. She lay still for a moment, conscious of her beating heart and the pulsating blood that echoed in her ears.

This was not as she had imagined love making would be. Before this day, she had had virtually no viable information given to her about sex and the expectations of a man and now she felt dirty and ashamed. She was a rag doll stuffed under a dirty sheet next to a fellow she really did not know. She curled her naked body into a fetal position and sobbed into the crumpled pillow.

Charlie was bewildered. "I reckon I don't know what t' say t' ya', Sara Mae. Didn't ya' like it? I was good wasn't I? Why are ya' cryin'? Stop yer cryin' now."

"Take me home, Charlie," she pleaded, unsure of why she wanted to be there.

"Jist a minute, now, sugah. Ya' need t' stay with me. We ain't done yet. I got t' take ya' t' a place ya' never been."

"What?" Sara had not the foggiest idea to what he was referring.

"Jist give me time, now, sugah. It's goin' t' be all right. It's goin' t' be jist fine."

With Charlie's lust satisfied, he did what he needed to do. If Sara was going to be his girl, he had to make sure she would stay. He shifted into a second round of seduction.

Wrapped in Charlie's robe, Sara sat on the divan, with a warm hot-buttered rum cradled in her hands. Midnight had joined her and was curled up next to her bare toes. Charlie lit a fire in the fireplace and leaned rakishly against the mantle looking deeply at Sara as though he could devour her. He had worked hard to acquire that dreamy gaze and he knew it was effective; it had served its purpose many times before.

After several drinks and banter filled with lusty innuendo, Charlie again seduced Sara, this time on the floor in front of the crackling fire. His skillful hands and mouth explored her body and she absorbed his caresses. She was naked and glistening when he finally brought her to that point of pleasure she had never imagined possible. She lay weakly in the flickering light flushing pink from the heat, the rum, and a place of confused delight.

Charlie's dimpled grin showed his approval of her performance. Tossing two blankets over his back, he lay beside her and stroked her hair and back until they both fell into a fitful sleep.

Chapter Seven

"Yer goin' t' be in a heap a' trouble." The words Sara most wanted to deny were the ones that swirled in her head when she awoke, stiff and cold next to the smoldering fireplace. It was early morning, the sky not yet light. Charlie lay sprawled on his back still deep in sleep. Sara watched him and that familiar feeling of apprehension reappeared. He looked peaceful and pleased. Why then did she feel the opposite? She felt grimy, dirty inside and out, and was cognizant that she was caught in a predicament she stupidly had not foreseen. She didn't like this man. She didn't like herself.

She stood carefully and tiptoed into the bedroom, careful not to wake Charlie. Her head was aching and she felt a bit dizzy as she stooped down to find her clothes which were strewn around the floor. A strange musky odor and an odd smell like bleach permeated her nostrils. Her panties promptly absorbed a slightly bloody stickiness from between her legs. She quickly threw on her clothes and grabbed her coat, checking herself in the scratched hallway mirror. "Yer a sight t' be seen!" she thought, as she opened the door and slipped from the house into a hazy dawn.

She had to get home. It was where she belonged, but she was afraid. Never in her entire life had she been away from the familiarity and security of her home over night. Her mind swirled with made up explanations and ridiculous reasons for her absence. Her mama and papa would be alarmed and fretting. They would be waiting for her, lights on, coffee cups in hand, murmuring their worries to each other. She could picture the scene in her head as she walked the mile to the familiar farmhouse. They would be angry, but they also would be relieved. They would smother her with hugs, and bombard her with questions. She would be happy. She would be scared. She would be searching for words to justify her behavior. She would welcome Mama's wrath. She hurried along clutching her coat tightly around her, listening to the rhythm of her feet crunching the frozen turf as her pace quickened. Home. It had never held such importance to her.

And then she was there. It was dark. No lights welcomed her. No one greeted her as she stepped onto the wooden stoop, and the door would not give in to her push. In Cam's Corner no one ever locked doors. She had never owned a key, but this door was closed tightly and locked. She peeked through the cracked glass in the door into darkness. No one stirred inside, if indeed anyone was inside. She tiptoed across the porch and peered around the side of the house into more darkness. It was eerily quiet and then she heard a rustle near the thistles and weeds that leaned against the structure. Panic. She pushed her body firmly against the wooden slats and squatted hoping to make herself smaller. A profound cacophony of silence enveloped the place again then and she listened with intensity. Nothing. Her small frame slid down against the wall until she was sitting on her bottom and a faint moan broke the quiet. It was her own forlorn whimper that soon escalated into

an uncontrolled howl. With head in hands, she wept with unrestrained abandon. She had never felt so alone.
Above her cries, she heard the rustle again. Light was beginning to ease onto the horizon and through blurry eyes she could see two tiny shining globes near the ground beyond the stoop. Cautiously making its way toward her was the mongrel dog that had adopted the farm. A sniveling muzzle was poked into Sara's cheek and she looked at the brown curly-furred dog as though for the first time. She touched the dog's head and it sat down beside her as if it instinctively understood the worth of unfettered companionship. It was a moment Sara would not forget.

The dog's ears periscoped forward suddenly and the fervent face alerted Sara to morning noises inside the house. "Thank the Lord," she thought, standing on wobbly legs to knock on the front door which creaked open to meet her.

Mama stood, still in her flannel nightgown, on the braided throw rug just inside the door. "I reckon yer wantin' t' do some explainin', Sara Mae," she said, "but I ain't in a mind t' want t' hear ya'."

"Mama, I . . ."

There were no words.

"God help ya'. Ya' look like the wreck a' the Hesperus. Ya' come in now. Clean yerself up. Then yer goin' t' have t' git yer things."

Sara stared into her stern face and tired eyes not willing yet to understand Mama's unveiled judgment and sentence.

"I kain't have no whore livin' under my roof," Mama continued. "Ya' been taught t' fear God an' live a good, clean life. Jist look at ya'. It don't take much a mind t' see what ya' been up t', an' I'm ashamed. I'm ashamed a' ya'. If ya' were little, I'd give ya' what Patty gave the drum, but ya' ain't little an' I can tell by the looks a' things that yer a real woman now. I made mistakes I reckon in raisin' ya' up 'cause this ain't how I was expectin' ya' t' turn out."

Sara could see her Papa seated at the kitchen table, eyelids lowered and his chin resting at the top of his chest. He reminded Sara of a stranded sparrow defeated by the swirling winds of a storm. He sat motionless and did not raise his head to look in the direction of the intense one-sided tirade that his wife was inflicting like a knife into his clearly wounded daughter. Papa was a man of few words and fewer actions. It was as if God had simply given him a place on earth to stop and sit a spell. He would not come to Sara's rescue, or to Mama's.

"I said, 'git in here now.' Git yerself cleaned up. I kain't stand lookin' at ya' no more like this. Now go on in. Make yerself presentable."

Sara numbly passed through the doorway and down the short hallway to her childhood room. She fumbled to take off her clothes. When they lay in a pile on the floor, she kicked at them and stomped on them hatefully. She would dispose of them somewhere, anywhere. She would never wear them again.

Soaking in a tub of lukewarm water eased some of her tension but looking down at her nakedness made her self-conscious even at this solitary moment. Mama was making her leave, and she would. She would go without resistance. She had been resisting Mama for a lifetime, but now she would let go. Mama was ashamed of her. Mama didn't want her there. Sara had gone too far this time. Shame was a burden she hadn't wanted to gift her mama, but she had and she was certain Mama did not have the gumption in her to forgive. "Judge not that thou be judged, Mama," she thought, and then stifled the notion that she had a right to recklessly throw scripture in her mama's path.

The stark realization that she'd been asked in no uncertain terms to leave Mama's house filled Sara with sorrow that sucked her empty. She couldn't conjure any identifiable feeling. When she had lost before, as when Addie was murdered, she had been racked with deep grief which released itself in sobbing wails that she had to bury into her pillow. She had shuddered unstoppably as she imagined Addie's fear and pain, but now, in a second round of loss, she felt numb. Sara knew she had made a naïve choice with Charlie, and she regretted it deeply, but ironically it was Mama who had granted her lessons in resiliency and strength. Mama had been an apt teacher. Sara had watched and learned and was instinctively cognizant of the fact she would survive. Gathering her willful wits and guarded determination she would make her own way now. With her meager belongings placed neatly in a wooden crate, Sara stared around the tiny room where she had grown up. It was the last time she would ever see it.

❧

Sara was presentable, as Mama had insisted, when she left the house. Her long hair glistened and she wore a respectable suit, creating an image that would help her secure a room in Mrs. Gibson's boarding house in town.

"I love ya', Mama," Sara managed as she left.

"Yeah, I reckon ya' do." Although the words were cold, Sara was sure she detected a slight crack in Mama's voice as she said it.

Sara savored her walk back into town, even though the box she carried began to cut into her hands and she shifted it awkwardly to alleviate the sting from its pressure. Walking gave her time to think, not that she welcomed some of the thoughts that were spinning in her head. *"Mama's real mad. She ain't never goin' t' forgive me. An' Papa? What 'bout Papa.*

He ain't said a thing! Now I got t' face Charlie. Don't want that! Wonder if he'll be sellin' at the Ford place t'day. Wonder if he's mad. Bet he's goin' t' be bustin' all over hisself. I'm a silly girl. Mama says I'm a woman now. Bet those folks at work goin' t' know what we done. They're goin' t' see it in my face. I kain't hide nothin'. I feel real bad inside. Maybe Charlie won't talk t' me no more. Jist as well. An' where's Midnight? Bet I won't see him no more neither. I want that little kitten, even if Charlie give it t' me. I want it. Hope Mrs. Gibson's got a' empty room fer me. God, I sure hope so."

Sara's disjointed thoughts ended with a phantom glimpse of Addie, blond hair blowing lightly in the wind, blue eyes intense. "What would Addie say 'bout all this?" she thought. "She'd prob'ly say I'm a mess."

"I miss ya' Addie," she mumbled out loud. "I miss ya' so much."

Mrs. Gibson led Sara to a small room at the back of the boarding house. It was modestly furnished with a double bed covered with a colorful handmade quilt, a squat wooden chest of drawers, a small desk and straight cane chair, a lamp with shade askew, and an ice box, atop which were a hot plate and a few pans. And it was clean. Mama would have said, "Why, it's clean as a whistle," but she'd still touch the shelves to see if dust was hiding there. Sara instinctively did the same, all the time thinking, "This'll be all right. Guess it's goin' t' have t' be."

"Bathroom's down the hall," Mrs. Gibson said. "Ya' got t' share with the two other folks what live down on this floor. An ol' gentleman, Mr. Foster. Got a brace on his leg. Polio it was. Walks real slow, but he's pleasant enough. An' there's Shirley Walters. She works at that Ford place too. Does the books, I think. Always chatterin' 'bout who comes in an' who goes out. She's a talker, that one. Suppose ya' better watch what ya' do 'round her 'cause she's full a' the gossip. She knows 'bout ever'thing 'bout ever'body."

"Well, I thank ya', Mrs. Gibson. I reckon this'll do real fine. Jist me an' maybe my kitten. Can I have my kitten here?" she asked, hoping for Midnight's return.

"I don't much care fer cats. Can take 'em or leave 'em, but I reckon if ya' clean up after it, an' keep it out a' my way, it'll be all right."

"I thank ya' so much," Sara said to Mrs. Gibson's back, because she was already out the door. Sara heard her plodding footsteps on the stairs that ran alongside the building. Mrs. Gibson had the second floor to herself, and above a third floor had three more rooms which were rented out nightly, or weekly, or even for a month or two. The first floor was for the permanent renters, folks like Sara who'd be staying for awhile. The top floor, though, housed a carrousel of characters, male and female, coming and going, all carrying stories in their stances, tales etched in their faces.

Sara set her box of belongings on the bed and began to sort through them. On top was her hand mirror with mother of pearl handle, a matching hair brush, a lipstick, some rouge, and a tube of mascara. She had four skirts, four blouses, two sweaters, and her favorite summer dress. At the bottom of the box were her undergarments, one pair of black patent leather high heels, a Bible, a dictionary, some lined paper, and a pen. Stuffed in the corner were two pairs of old black cotton stockings. She had worn her brown flats and her navy blue suit under her flimsy black cloth coat. She'd have to take a little of her pay to buy a few necessities at the five and dime or the Kroger store. Food wouldn't be too much of a problem though. She wasn't much one for breakfast, she could make a sack lunch to take to work, and a home cooked supper was provided by Mrs. Gibson in the kitchen at the back of the second floor. Sara would learn to welcome the camaraderie created when the boarders all settled in for their evening meal.

Sara began arranging her belongings in the chest of drawers, laying each item neatly one on top of the other to eliminate wrinkles. She liked things to be in order. Mama never liked a mess either and used to pride herself on a freshly waxed linoleum floor and windows cleaned with newspaper and vinegar. "If ya' expect yer life t' be in order, ya' got t' start at home," Mama would say with conviction.

Though Mama was apart from her now, Sara found her by her side. She bristled at her own inability to leave Mama at home. From childhood, she had been infused with bits of homespun wisdom and made up truths generated and delivered authoritatively by Mama. "She's done made a nest up in my mind," thought Sara. "Kain't git her out a' my head. Got t' though. Got t' move on."

Sara physically tapped the sides of her head with the palms of her hands. "Ya' go on now, Mama. I got things t' do," she said aloud.

<hr />

Sara spent a quiet Sunday wandering around her little room, moving this and adjusting that to make it her own. She spent long minutes looking out the window at the clothes lines that sagged and flopped in the cold late winter wind. Mrs. Gibson took in laundry as part of her boarding service and on Monday morning the lines would be laden with damp clothes that had been wrung through the old wringer washer and pinned securely with wooden clothes pins. The ancient maple trees beyond the clothes line had been stripped bare and leaned a little this way and that in the erratic breeze. The sky was a cold silver-blue over which thin white cirrus clouds stretched threatening even colder weather and perhaps a little rain.

Sara napped restlessly, interrupting her sleep with thoughts about her tomorrow at the Ford dealership. She feared seeing Charlie. She imagined every scenario possible.

"*Why, Sara Mae Jenkins. What in the world have ya' been up t' all weekend?*" he might say, smiling radiantly, revealing the familiar dimples that were deep diminutive cavities in his cheeks. His question would make her blush and the accounting girls would be watching.

He'd march up to her counter, slap his hand down startlingly, stare into her face, and then lean aggressively toward her. With a scratchy whisper, he'd assert, "*Yer a bitch, Sara Mae. Yer no good.*" She knew she would cry then.

He'd slide up to her counter, and with eyes wide and innocent, say, "*Why, Sara Mae. Ya' done gone an' broke my little heart. I reckon I kain't live one more minute without ya'.*" This lie would not be lost on Sara. She'd been silly and naïve, but she also had been quick to discover that she need not be a victim of her own egotistical misguided actions.

He'd touch her arm, escort her to the door, step outside, and say as earnestly as he could muster, "*Sara Mae. I've been s' worried 'bout ya'. Why'd ya' slip out on me, sugah? We had a good time, didn't we? I need ya', Sara Mae. I still want ya' so bad.*" She would momentarily find herself falling for his charms again, but she would catch herself just in time.

Maybe he'd glance fleetingly at her and then twist his head away. He'd march into the dealership like he owned the place, flirt for a time with the accounting girls, and then strut out to the car lot.

None of those things occurred when Sara saw Charlie on Monday morning. He simply walked into the dealership, dressed sharply in his blue suit. As he always did, he was pleasant and handsome, greeting the other salesmen, and winking at the accounting girls. He did not look her way.

She watched him hand a small box to one of the mechanics, whisper something in his ear, and then walk into the manager's office. Sara could feel her face warm suddenly, and was conscious of a noticeable intensity in the volume and measure of the accounting girls' banter, but the merciful ring of the phone redirected her attention. "Cam's Corner Ford," she said with false cheerfulness. "How may I help ya'?"

The day went by quickly, and although Charlie passed through the showroom several times, he did not give Sara the time of day. She was strangely grateful for his arrogance, and by afternoon, she was breathing more normally and greeting customers as usual. The dealership closed promptly at 6:00 p.m. each day and on this cloudy, cold afternoon, Sara was more than ready to go home, to her new home, just a block away. She was conscious of having held her body tensely all day. Her neck was stiff and her shoulders ached as she reached for her coat that hung in the cloakroom. As she headed for the door, she glanced once more at her counter to make sure it was in order and noticed a box there. It was the one she had seen Charlie carry in that morning. She hesitated by the counter, looked around guardedly, and opened the box. When she peered into it, she was flooded with gratitude. Curled inside was Midnight, quietly resting on one of Charlie's handkerchiefs. She had her kitten. She would have hugged Charlie right then if she had seen him, but fortunately he already had disappeared into the evening dusk. It dawned on her that there could possibly be an element of good in his otherwise questionable character, but she hastily pushed that notion away from her thoughts. She had to stay mad. She wouldn't trust herself with him again. He had taken from her, but as she looked at the moist kitten eyes, she realized he had given her something too, much more than just a cat. While she would have loved to shout angrily that he had taken her innocence, she knew she had given it more freely than she would like to admit. Taking and giving created a tentative balancing act. It was suddenly glaringly clear to her. To keep herself in balance, she would have to take every experience, every memory, good or bad, and own it. She may not need to hold it close, but it couldn't be tossed aside either. The very person she had become had been under construction for many years. She had the choice. She could pick away at and destroy who she was, or she would become her own architect and add on to her own inimitable self.

Chapter Eight

The dreary days of winter seemed to make time crawl, exhausting everyone's energy and putting an edge on the dispirited people of Cam's Corner. Even on Valentine's Day, pallid pink seemed to dominate the vivid reds that represented love. Sara exemplified the times. The ill-fated relationship with Charlie had dipped to even further depths. Ignoring her was acceptable, but his bruised ego had led him to brutally launch into a desperate effort to malign her. Rather than talking to her, he made sure the mechanics in the shop and the salesmen on the floor knew she was easy. She became the recipient of off-color comments that stung severely. The accounting girls were privy to the gossip and giggled in her presence. She pulled into herself, but was able still to perform her job with aplomb. Though she was disheartened and dejected inside, she greeted the customers with manufactured joy and enthusiasm. She was the actress she had always hoped to be. She found strange satisfaction in this feat. After the days ended, she would walk home alone to her little room and the kitten that welcomed her with unqualified affection. It was in this little room that Sara found solace and began to make peace with herself.

Suppers with Mrs. Gibson and the others provided a respite from her never silent, ever active mind. Mrs. Gibson was a good cook who ate like a man. Her wide round belly was proof that she had enjoyed more than a few hunks of buttered corn bread or mashed potatoes smothered in gravy. Whether she fried chicken, made a beef stew, or baked a ham or roast, she made gravy. It was a mainstay. She cleaned her plate until it shone, sopping up every morsel with a homemade biscuit or hunk of bread. And then there were the pies – cherry, apple, apricot, mincemeat, and pecan, Sara's favorite. Mrs. Gibson wouldn't let anyone escape her kitchen without a hefty slice of pie. She was not a wealthy woman by far, but found intrinsic delight in giving through her gastronomic efforts. Sara figured it was a way for her to show love. She had no one else.

Joining Sara at Mrs. Gibson's table nightly were Mr. Foster and Shirley Walters. Mr. Foster took his sweet time working his way up the staircase to the second floor every evening, but he wouldn't accept help from anyone. Working his disability to an advantage didn't suit his character. Only under the most unusual circumstances would he accept a hand. He preferred to manage alone. He would proudly hobble into the kitchen, smiling broadly and perspiring slightly even in the cold. "One more mountain behind me," he'd say, and flop into a chair propping his crutch up next to him. He was full of stories of his youth, when his only concerns were stoking the fire in his daddy's cabin, hunting rabbits in the early morning mist, or frittering away a lazy afternoon down at the creek. He'd leave school most days at recess and amble down the banks of Turtle Creek to fish, or to swim in the deep hole that had formed at the base of a huge oak tree. "Had t' watch out fer snakes once in awhile," he'd say, "but other than a close call or two with a moccasin, it was heaven on Earth." When he was fifteen, he contracted polio. A year-long stint in the county hospital welfare ward saved his life, but left him with a twisted hip, a withered leg, and no daddy. He'd been on his own since he was sixteen. With a little help from the government, and Mrs. Gibson's charity, he had lived in the boarding house for thirty years. He was forty-six and looked sixty with graying hair and deep furrows in his forehead and cheeks. The bent back and hobbled leg added to the caricature of a broken man, but he was far from that. His unique spirit carried him. "Thank ya', God, fer another day," he'd say, and he'd mean it.

Shirley Walters, on the other hand, was, as Mama would have said, "a handful". She and Mr. Foster stepped on each other's words trying to get the floor. While Mr. Foster would issue his tales with genuine, though sometimes belabored detail, in a monotone, Shirley's voice would rise and fall breathlessly as she spread her gossip. She embellished her stories, rolling her heavily mascara laden eyes, and gesturing excitedly. "What a tattletale," Sara thought, and made up her mind to keep her distance from Shirley. Nosy people had always annoyed her and vexed her more subdued demeanor. Shirley was a big shot at the Ford dealership, managing the accounting department with quick-tongued barbs that put the younger girls quickly in their places. She had embedded herself as the company's finest bookkeeper having worked her way into her position of authority over twenty years. She was a ruthless boss who manipulated her "girls" with threats of gossip, and who had an affinity for the ones who modeled themselves after her. She knew everyone in town, especially if they owned a Ford. She was privy to private information few others had, and she used her knowledge as leverage whenever she needed to do so. In Sara's position as the counter girl, she could keep her distance, but she had learned to watch and to keep quiet when Shirley was around.

Even at supper, Sara offered little in the way of conversation. She actually enjoyed the daily dramas that the two other boarders provided. Mr. Foster approved of Sara's silence, construing it as her interest in his ability to weave a tale. Shirley Walters dismissed Sara as aloof and shy. Though she had heard Charlie's gossip, she recognized the source, and questioned its validity. To her, Sara was a detached and uninteresting girl who didn't rate her time. For Sara, that was a blessing.

With supper over, Sara would retreat to her room and cuddle her cat. Midnight had left his kitten phase behind and had grown into a handsome strapping feline. He strutted across the room, stretching his legs and demanding attention that was always forthcoming. Sara would pet him to sleep, and he would curl up or stretch out on the pillow next to her. In these quiet times, Sara's thoughts would venture to her mama and papa.

In the months since her exile, she had not visited her old home and had not been invited. She did see her mama from a distance on a cold Sunday morning in early March. A single day of bright blue sky and brilliant sun had pulled people from the doldrums and the congregation at Bethel Baptist Church had bulged, singing to the glory of God. The next day, the town was blanketed in eight inches of wet snow. The radio broadcasters spoke of the ominous weather with reverence and boasted that records throughout the South had been broken. Sara trudged to work in snow above her ankles, being careful not to fall. When she reached the Ford dealership she pushed through the doors into the welcome warmth, and into the arms of Charlie. He held her close, breathed into her hair, and spoke of love. "I love ya', sugah. I'm wrecked without ya'. Holy Jesus, Sara, let me have another chance."

Sara froze in his grasp.

"No, Charlie," Sara gasped, frightened by his presence and by the otherwise eerie silence of the building.
"Nobody's here, sugah. It's jist us. Nobody's comin' in t'day. It's jist us. Me an' you, like before. Ya' got t' let me have ya', Sara Mae. I ain't had nothin' else on my mind."
His lips were on her then, and he pushed her recklessly to the ground. She squirmed from his grasp and ran toward the door, but he grabbed her from behind, dragging her to her knees, and twisting her toward him. Her heart was pounding in terror as his strength overwhelmed her.
"Let me go, Charlie. Please. I'm tellin' ya', stop." Sara was trembling, and pushing with all the strength she could gather, but it was of no use. "Oh, God, please," she said to no one.
When it was over, Charlie stood up and looked down on her. "Thank ya' sugah. That was real fine," he said, his mouth distorting cruelly as he hitched up his trousers.
Sara could not look at him. She crawled on her knees to the safety of her counter and leaned against it adjusting her clothes and wiping her face. She heard the door open and close and she sat still, silent, and alone in the muted grey emptiness of the showroom. Seconds passed, and then minutes. Finally she stood and faced the door just as Shirley Walters brushed through, snow swirling through the entrance with her. Shirley stared at Sara's anguished face.
"What on Earth?" she said. Her image seemed to steam in the warming room. "What happened t' ya', Sara? Yer a sight!" She stopped speaking for a moment. One could almost see her thoughts churning. "Didn't I jist see Charlie out an' 'bout on the lot? He was 'bout t' git in his car when I seen him. Was he here, Sara?" She answered her own question. "Ah, he was wasn't he? What'd he do t' ya', Sara? Ah, ya' poor girl."

Sara had no choice but to fall into Shirley's arms. It was not a place she had ever wanted or expected to be, but for now it had to do.

※

Finding Sara that morning did something to Shirley. She would always be a relentless big mouth. She knew and even embraced her character, but on that snowy morning when she walked into the showroom and found the stricken girl standing mutely before her, she was overcome with a feeling she had never before had. No one had ever needed her in her life, but at that very instant, Sara did, whether she wanted to or not. Shirley was far from nurturing in her own view, but instinctively, she did just that. Cradling Sara in her arms, she guided her into her private office and pushed her gently into a wide leather chair. Once she was seated she scurried to the bathroom returning with a warm wet towel. She placed it in Sara's hands, "Use it on yer face, Sara. Ya' need t' calm yerself down. This'll help."

She turned then, lifted the phone, and called the sheriff.

Sara was interrogated as though she were a criminal. The sheriff who arrived in Shirley's office offered little in the way of comfort or consideration to the shivering girl. Sara recognized him as the man who had presided over the Gilbert affair years before. He was tall, and slightly overweight with a shirt that stretched over a taut belly. He was curt and gruff showing yellow, tobacco-stained teeth when, as she perceived it, he attacked her for the second time that day. Of course he didn't see it that way. He was doing his job as he saw fit. He leaned back on Shirley's desk, inconsiderately shoving papers aside as he directed a bevy of questions at Sara. "Why were ya' alone here? Were ya' waitin' fer someone? Was Charlie the man ya' were waitin' fer? Did he really surprise ya' or were ya' expectin' him? Are ya' tryin' to git him in trouble with the law? Did ya' engage in this action willin'ly?"

He looked at Sara squirming nervously in the chair and continued to question her ruthlessly. "Are ya' tellin' the truth here, young lady? Do ya' even got a notion a' what rape is? Do ya' understand the charge yer tryin' t' make? How old are ya' anyways?" Sara insisted she had told the truth, but the intensity of the questions brought on a new onslaught of tears.

"Them tears ain't goin' t' help yer case much with me, so stop yer snifflin'. I know yer the Jenkins gal an' I hear tell yer mama's done with ya'. Kicked ya' clean out a' the house, I hear. What'd be her reasonin' ya' reckon? It's mighty clear t' me it has somethin' t' do with how ya' been behavin'. So I'm tellin' ya' one more time. Ya' better be tellin' the truth."

"I am," Sara muttered.

"What ya' sayin', gal?"

"I said, I am," Sara nearly shouted.

"Well, the doc's goin' t' have t' confirm that, an' ya' know what that means, so ya' better be thinkin' twice 'bout what trouble yer causin'."

Sara stared at him wide-eyed, astonished by the bruising treatment she was enduring. Shirley could hardly contain herself. She was livid. Having doled out more malicious rumors than she could count, she always felt her victims had it coming, but this was wrong. Maybe because she had found Sara first; maybe because she knew the kind of man Charlie was; maybe because she had made the call to the sheriff; maybe because she cared for once, she found her voice. "Sheriff, with all due respect, Sir, ya' ain't bein' fair."

"I reckon it's none a' yer affair, Shirley," he snapped back. "An' what would ya' know? Ya' ain't exactly been the gospel a' truth yerself, if I understand correct-like. Are ya' in on this with her? Ya' two got somethin' in fer ol' Charlie there? Wouldn't put it past ya'," he alleged.

Shirley bit her lip to quiet her tongue. She darted past the sheriff and stood like a statue in the still showroom imagining the venom she could spit if the man inside didn't have the law behind him. She had been angry before, and felt fury's grip tightening her throat and silencing her. The verbal assault leveled at her personally was acid to her stomach. She wrapped her arms around herself, an unconscious self-comforting action, but next to her gut she clinched her hands into hard fists. It was all she could do to stifle a scream.

Inside the office, Sara had dissolved into a mess of tears and snot. The sheriff had belittled and harassed the girl until she caved. She would not press charges. "I need t' go home, now, Sheriff," she managed.

"Well git on, then," he responded, "an' try t' keep yerself out a' trouble, would ya'? I got better things t' do with my day then t' fool around with the likes a' you."

He stalked out of the room, passed Shirley standing in the shadows, and cast a hateful glare over his shoulder at her. "Let this be a lesson t' ya', girl," he said, knowing she had heard and not expecting a response.

Shirley mentally collected herself, gathered Sara's things, and Sara herself, and the two walked silently out the door onto the dirty sidewalk snow that had been smashed down by human traffic. The woman and the young girl held mittened hands like children and silently sloshed home together. Both of their lives had shifted and they were inexorably bonded, distinctly disparate women who before that day could not have fathomed a friendship.

At the boarding house where they lived, Shirley and Sara began to breathe a bit easier. In the safety of her room, Sara's words tumbled out with abandon until her emotions had been stripped bare. She told Shirley every detail of her encounters with Charlie, from the innocent beginnings to the vicious end. When she had no more words, she rushed out the door and vomited on her knees into the snow. Shirley held her hair out of the mess, and then gently guided her from the icy cold back into the warm little room. A wide-eyed Midnight watched from his pillow and settled down only when Shirley had helped Sara into bed and said good night. Impulsively Sara nearly asked her stay, to not leave her alone, but the words caught in her throat as she thought suddenly of her absent mother. With the bittersweet memory playing in her mind, Sara recalled Mama's vigilance the night of the Gilbert murders, and although sadness suffocated her, she had no more tears to offer.

"'Night, Shirley, an' thanks," she managed as the light snapped out and the door shut. Her head sank into the soft pillow and she willed sleep to follow, but rather than the comfort of her dreams, she stared into the dark until morning dawned.

Shirley Walters did one more thing for Sara Mae Jenkins. She saw to it that Charlie never set foot in the Ford dealership again. If she could have, she would have had Charlie banished from Cam's Corner altogether, but her power only extended to the boundaries of the dealership. She had what she called a heart to heart with the manager, Mr. Mason, telling him in no uncertain terms about Charlie's conduct both with Sara and with her girls in accounting. Unlike the sheriff, who had looked the other way, Albert Mason listened. Shirley filled him with details of myriad complaints the accounting girls had made concerning Charlie's unwanted advances, gross gropings, and tactless remarks. She painted him clearly as the monster he had become. Mr. Mason knew about the alleged rape and although he could not at first believe his best salesman could do such a thing, Shirley set him straight on the matter in nothing flat. The intensity of the attack on his favorite little counter girl made him uneasy and his thoughts drifted to his own innocent adolescent daughters. Shirley made sure he comprehended every facet of Charlie's overtures toward Sara, his manipulation, and his all too apparent calculated plan to deflower her. She ended with a description of the ruthless rape that Sara had endured. Her gift for embellishment did not play into her assertions. She simply reported the facts.

Albert Mason listened because he thought highly of Shirley. He had employed her for twenty plus years and knew he owed much of his wealth and success to her behind-the-scenes management of company transactions. He'd often boast, "Why, Shirley's my right hand man!" And he would laugh at his own misguided joke. "Don't know what I'd do without her. When she's not talkin' her head off, she sure gets crackin' an' does a real fine job, an' she's honest as the day is long."

He was right about that. Though Shirley held others at bay with her corrosive comments and sometimes bitter outlook, she had character. "She's a character with character," Mr. Mason would chuckle in her defense if an employee or customer complained about her crassness or her brusque manner. Sara had often marveled at his dedicated allegiance to Shirley, having watched their interactions from a distance. Only after her own recent connection with Shirley was she able to understand his almost reverent affection for her. Albert Mason was a pillar in the community with a lovely wife and four accomplished children, but Sara guessed that beneath that façade he was likely in love with Shirley. It was never spoken and neither would have ever acted on it, but their admiration for each other was clear.

Albert Mason delivered the news of Charlie's dismissal to him face to face, man to man. He felt he owed Charlie that much. Charlie's absence at the Ford dealership would have an impact on the business for a time, but Albert knew that when one person sank to the bottom or disappeared altogether, another would rise or seep in to fill the spot. He would miss Charlie's aggressive salesmanship, but after absorbing Shirley's story, the thought of Charlie on his premises was repugnant to him.

"Yer not goin' t' be welcome at my business any more, Charlie," he had told him, sadly, and the emotion that washed over him was indeed sadness, not because he was losing a once established friendship, not even because his business would be affected adversely, but because Charlie was a sick man, a man devoid of integrity, a man who could offer nothing but pain, a pain fueled by his own egotistical, destructive intentions. Albert was disgusted with himself as well. Why had he not seen this side of Charlie? How could he have been so blind?

Charlie's reaction was predictable. His face flushed red and his eyes quivered and darted to Albert's solemn face and then beyond into the foggy air behind him. Lacking the ability to focus, he lit then again on Mr. Mason's face, shuffled his feet nervously, and leaned closer, "This is 'cause a' that little bitch, ain't it? She put ya' up t' this? I should a' knew this was comin'. Yer goin' t' regret this, Albert."

"No, Charlie," Albert said calmly, "I will not. I do not regret this. Ya' can stick t' yer story. I'm not 'bout t' stop ya' doin' that, but I can stop ya' from dampenin' the doorstep a' my business ever again. I came here t' offer ya' a courtesy, but it looks like ya' don't have it in ya' t' be civil, so ya' go on 'bout yer business, an' I'll take care a' mine. A box with yer things'll be delivered t' ya' this afternoon. Take a look at yerself, Charlie. Ya' need t' take a good, close look. Ain't nobody goin' t' have t' face ya' in the mirror but yerself."

He left then, left Charlie standing in the door frame, a picture of rage and foul malevolence.

Chapter Nine

With the advance of spring, and Charlie's absence from the Ford dealership, Sara began to feel a sense of tenuous comfort. She had gained a new friend in Shirley and new respect from the girls at work. The incident with Charlie was an odd way to earn recognition, but people treated her differently. Whether it was due to compassion, awe, or just curious interest, Sara had risen to a new status with a reputation for courage and a new-found popularity that she lapped up like a hungry puppy. She sparkled at work, was energized at home, and even laughed at her own boldness when she butted into the conversations at Mrs. Gibson's supper table. Mr. Foster and Shirley suddenly had another person in competition for the floor. "But, but, but . . ." she would interject until she had her say. Supper was her favorite time. She looked forward to the animated conversations and senseless debates that never ceased and always entertained. She was certain the others at the table felt the same.

Shirley was the first real friend Sara had had since Addie's death, and while she loved the companionship of the older woman, an inkling of fear tiptoed around her mind at times. She remembered her promise to herself never to let anyone close to her again. Addie's death had been almost too much to bear; and there had been other losses too. Mama was one, and Papa too, really, although they had never been close. Mama had rejected Sara completely it seemed. Early on, Sara had attempted to communicate, but her letters and phone calls were unanswered. The letters were never returned though, so she retained a morsel of hope that Mama would renege on her ostracism and call her home.

"Come on back, Sara Mae," she would imagine her mama saying. "I reckon ya' learned a good lesson, s'ya' need t' come on back home where ya' b'long. Yer daddy an' me'll be waitin'. We'll have supper ready. Bring yer things with ya'."

Yet her muddled musings did nothing but confuse her further. Even in her dreams her mama would appear. *Wearing the navy blue voile dress she saved for Sunday church services, Mama approached Sara as she sat alone on the cold, empty steps of the court house where Papa used to sit. She tapped her on the shoulder, startling her for a moment, but the fear melted immediately into relief and joy. When Sara turned and looked into Mama's eyes she could see she'd been crying. Mama never cried. Why was she crying? "Come on home, now Sara Mae," she said softly. Sara reached for Mama's outstretched hand, but she vanished in front of her. She heard laughter from far away, and then she heard a sobbing child.*

The laugher disappeared with the dream when Sara sprang up suddenly wide awake. The sobs, however, were real. They were her own. A variation of this dream was replayed in Sara's subconscious almost nightly. As a result, she suffered the rejection and the loss of her mother over and over again. The dreams were ominous and disturbing, in clear opposition to the serenity Sara had begun to enjoy in her daily life.

Sara shared her dreams with Shirley and Shirley listened just like Mama used to do. The difference was, however, that Shirley did not judge. She just heard, and that in itself was comforting. No one except Addie had ever just let Sara be Sara. It stood to reason, then, that despite the age difference the two women had become fast friends. They would talk well into the night, they would shop on Saturdays, they would walk to work together, and they would even share the current gossipy news that continuously circled among the accounting girls, the salesmen, and even the mechanics at work. In the evenings they often would meet for a game of gin rummy. Sometimes Mr. Foster and Mrs. Gibson would join them and the competition to win became as spirited as their supper conversations.

"Why ya' ol' skunk!" Mrs. Gibson would say playfully accusing Mr. Foster of cheating.

"Well, I'll be darned, Shirley. Ya' done gone out on us again!" Mr. Foster would moan mockingly and thump his crutch up and down on the floor in protest. "Ya' make me s' mad I could spit!"

The jabs were all in fun though. The warmth and harmony lasted well into June when Sara was delivered a blow for which she was mercilessly ill prepared.

On the last day of spring when the days were lengthening and the evenings retained the warmth of the sun, Sara's thoughts turned to home. Shirley had left to visit old friends in Memphis, so Sara's evenings were spent alone with Midnight purring in her lap or rubbing relentlessly around her ankles. The nights were balmy now and Sara liked to lie on the top of her bed without covering herself. Crawling into sheets that felt damp from the heavy humid air made her uncomfortable and edgy, exacerbating her troubling dreams. On a particularly quiet night, Sara heard shuffling in the hallway, muted voices, and then a low tap on the door. She was startled, but not afraid.

"Yeah? Who is it?" she asked.

"Sara? Ya' awake?" It was Mrs. Gibson's voice.

"Yes, Mam. I am," Sara answered.

"Need t' talk t' ya' fer a minute, honey," Mrs. Gibson said through the door.

"Be right there," Sara answered as she slipped into her pink chenille robe. Her stomach lurched with instant apprehension and she could feel her heart begin to pound more heavily as she opened the door and saw Mrs. Gibson with that awful sheriff standing behind her.

"Honey, sheriff needs a word with ya'," Mrs. Gibson said. Her face was drawn and concern was written in deep lines of ashen grey and pale pink. A rosy tinge had reached her cheeks and she bit her lip without realizing it.

The sheriff got to the point.

"Yer mama's dead," he said bluntly. "Yer papa woke up with her cold beside him this mornin'. Don't know the cause. Doc Miller spent a spell over t' the house but I reckon they done took her t' the morgue, basement a' the hospital. Yer papa's done left the place. Said he kain't be there without her. He was shakin' real bad. Reckon he didn't know the goodness what he had right before him. Yer mama was a real fine woman, I hear tell, an' yer papa was howlin' real sad-like when I seen him last. Don't know where he high-tailed it t' but reckon he'll turn up come t'morrow. Been takin' care a' the death scene purty near all day, but reckon'd ya' needed t' know yer mama's gone now. Did find her Will stacked up with her Bible an' some other papers. Judge'll be readin' that in a day or two."

The sheriff babbled on inconsiderately without the slightest concern for the anguished young woman in front of him. "Yer a big girl now. Yer goin' t' have t' make the best a' things an' git on with it."

"Things" or "it" were empty words that mirrored how Sara felt inside. She stared blankly at the sheriff and an indiscernible volume of hate bubbled up into her throat and caught there. She couldn't say a word, but in her mind she wanted to lash out at the callous, indifferent man standing before her. Replacing the immediate void of emotion was a quickly escalating combination of rage, shock, and sadness that were released in her hands that twisted into fists. She began beating her pillow viciously.

Mrs. Gibson reached for the girl and tried to soothe her. She looked up at the officer before her with a questioning look. "What must I do?" she thought silently delivering the words with her eyes.

A blank stare met her sad eyes. The callous retort would never leave her memory. "I reckon I ought not be privy t' this outburst," the sheriff said to Mrs. Gibson. "I'll be movin' on now. Got more pressin' matters."

And he was gone.

Mrs. Gibson, spelled from time to time by Mr. Foster who had heard the fracas and had hobbled down the hall in concern, stayed with Sara throughout the night. She bathed her face with warm towels, provided hot tea, rubbed her back, and even petted Midnight who would not leave Sara's side. Mr. Foster stood by, numb with lack of sleep, but honorable in his assumed responsibility to support the two women.

The next day, Mrs. Gibson accompanied Sara to the homestead, just to look. They walked silently. The beauty of the day, the first day of summer was stunning. The sky was deep blue and filled with puffy white cumulus clouds that floated along, connecting, separating, connecting, separating, in random arrangements that drew pictures in the sky. The fields next to the road were deep green, a color that would be sustained with summer rains. Birds were flitting about busily tending their nests, while a red-tailed hawk positioned itself on a telephone wire, staring intently at the ground below, seeking its next tasty morsel. Cows, black and white giants, ruminated contentedly in grass that rubbed against their legs as they moved slowly in the intensifying summer warmth. They would gather soon at the base of the maple trees that lined Turtle Creek and lie there basking in the cool, avoiding the afternoon heat.

When they reached the house, Sara began to sob softly, but the cries were more for the place than for the people who had lived there. This is where she had grown up. She walked completely around the house, gazing at the weathered wood, the chipped brick fireplace, the cracked front door window, and the slanted addition that had housed the tiny bathroom at the back of the house. She recalled Mama's joy when the bathroom had been completed and the outside outhouse torn down and plowed under. No more wandering to the back yard on cold mornings and no more slop jars under the beds. It was a wonder to behold for Mama who had never enjoyed many luxuries in her life.

Sara finally settled on the front stoop. She did not want to enter the house, and could not have anyway, for three boards had been nailed across the entryway; a swash of black paint warned "No Trespassing" in crooked letters. She gestured for Mrs. Gibson to join her and the two sat for a few minutes in silent companionship. As they looked out on the abundant weeds that covered the front yard, Sara heard a familiar rustle coming from the side of the house. She turned to see the mongrel dog slowing inching her way. Mrs. Gibson noticed it too and immediately grew concerned. She wasn't afraid, but worried.

"Is this yer dog, Sara?" she asked.

"Well, yeah, I guess it is. He jist come 'round here years ago, a stray, an' jist stayed on," Sara explained. "He's a' ol' boy. Real sweet though."

"What's goin' t' happen t' him now, I wonder," Mrs. Gibson mused.

"Don't know. Reckon he'll find a new spot t' settle or jist go off. Kind a' sad though."

"Kain't we take him back t' my place?" Mrs. Gibson surprised Sara with her question.

"Sure. He don't really b'long t' nobody. Mama used t' feed him scraps. Never let him in though. Smells like heck."

"I'm a' ol' sap when it comes t' dogs," Mrs. Gibson said then. "Used t' have a' ol' Collie dog. Lived t' be fifteen. Then it up an' died one day an' I been without ever since. Maybe this ol' boy could fill in fer a spell. Reckon he don't have a lot a' years left, but he'd be a nice figure on the back porch."

Mrs. Gibson really did like dogs, but she also thought having this particular one around the boarding house would give Sara a touch of the familiar, and she'd enjoy its company too. The dog was all too happy to have some companionship and cheerfully accompanied them back to town where he did indeed become a fixture on Mrs. Gibson's back porch, absorbing affection from everyone who passed through her back door. Mrs. Gibson was the best thing that ever happened to that old dog and the dog knew it.

Sara's mama's Will was read a few days after her death and burial in the county's welfare cemetery. She left her house and lot to the Bethel Baptist Church. Papa got the rickety old truck, and Sara was willed Mama's old tattered Bible, a gold locket devoid of photos, and two hand embroidered pillow cases.

Sara moved away from Cam's Corner in the early fall when the winds were balmy and the sun dimly glowed through hazy skies. Without her mama, she had nothing to hold her there and although she had never been a terribly ambitious person, she knew what a dead end was. She was going nowhere there. Cam's Corner, complete with its characters, villains, friends, and family had formed her. It had given and taken. It had provided her a birthplace, folks who loved her as best they could, and a few friends, some of whom were snatched away ruthlessly and others who were placed in her hands compassionately. It had swallowed her youth and had spewed her into adulthood in a cold, hard, pitiless manner that had softened her sensibilities but had hardened her edges.

She said a sorrowful goodbye to her boarding house friends, crying into Shirley's neck until it was wet with her tears. Mr. Foster leaned on the door frame for support looking as if the whole world had come to an end. His eyes glistened, his lips quivered, and his knuckles blanched on the head of his crutch as he fought to keep his balance.

"I'm sure goin' t' miss ya', Sara," he said earnestly.

"Ya' jist don't have t' go." Mrs. Gibson added. "Ain't this been a good home fer ya'?"

Sara shook her head in agreement, but said, "Ya'll have been the best, an' I kain't thank ya' enough, but somethin' inside is tellin' me t' move on. I kain't stay here no more an' chance seein' my papa out at the courthouse makin' his home on the steps there or tossin' his blanket in the dime store doorway fer an evenin' nap. It jist don't sit well with me. An' Charlie's still hauntin' the corners a' town. Seein' him turns me inside out. My mama's gone now an' I didn't git t' say my good-byes. I jist want t' go somewhere new."

She reached then for Midnight and her sobbing racked her to her core. She would have to leave him too. Shirley would take him and eagerly so. She had developed a genuine affection for the big black cat that had taken to wandering from Sara's room to hers searching for warmth and cuddling. She would give it all the love she could. Shoving Midnight gently into Shirley's arms, Sara turned then, picked up her overstuffed suitcase and walked down the hallway and out the door into the filtered sun.

She did not look back.

Part Two

Chapter Ten

Sara Mae Jenkins gave her daughter many gifts, the first of which was life. A tiny baby girl was born two years after Sara had left Cam's Corner in a tiny room in the east wing of Mercy Hospital on the outskirts of Nashville, the result of an ill-fated love affair with a soldier stationed in Smyrna. Sara had revealed this much. *"He was s' handsome I was likely near t' swoon jist lookin' at him. One glance from him could git under my skin like nothin' else could. He had a shaved head, a' course, 'cause he was duty-bound, but his brown eyes, ah, they twinkled, an' they sparked with gold flecks when the light was jist right. He was a real gentleman. Brang me flowers, opened doors, an' he'd hold my hand in the park or slide his arm over my shoulder at the movie. Times like that would make my toes curl! I reckon I fell fer him 'cause he was s' simple an' sweet. One day he met me with a sweepin' bow an' kiss on the hand s' soft I had t' look t' see if it was happenin'. An' he was always good fer a quick peck on the cheek, or a wink an' a grin. He was a boy in a man's body I reckon, an' I let my guard down."* Sara had fallen for him despite the intentional caution she had imposed upon herself just a few years earlier.

Orders to Europe interfered with the courtship and despite definite qualms Sara and her beau slipped into Sara's single bed one warm summer night in August and made love. Three months later, on the day after he was bussed to Chicago for a flight overseas, Sara realized she was pregnant. Her young soldier never knew that his baby girl was born on the first day of summer the following year. Sara named the infant Sheila Masie Jenkins. Shelia because Sara just liked it. Masie, because it was akin to Mason, Sara's first boss, who had given her a chance and had believed in her, and Jenkins because it was Sara's birth name. It was one thing they would share for a lifetime.

Sara and her daughter were a twosome, by fate and by choice. Through the years of Sheila's childhood her mother nurtured and cared for her. She read stories and made up stories. She sang songs. She drew pictures. She taught her daughter to be proud. "God made ya' perfect, Sheila. He don't make no mistakes, so feel good 'bout yerself," but then she would add another thought. "Pride's a sinful thing, Sheila. It don't help ya' 'long much in life."

Sara was full of her own versions of what wisdom was, but it could have been debated whether she really believed them all herself. Her own mother had been infinitely preachy she recalled a bit resentfully, but ironically, and somewhat subconsciously, she was carrying on the tradition whether she liked it or not.

In spite of all the maxims and principles she imposed on Sheila, her little girl listened more often than not. She'd kick a few ideas into the wind, but if the truth be told, her mother was right time and again, and Sheila believed she delivered her version of reality as she saw it, right or wrong. So because she listened and because she believed in the goodness of her mother, they became best friends. Of course Sheila had her own group of pals at school – Sharon, Elaine, Joan, and Melanie, but she always enjoyed being home with her mother. In the spring they planted gardens and smelled flowers and in the summer they picked strawberries and blackberries to make jam that never quite jelled. It always seemed to boil up into a syrupy mess that they'd look at skeptically, but enjoy anyway, pouring it over pancakes or slathering it on hot biscuits. One summer they adopted a kitten and named it Sunny. The furry little orange ball was offered up for free in a basket at the Kroger store. When Sara saw the kitten she oohed and ahed, looked at Sheila with sparkling eyes, and snatched it up and into her arms. It inched its way with tiny claws to her neck where it purred itself to sleep. Sara was crazy about cats and with Sunny to love and entertain them, Sheila followed suit.

Sara Jenkins was a hard worker. She had a good job at the J. J. Newberry store managing all the girls who ran the cash registers or served up lunch plates piled full at the sit-down counter. And she ran the boys too, making sure they combed their hair, tucked in their shirts, wore their belts, and stocked the shelves with care. She couldn't stand to see a messy shelf when she perused her tiny domain. She had worked her way up from a luncheonette waitress to assistant manager because she was sharp as a tack and good with people. She could tell a shop lifter off with her eyes and was quick to establish a reputation for perfection. The J. J. Newberry store was stocked to the brim with all the items a person could want, from wooden spools of colorful cotton and silk thread and countless swatches of bright, gaudy material, to nail polish and make-up. Along the back wall were shovels, rakes, hammers and other tools that would make a man's heart sing. And the modern woman of the day could find mops, brooms, and cleaning supplies galore. There was an ample assortment of fishing equipment and sporting goods as well as stacks and racks of cheap clothing that sold quickly to families who were watching their pennies.

While her mother worked, Sheila was at school. Sara was a stickler about school. She told her little girl that if she wanted the good things in life, she needed to be educated. Sheila didn't let her down. She liked school and learned what she needed to know from her teachers; when at home, she learned much more from her mother. Sara wanted Sheila to be smart and strong and sure. She was an adoring mother, and as the years passed she and her daughter saw eye to eye more and more. They shared thoughts and fears and dreams. More than a few times a faraway look would overshadow Sara's face.

"One a' these days, Sheila," she'd say, "I'll have a nice big house fer ya' t' play. Ya'll have yer own room an' a big ol' canopy bed with a pink an' white satin bedspread. Ya'll have teddy bears an' dolls an' all the things a little girl could ever hope t' want."

Yet the years sprinted by and Sheila was quickly beyond dolls and bears. She just wanted to know about life and love. She was inquisitive about her mother's life too, so would ask, "Mother, what was it like when ya' were little?"

Sara evaded Sheila's questions focusing instead on the young face before her. "What are yer thoughts? What are yer dreams? What d' ya' want t' be when ya' grow up? Are ya' happy? Would ya' be happier if we lived in a big ol' house in the country? Why d' ya' want t' know s' much 'bout me?" Sheila had to beg and beg for a glimpse of her mother's past, and in time Sara relinquished the gift of her childhood. While she was silent about much, she delivered what she could.

When her mother reviewed her early life she described Cam's Corner's charms and appeal in detail. Her eyes would beam to the ceiling as she told of crisp winter mornings that formed ice crystals on the window panes, of the smell of hickory chips and cedar logs that raged and burned until they fell into powdery ash, of the fresh spring fragrance provided by crocus, freesias, lilac, and budding roses, of sultry hot summer days where simply moving made her sweat, and of the fall when an avalanche of color – reds, yellows, golds, maroons, and innumerable shades of browns and greens – were candy to her eyes. She talked about traipsing down to Turtle Creek, skirting the voluminous cow patties that dotted the pasture adjacent to an expanse of pussy willows and thick thickets of brambles and weeds where snakes and sparrows, hawks and skunks, field mice and jack rabbits lived in anxious harmony. She remembered the sky mostly. At night she would lie on a blanket in the yard or lean against her mama's knees on the front stoop and gaze at stars, bright and flickering, too many to count. Fire flies would flit about in the dusk, beacons of energy that she would capture and stuff into a mason jar, just for fun. On a summer day, fluffy cumulus or wispy cirrus clouds would play in the sapphire sky. In winter the clouds would darken, sliding together to form a damp grey nimbus mantle that pelted rain and sometimes offered flakes of snow that would flutter around in airy disarray or pummel down heavily, sticking to the cold ground and drift along the sides of the houses and hillsides. Sara could paint nature's pictures in Sheila's mind better than anyone else. She would listen to the lilt of her mother's voice and watch the widening of her eyes as she embellished Cam's Corner's allure. While Sara vividly remembered the beauty, Sheila sensed Cam's Corner held repugnance for her as well.

"Cam's Corner was a little spot in the road," her mother would say. "Full a' prideful, church-goin' sinners who didn't know right from wrong sometimes. My own mama was one a' 'em. Oh, I loved her, but she must a' determined before I was born that she was right, no matter what. I had t' live by her rules or she'd git the switch. We could disagree on jist 'bout anythin' an' I'd want t' argue but it didn't do me no good. She'd always have the last say. An' my papa would jist sit back an' watch. He never said nothin'. Or he'd go off somewhere, usually t' the courthouse with a bunch a' other bums. He'd lean back on them stone steps, rain or shine, an' stare off int' nowhere. He was a thinker, that man, but he never done much action with his thinkin'. Fer Mama, I reckon he was a disappointment, but she'd take him back ever' time he'd wander home. 'I'm so hungry, Emma, my stomach thinks my throat's been cut,' he'd say. She'd feed him an' he'd do a chore or two t' thank her. She ruled the roost though an' it must a' cut int' his soul 'cause he was a spiritless man. 'No backbone,' Mama would say."

"We buried Mama in the cemetery outside a' town, Papa an' me. Jist a few folks come by t' pay their respects. Papa didn't have much t' say t' me. Reckon he thought I was the cause a' her dyin'. Maybe so, but I ain't apt t' dwell on that nonsense. Mama died defendin' her way a' thinkin'. Wasn't nobody goin' t' change that."

Sara would talk in riddles sometimes, never quite finishing her tales, leaving her daughter wondering and confused. What Sheila did know, and believed was true, is that when her mother left Cam's Corner she had hoped to leave behind the memories that had set up house inside her. Besides burying her mama, she had lost a friend, "in a senseless act a' human conduct gone awry," she'd say, but she'd end it there. Her friend was Addie. She revealed that much, but when she lingered too long on her recollections, Sheila could actually watch her face fall, eyes directed downward, mouth drawn and tight, and her chin dipping into her neck. Her body would tense and then she'd change the subject.

"Had some nice friends when I lived at the boardin' house," Sara said. "They're gone now, but we had some times t' remember. Little treasures they were."

Sheila loved it when her mother recalled the good times because she could recreate memories so vividly that the two of them would lean into each other as though they were right there enjoying the warmth of the moment again together, or they would fall into ripples of laughter as she remembered the antics of her boarding house companions or her cat she called Midnight. Her friends had taught her loyalty and compassion and thoughtfulness. They had also given her courage to survive the bad times too. "Whenever I'm feelin' blue," she'd say, "I recollect my times with Shirley or the courage a' ol' Mr. Foster who must a' been in pain pretty much from sunrise t' sundown. He wasn't one t' gripe 'bout nothin'. He was crippled ya' know. Think it was the polio, an' he was jist happy t' be breathin' in the good air. An' Shirley? Well, I reckon I learned more from her than anyone else a' 'em. In the beginnin' I seen her as a loud mouth an' a hateful gossip but when the truth be known, she was a jewel, jist like a perfect gemstone. Why Mr. Mason, who owned the Ford dealership, thought the world a' ol' Shirley, an' after a spell, 'specially after she helped me over a bad spot, I had t' set aside all my notions an' give her a chance. An' she give me one too. If the truth be known," she added, "she was jist like a sister. Least I think she was like that bein' as I never had no sister, no brother neither. But I wouldn't a' traded Shirley in a month a' Sundays fer anythin'."

"Not all folks are good," she'd unexpectedly say. "Had t' learn that the hard way an' bein' intelligent an' bein' smart 'bout folks jist ain't the same. Guess ya' got t' take the bad with the good, but the bad ones can sure sour yer soul." Sheila would watch her face darken as she dredged up unwelcome thoughts, but she would say no more. Sheila suspected her sadness had something to do with a love story, or the lack of one, but putting the puzzle pieces together was impossible. Now and then her mother's facial expressions betrayed her, because beneath a wan smile that encouraged a belief that all was well, she would gaze out the window for minutes on end. Her eyes would moisten and then close, her head would tilt to the side, and her mouth would twist tight to hide quivering lips. What Sheila was not likely ever to understand was that at those moments she was suffering from the inexorable sting of an intense and terrible time that had left a permanent wound.

Sheila would feel bad for her mother then. She wanted to comfort her and take care of her at times like these. It was a troublesome instinct that she would have to conquer some day.

While Sara had her moments of sadness, most of the time she would keep herself very busy. She was wrapped up in her work and in Sheila's affairs. She loved hearing about school, about friends, even about her daughter's budding interest in boys, but as Sheila grew older, she began to notice edginess to her mother's questions.

"Where ya' off t', Sheila? I want ya' home before dark. Are there goin' t' be boys there? Is Sharon's mother goin' t' be at her house? I'm not too sure 'bout that woman's motherin' skills. An' that awful Donna Lynn ain't goin' t' be there is she? She's a bundle a' trouble waitin' t' happen, the way she dresses, skirts too short, knees showin' above her socks. Buys her mascara at the J. J. Newberry by the bushel. Yer judged by the company ya' keep ya' know," she'd say, wearing out the overworked adage. "Be careful, now, young lady. I mean it."

Sheila had just turned fourteen. She was really just a girl, but her mother explained in no uncertain terms that she had become a woman now and had to be very careful. A patch of dark blood in Sheila's underpants was something of a surprise, but after a heart to heart she understood. The new awareness made her feel grown up and satisfied, but it was like a stomach punch to her mother. Worry suddenly seemed to be Sara's constant companion sitting on her shoulder like an injured hawk. She became a little more distant and much more vigilant and so inquisitive Sheila began to resent her prying.

"Ya' have t' be s' cautious, now, Sheila. It's s' easy t' git pregnant. Ya' need t' be real watchful a' yerself, an' the boys 'round ya'."

Sheila grew so nervous about getting pregnant, she wasn't sure she'd ever talk to a boy, much less let one touch her. And what about being married some day? She could never let a boy see her naked. She began to feel self-conscious and a little bit embarrassed about her growing breasts and curving hips that were accentuated in the short skirts that were becoming the rage.

Her girlfriends were a Godsend. Before their slumber parties Sharon would slip cigarettes from her daddy's pocket and they'd all try a fag, as they called them, sucking in the smoke and sophisticatedly puffing it out the way they'd seen in the movies. Elaine and Sheila would cough until they choked while Sharon blew perfectly rounded smoke rings into the air. She'd been practicing. They drank Coca Cola by the gallon and ate bags of Fritos dipped in melted Velveeta cheese. They donned their baby doll pajamas, rehashed the latest gossip from school, and chattered into the night about all the boys they thought were cute, and the hoods who made them feel creepy. Elaine was crazy about Billy, Sharon was going steady with Joe, and Melanie, Joan, and Sheila were just looking. They all shared newly found interests in their changing bodies, boys, and sex. The girls all laughed when Sheila told them she used to think babies came from kissing, but Sharon set them straight. Sharon would draw pictures on a paper explaining just how babies were made. The x's would go here and the y's would go there. She was a genius in anatomy and physiology. She knew everything! The rest of the girls listened respectfully and vowed together that they would be virgins until they were married.

Sara provided Sheila with Kimberly-Clarke pamphlets that explained the menstruation cycle and she was relieved to find her girlfriends equally as interested as they poured over the pages, giggling and blushing even with each other. Sharon was more aloof. She had been having a period since she was eleven. She seemed almost arrogant occasionally waving her maturity like a flag.

In March when Elaine was shuffled off to live with her grandmother in Chattanooga, Sharon didn't bat an eye, but Melanie, Joan, and Sheila were openly agitated and troubled.

"She's goin' t' have what she wants now, I guess," Melanie said. "I told her Billy just wanted one thing an' she gave in. Why'd she do it? She swore t' me she wouldn't."

Melanie shook her head feeling deceived by the new revelation.

"She just always wanted somethin' t' love an' now she's goin' t' have her own little baby," Joan added trying to justify Elaine's predicament.

"Reckon she's goin' t' be stuck with that responsibility for a long, long time, 'less she gives it up, but she's not likely t' do that. Her daddy might make her though. Elaine's folks don't like t' be singled out, an' right now ever'one's lookin' their way. Saw her mama yesterday an' she wouldn't even look my direction. Suppose she's too embarrassed by what Elaine's gone an' done." Sharon had a way of slicing into a person's character seeming to enjoy the festering aftermath.

Sheila was on the verge of saying how much she wanted to give Elaine a hug and tell her she'd be fine, but Sharon's comment had silenced her. When the afternoon fell into evening she hurried home with the shocking rumor on the tip of her tongue.

Her mother was undone by the news of Elaine's pregnancy when she told her. At first Sheila thought she was just projecting the fear of the same fate on her and she coiled in anger.

"Well, it's not me!" she said, resenting her mother's accusing attitude.

"Ah, Sheila. I know. I know. But she's s' young. Jist fourteen."

"Fifteen!"

"She's still s' young an' she's goin' t' have the burden a' that child with her whether she keeps it or not. Givin' it up won't be easy, but I suspect it might be best. Havin' a baby takes yer freedom from ya'. Ya' got t' give ever'thing t' the baby an' more often than not, nothin's left. I know, Sheila. I been there." Sara's body stiffened suddenly and she stopped speaking. She stretched her arms in Sheila's direction though she was much too far away to touch. She most certainly had seen the stricken look on her daughter's face because she rapidly began to backtrack. "Not that I ever regret a second a' havin' ya' in my life. It's been a blessin' an' I wouldn't trade ya' fer anything. It's jist that havin' a baby causes a big change in yer life. A big change."

Sheila stared at her mother not wanting to believe what she was hearing. Did she mean it? Was a baby a burden? Had she been a burden? She was suddenly awash in the realization that her mother had suffered the same dilemma years before that Elaine was faced with now. Her mother had had a baby out of wedlock. She had never really given much thought to the way she and her mother lived. They had each other and that's all that seemed to matter. She didn't miss having a daddy because she'd never known one. Her daddy didn't have a name because her mother had never revealed it and where he lived was a mystery too. Sheila and her mother had always been such companions, such pals. The thought that her mother might ever have rejected her or resented her had never entered her mind. Considering either as a possibility made Sheila shudder inside and she looked at her mother anew.

Sheila's lingering stare was lost on her mom. Sara had turned her back and had busied herself scrubbing the stovetop in a fury. She attacked the minuscule spots of grease that had settled there with an intensity that immediately calcified her thoughts. She remembered her mama saying, *"Git busy, Sara. It'll take yer mind off a' yer troubles."* She had taken that directive to heart and discovered that as long as she could attend to the mundane and the manageable, she would be safe. The ability to focus had been her defense for years. When dark memories seeped into her mind, she would use her power of single-minded concentration to sustain herself. Every action in her life was controlled and her practiced perfection was evident in the image she presented to others. Always neat as a pin, carefully coiffed, and tactfully made up, she had established her reputation as a composed, self-possessed woman, a far cry from the naïve girl who had bumbled through her adolescence in Cam's Corner. Sara had made an effort to improve her manner of speaking, just as her high school elocution teacher had drilled; she had worked hard in her job, giving even the most routine or dreary task her best effort; and she knew when to listen and when to offer a suggestion or greeting. She had an intelligent, lovely daughter whom she had raised completely alone and on whom she had doted. She had earned the respect that had escaped her in her early years, and now rested in her hands like a beautiful hand-picked bouquet. And yes, she was proud of herself.

Chapter Eleven

As the days of spring began to warm, the relationship between Sara and Sheila cooled even more. Sheila began to spread her wings a bit, staying at Melanie's a bit too long, or meeting a boy after school on the bleachers by the football field. By fall she had been kissed often and had experienced the covert pleasure of lying and getting away with it. If she entered the house smelling of cigarette smoke she would face her mother's wrath.

"Sheila Masie Jenkins, have ya' been smokin'?"

"No, Mother."

"Don't ya' lie t' me young lady."

"I said 'no' an' I mean no." Sheila would level her eyes at her mother and spit the words at her.

"I smell smoke." Sara would not be deterred.

Whether she had smoked or not, Sheila always denied it. She conveniently used Sharon as the culprit. Sara knew Sharon smoked like a chimney. Whenever she entered their apartment, her White Shoulders perfume would permeate the air with an immediate jolt, but once the fragrance had settled, the tinge of cigarette smoke became evident. Sheila milked the fact on a regular basis.

"Sharon was smokin' in her bedroom as always. It gets on ever'thing, Mother. I did not smoke."

Such interactions had become typical. Sheila hated being home when her mother interrogated her, and Sara detested the pouty, inaccessible demeanor of her daughter. The warmth and engaging chitchat that had dominated their past had lapsed into daily clashes and conflicts of wills. Sara was beside herself with concern.

"Elaine's back," Sheila informed Sara one late afternoon. "Came back t' school t'day."

"How's she doin'?"

"She's fine," Sheila lied, because Elaine did not seem fine. She had put on pounds that had unflatteringly settled on her hips, and under her short skirts her legs were chubby and pasty white. Sara would have called her pleasingly plump, but in the eyes of Sheila, Melanie, Joan, and Sharon, she was just plain fat. The four girls had gathered in the bathroom at school to sneak a cigarette and discuss Elaine.

"I hate t' chew her up an' spit her out," Sharon said smugly, "but she looks nasty. She used t' be s' darn cute, but now . . ." Sharon sucked on her cigarette while Melanie finished her sentence.

". . . she's fat! An' her face! Did ya' look at her face? It's blotchy an' red. Looks like she needs some foundation, an' a little lipstick would help."

"Her hair's a mess too," Joan added. "It's real stringy now. Used t' be s' pretty when she curled it. Remember, she used t' brush her hair ever' day? 'One hundred strokes a day,' she'd say."

"I feel real bad for her," Sheila added. "Maybe we should talk t' her an' help her. Maybe she doesn't want t' think 'bout what she used t' look like an' how she took care a' herself. We could remind her."

"It's what she looked like prob'ly got her int' trouble in the first place." Sharon was matter of fact. "Billy went after her 'cause she was skinny an' pretty an' well, easy, I guess."

"I don't think she was easy!" Melanie argued.

"Well, what would ya' call it then? She's the one that got herself in trouble, an' frankly, I don't think we're the ones that need t' pick up the pieces." Sharon was ruthless.

"Well, I don't want t' ignore her completely," Sheila said.

"I'm with you, Sheila. We were her best friends. She's been mopin' 'round the hallway an' was alone at lunch. Saw a bunch a' hoods eyein' her," Joan said.

"That's what I'm sayin', Joan," Sharon continued. "Her reputation's ruined an' I'm not sure I want t' be associated with a girl like her."

"She was a friend," Sheila said simply. "I'm goin' t' try an' talk t' her."

"Go ahead, Sheila. See where it gets ya'. I don't want t' have nothin' t' do with her." Sharon had made up her mind. She was the judge and jury.

"You're prob'ly right," Joan said sadly, tightening her golden pony tail and looking into the scratched bathroom mirror at her own sweet, round, dimpled face.

"I am. Got t' go. Bell's goin' t' ring."

Sheila watched Sharon push through the door, flipping her mass of dark curls with her hand. She was always quick to escape the smoky bathroom first, innocently walking to her locker before the hall monitor came in to chastise, "Who's been smokin' in here?" It was as routine as the bell schedule.

At home that evening, Sheila helped her mother with dinner, washed the dishes, and tidied the kitchen. Sara had retreated to the living room and was curled up on the divan with Sunny at her feet and a tattered copy of *East of Eden* in her hands. Steinbeck was her favorite author and she loved to escape into his stories. He took her to places she had never been and she never tired of his rich description and painstaking detail. A whole day could be stolen by Steinbeck if she let it. Tonight, however, he would be upstaged by her daughter.

Sheila walked slowly into the dim room that was illuminated only by the two lamps that stood like sentries at the ends of the divan. She looked tenderly at her mother who looked so pretty in the filtered golden light and flopped down beside her. She scrunched up as close as she could, laying her head on her mother's shoulder. "I love ya', Mother," she said.

Sara was a bit astounded by this unusual act of affection, but embraced it with delight. She was immediately consumed with an intense wave of emotion that buoyed her spirits but also alerted her that something could be amiss. Shelia had been distant for too many days to count, and this welcome demonstration of warmth both pleased and frightened her.

"I love ya' too, Sheila Masie Jenkins, more than tongue can tell." She realized at that moment that, with the exception of the name, the exact words had been spoken to her by her mama many years before. Her throat tightened then and tears welled in her eyes. "Don't cry," she ordered herself.

The two sat together in a tiny huddle for a long time. Sara waited silently for Sheila to begin to talk. She wanted her to make the first move. After all she had initiated the interaction and in an unusual act of deference, Sara remained silent. This scene had to be directed by her daughter.

Finally, Sheila began.

"Elaine came back, an' nobody's talkin' t' her. Sharon hates her now. Joan an' Melanie think she looks awful, an' she does, but she was our friend. I feel bad. Sharon says she's easy. Says she's got a real reputation now an' won't have nothin' t' do with her. I feel bad."

"Ah, Sheila, you're wantin' t' patch her up an' make the past disappear, but honey ya' kain't be takin' that on. I'd say she was a child, but she ain't any more. She's got her own child."

"No. She doesn't have it. Her daddy made her give it up. Don't even know if it was a girl or a boy. They took it from her an' put it in the orphanage over in Smyrna. Guess somebody's goin' t' adopt it."

The mention of Smryna conjured memories that jabbed at Sara's heart, but she pushed the sensation away and said, "An' does that bother ya'?"

"It does. What if ya'd done that t' me?" Sheila plaintive voice literally filled the room with despair, as anxious imaginings overwhelmed her. She pulled back then and looked her mother full in the face. Her beautiful brown eyes were afloat in tears and the golden specks that always sparkled in the sunlight did so now, illuminated by the lamp's filtered glow. They were her father's eyes. Sara had never been able to escape the memory of him. Her baby's eyes had darkened quickly from blue to brown and by the time she was a toddler they would flash with happiness, frustration, anger, or excitement. No matter the moment, the eyes captured the emotion. Now was no exception. Sheila's face was intense and alive, bearing down on her mother with concentrated focus.

"Honey, I could never have let ya' go. When I heard yer little cry, a yelp really, I knew ya' were my little girl an' we'd tough it out through thick an' thin. I was by myself back then though. Didn't have no parents makin' my decisions fer me, an' yer father had gone off t' serve the country. I didn't have the heart t' tell him 'bout ya'. Thought it would be a mistake. But Elaine's got her folks, an' they took the matter int' their hands. I reckon maybe they're goin' t' regret the decision, though in some ways, like I told ya' before, could be the best thing. Elaine's jist a child herself an' I reckon her mama didn't want t' raise another, 'specially not under the circumstances."

Sara stopped for a moment then, looking at the girl, her precious daughter beside her, and realized the truth of the moment. The hugs, the tears, the emotion were not about Elaine. They were about the two of them. Sara touched Sheila's face tenderly and then took a wide lock of her long brown hair and began to comb it with her fingers. She did so for a long minute and Shelia allowed it. Sara was aware that she had a chance, and perhaps even the duty now, right at the very moment, to tell Sheila some truths that had been lurking in her memory for years. She had never before dared to do so.

"I love ya', Sheila. Can't imagine lovin' anyone or anything more. Guess that's why I never wanted t' share ya' with nobody. Couldn't imagine bein' with a man who wasn't yer father. I see yer daddy ever' day when I look at ya'. Yer eyes are his eyes, an' yer smile, it's the same too. I see him when ya' smile, an' that's always been a nice thing fer me. I never got t' be with yer daddy fer long, but I want ya' t' know that at the moment ya' were created, there was love. I have yer daddy's name, locked up with my papers, an' I know his home was in Indiana, not real far from South Bend. We wrote back an' forth fer some time, but lost touch in a month or two. I reckon he was too tied up with his duty an' before I knew it, I had ya' here in my arms. Cute little baby ya' were. Born with a mess a' dark brown hair an' those deep blue eyes that changed on ya' real fast. Used t' put ya' in the buggy an' push ya' down the street t' the park an' back. Only way t' get ya' t' sleep sometimes. Ya' got real cranky 'cause a' the colic, but by winter it was better. I'd bundle ya' up an' we'd go t' the park or jist walk fer a spell. When it snowed the flakes would land on yer eyelashes an' ya'd bat yer lashes wonderin' what in tarnation was happenin'. Ya' were a cute little baby an' a funny little girl, always busy with yer dolls an' yer tea set. Ya loved that tea set an' ya loved yer babies. Sometimes ya'd make a bed fer them under the big maple got cut down a few years ago. I hated t' see that ol' tree go, 'cause I remember ya' there, tuckin' blankets 'round yer babies t' yer heart's content. Sometimes ya'd get t' playin' an' ya'd forget t' come in t' pee pee, an' ya'd have t' go s' bad, ya'd jist squat. Ya'd look s' uncomfortable, an' I'd have t' go help ya' int' the house. Had t' clean up a few accidents, but ya' outgrew that condition, thank the good Lord."

Sheila was enthralled. She'd never heard her mother reminisce about her like this. It was like magic to her, filling her with delightful visions that she created in her head. It was another present, a gifted glimpse of herself and her mom in days she could not possibly have remembered. She could envision her mother dressed in an airy, summer dress, pushing the buggy straight ahead, intent on her mission, her hair lying on her back in limp curls; or Sara would be trudging through thick wet snow, pausing to adjust her baby's blanket, and humming a tune that had become lodged in her mind. She could see herself, too, squatting in the yard, a look of painful confusion on her little face. These were pretty little pictures that made Sheila smile her daddy's smile.

"There ya' go, remindin' me a' him again with that look."

"Was my father yer first boyfriend?"

It was a question Sara had feared would come someday. She could say, "yes," and be done with it.

"No," she said, surprising herself. "There was another person, not really a boyfriend, jist a man who turned out t' be a real bad so an' so. An' I was pretty stupid 'bout him too. I didn't know how t' recognize that he was jist flatterin' me t' beat the band. Reckon he's off still doin' the same thing t'day, though he'd be an ol' codger an' I don't reckon he's got much left under his umbrella these days. But, if the truth be told, he hurt me real bad back when I was jist a little older than ya' are now. I was real young then, an' didn't know much 'bout the world, 'specially 'bout a man like he was. Real rotten fella. It ain't really a story I want t' recall, but reckon yer old enough. He's kind a' what makes me worry 'bout ya, Sheila. I want t' protect ya' from what I had t' go through an' that's why I tell ya' t' be smart an' watch yer p's and q's. Ya' jist have t' be real careful 'round some fellas."

Sheila was silent for a moment, letting her mother's words settle, aware finally why her mother had been so intent, so meddlesome, so bothersome to her. "Love doesn't always look like love," she thought and then said aloud, "Thank ya' for tellin' me 'bout this. An' I'm real sorry 'bout what happened t' ya'. But I'm real glad ya' met my daddy, 'cause here we are!" Sheila cuddled again as close as she could get and then she asked, "What do ya' think I should do 'bout Elaine? Should I talk t' her an' be her friend again or should I stay away from her like ever'body else is doin'?"

"If I were you, I'd be her friend, but that don't mean ya' have t' be with her all the time. Jist be nice, like ya' are. Jist be yer nice, sweet self, an' that'll be enough."

"I'm not sure, Ma." It was the first time Sheila had ever called her Ma, but it tickled her and made her happy. She took the opportunity to have the last word.

"Talk t' me Sheila Masie Jenkins. Ya' got t' talk t' me 'bout things. I git scared. I may be yer mother, but I've been a young girl too. I reckon I know a little a' what yer beginnin' t' come across whether it be a boy an' the fluttery feelin' ya' get when yer with him, or whether it be t' decide 'tween right an' wrong when it comes t' yer friends. I maybe kain't understand all yer goin' through, but I'll try my darn best."

A tight embrace ended the conversation. Sheila said goodnight and headed to bed, flashing her extraordinary smile into the darkened room. Her curious doubts and conjured anxiety had been satiated. Sara watched her go, and then slowly opened her novel again. Her thoughts would not allow her eyes to focus though. Instead, she closed her lids and let herself cry, a soft, silent release that had been a long time coming.

Chapter Twelve

"Pussy! Hey you, pussy!"

Sheila reeled around looking for the direction of the screaming voice. Was it directed at her? Was it meant for Elaine who was a few yards ahead of her?

The two girls had just left the Buttercup Diner where they had been sipping cherry cokes and munching potato chips dipped in catsup for over an hour. Sheila had invited Elaine there just to talk, and although Sheila attempted to be animated and friendly, Elaine was restrained, lapsing into uncomfortable silent stretches. Sheila had hoped to make Elaine comfortable in the familiar setting of the Buttercup Diner where they, Melanie, Joan, and Sharon had spent many happy hours. It was a cozy café and friendly Miss Baker, the owner, had welcomed the girls and enjoyed eavesdropping on their adolescent chatter. She had run the place on her own for twenty years. She made her own doughnuts and pastries, serving them with hot cups of coffee or tea on pretty, intricately-flowered china plates that were completely covered with cracked veins but were still usable. Miss Baker was soft, round, and jovial, welcoming her patrons from early morning until late afternoon when she'd hustle the last hangers-on out the door and pull down the sash in the front window. Sheila had been the last patron that day. She had given Elaine a quick, awkward hug and said good-bye.

"See ya' at school. I want t' buy somethin' for my mother," she said, secretly wanting to put a little distance between herself and Elaine. The unexpected effect of the get-together bothered her and garnered feelings of insensitivity and guilt. "Why I'm no better than Sharon," she thought, "In fact, maybe I'm worse for bein' a fake." She had wanted to patch up the old friendship but her efforts had fallen flat. It had been an uncomfortable hour that resulted in Sheila's babbling about nothing, and Elaine's detached silence. Elaine had changed. Sharon was right about that.

Sheila bought a tiny paper bag chock full of doughnut holes for her mother knowing they would make her chuckle with delight. When she closed the diner door she saw Elaine ahead on the sidewalk, her dirty blond hair hanging limply down her back and her pale legs clearly visible in the growing dusk.

"Pussy!" she heard again.

Sheila looked around again, angered by the nasty, unwelcome greeting. Who would say such a thing? And to her? To Elaine?

Ahead she watched Elaine march on, head down, shoulders hunched, and arms hanging like heavy limp ropes at her side. If she had heard the expletive, she was ignoring it.

Suddenly she saw a beat up, black Ford truck barrel out of the ally between the J. J. Newberry store and old Sam Harris's Shoe Store. "Hey, pussy! Got somethin' waitin' fer ya'!" a voice hollered in her direction, and then again at Elaine as it sped by her.

She was startled and gasped involuntarily. She and her former friend had been hatefully lumped together just by association. It degraded her and made her feel queasy and stupid. Sharon had been right about Elaine's reputation, but did she really deserve this kind of treatment either? She was certain to have another heart to heart with her mother, and soon. She slipped into the J. J. Newberry store and edged her way up the narrow stairs near the far back entrance to her mother's tiny office. She was relieved to be in the warm cluttered cubicle above the store and happy to know she'd be going home with her mother, not alone as Elaine was.

When Sara was satisfied that the store had been completely closed and carefully locked, she and Sheila made their way home. They hopped onto the city bus that would take them the two miles home and as Sheila settled into the seat by the window, she saw the black truck rumble by in the opposite direction. She shivered.

At home, Sheila relived the events of the afternoon. The conversation in the living room a few evenings before had unshackled her anxiety and subdued anger, leaving her free to talk, and talk she did. Sara welcomed the change and listened well. She was equally appalled by the vile words that had been hurled at Sheila and Elaine, but quickly labeled the perpetrators as asinine, thoughtless adolescents, and shelved them as ignorant fools to be ignored. "They're jist no count good-for-nothin's who were jist spoutin' off," she told Sheila, although a measure of apprehension nagged at her uncomfortably.

Sara was troubled about what Sheila had told her and was especially uneasy about Elaine. Should she take a chance and talk to her mother? Elaine's mother had always been friendly when they had met before but she was a silent woman who seemed to find even the most meager conversation painful. And, beyond that, interference in personal matters was an affront to the ways of the South. To do so might do more harm than good and actually lead to more trouble than it was worth. Surely Elaine's mother knew her daughter had become withdrawn and sad. Surely she could see how her appearance had fallen into disarray. How could she help but notice the difference in the way Elaine acted and carried herself now that she was home again? Sara cautioned herself though. She would wait. She would mind her own business.

Worry had become an unwelcome and constant companion. She was troubled about the day's revelation, and concerned about Sheila and her friends who were growing up in a worrisome world, explicitly explained and detailed by the daily bombardment of often sensationalized news. She had grown up in a much more uninformed and innocent time and sometimes resented the onslaught of information that shrank the world and put reality on their doorstep. Bad things happened. She knew that first-hand and had the mental scars to prove it, but the incessant and rapid dissemination of news, good and bad, brought things too close to home.

❧❦❧

Sara set off to work on Saturday in the late morning as usual. Saturday was the busiest day for the J. J. Newberry store and her presence was a must. She would often say, "Saturdays are s' busy an' the store gits s' noisy I can't hear myself think sometimes," but she actually loved the hustle and bustle that kept her hopping. Sheila had taken to joining her in the office from time to time, helping file papers and answering the phone. Sara loved hearing Sheila's voice, "Good mornin'. J. J. Newberry's. How may I help ya'?" It reminded Sara of her first job as the counter girl at the Ford dealership in Cam's Corner and she couldn't help but be proud. On this day, however, Sheila stayed at home. She had not fallen asleep easily as events of the previous day were stubbornly replayed in her mind. She had tossed and turned for hours until falling finally into a deep sleep. She was still snoozing when Sara tiptoed in to say good-bye. "Will I see ya' later?" she asked.

"Yeah. Maybe. Prob'ly."

"Take the bus if ya' come in. Don't want ya' walkin' with what happened yesterday."

"Don't worry." Sheila said sleepily. "I will."

Sara had been gone for only a few minutes when Sheila heard a heavy pounding on the front door of the apartment. She was startled by the thumping that would not cease. Had she heard a simple knock on the door, Sheila may not have been so upset, but the immediacy and intensity of a fist hitting the thick wooden door left her shaken. Once she had disentangled herself from the mass of blankets, she stood barefoot on the blue throw rug that was beside her bed shaking from her very core. She reached for her shaggy pink robe and threw it around her, tying it tightly in a knot at the front. The pounding continued. Who would be knocking like this? She was almost too afraid to move, but crept to the door that was still vibrating from its beating. And then, it stopped. As suddenly as the pounding had started, it stopped, and all was silent. She reached for the sheer curtain that covered the tiny window adjacent to the door and peered out. What she saw terrified her so badly that the throbbing in her head and heart literally mimicked the incessant knocking. Running across the street were two tall, thick figures, both dressed in solid black from head to toe. From her vantage point she could not determine who they were but that point was immediately trumped when she saw them heave their bodies clumsily into an old black Ford truck, the same one that had sped by her the day before. She slid to the floor in panic. She could hear the revving of the truck's engine, and then the clatter of scattering gravel bouncing under the truck's undercarriage as it raced away toward town. When it was gone, in the quiet of the room, she listened to the only sound she could detect, the pulsating blood in her ears that kept beat to the hammering of her heart.

After some moments, she gathered herself enough to crawl to the phone. She dialed her mother's number at the J. J. Newberry store and waited, listening to the dial tone that seemed to have been activated in slow motion. It was her mother who thankfully answered.

"J. J. Newberry's. How may I help ya'?"

"Mother! Ma! They were here!" she stammered.

"Who was there?"

"Them. The boys from the truck, from yesterday. Mother, they were poundin' on the door. I was afraid they'd knock it in. Ma, I'm so scared."

"I'm comin' home." That was the only thing Sara said as the phone slipped from her hand and fell askew into its cradle.

Sara was in a panic herself by the time she reached the door of her apartment. There had been no bus available, and she had no car, so she had begun to run in flats that were too tight and a slim skirt that restricted her stride. She brushed by Ray Ellis, the manager, on her way out. "Got t' go home," was all she said verbally, but in her face alarm was written in a rosy flush.

Before she had run three blocks her boss pulled along side her in his white Cadillac sedan, and ordered her in.

"Git on in here, Sara. I'll take ya' home. What in the world happened?"

Ray Ellis ruled over his store with strict authority and was often gruff and uncompromising to his employees, but concealed beneath his stern demeanor lay a caring and considerate gentleman. He had grown up in the South and knew both how to manipulate and how to influence. Everyone who was acquainted with him knew he could be forceful to the nth degree, but he also knew his manners and was acutely aware of right and wrong.

Sara was shaking so badly in the car, she could not even speak, and when she and Ray arrived at the door of the apartment and she tried to talk, her voice was quivering so much that the words spilled out in a garbled jumble. *She was back suddenly in the Ford dealership so many years before, trying to scream, trying to stop the inevitable. Her throat was dry and her breath caught, allowing no sound to escape except for a guttural wail like the howl of a trapped animal. With the events of the morning her brain had released the memory of that horrid time, and the intense buried emotions were let loose, tumbling one over the other with abandon. She could not speak. She was powerless.*

Shelia was waiting and opened the door wide, throwing herself into her mother's arms but Sara was so weak that she could only clutch at her daughter and she cried openly. Sheila responded with one tight hug and countless kisses. Both were so relieved in the precious moment to be together that they ignored Ray Ellis who had gently closed the door behind them and was watching patiently. When he felt the time was right, he lifted Sara gently by the arm, took Shelia's hand, and guided both to the divan.

"What in the world has happened?" he asked for the second time. He was not comfortable with prying. It simply didn't fit his style, but he wanted to get to the bottom of whatever had caused such a scene, and fast.

As Sara held one of Sheila's hands, she patted her face dry with the other. Sheila also calmed enough to explain what had occurred both the day before and that morning. Ray listened intently as Sheila detailed events as she remembered them. Sara helped jog her memory when she stumbled and searched for words. Sheila talked about her friend, Elaine, about being at the Buttercup Diner, and finally about the black truck following them through town. "These boys in a black truck followed us," she said, "an' they were yellin', 'Pussy, pussy!'"

Sara winced when she heard Sheila articulate the word with such passion and anger. "Girls are s' bold these days," she thought and blushed uncomfortably in the dim light. She was embarrassed enough about having lost her composure on the way home, but the reason she had fallen apart so completely would remain her secret. Divulging her tormenting past to either her daughter or her boss would have been mortifying.

Ray Ellis absorbed the word pussy like water off a duck's back. He was a man's man, and could curse with the best of them in the right circumstance, but he was astute enough to understand the underlying threat that certain words suggested and that had been imposed on Sheila and her friend.

"Yer goin' t' have t' report this," he said.

"But, it's jist words now. Nothin's really happened," Sara replied.

"Terrifyin' a young girl home alone isn't nothin'? I beg t' differ, Sara. I believe ya' need t' tell the authorities, jist t' be on the safe side. Won't hurt 'em t' know."

"Am I overstepping my bounds by interfering?" he wondered to himself. Maybe so, but the nagging affection he felt for Sara Jenkins made him instinctively want to protect her, and her daughter.

"I reckon yer right," Sara said to Ray, pulling Sheila closer to her.

"I guess we better do this," she added, this time to her daughter who had grown silent. Sheila's eyes, which had been cast down, looked up at her mother and she nodded affirmatively. Her striking brown eyes still glimmered with tears, but the golden flecks sparked with a fresh determination. She and her mother both recognized they were in a predicament that was too big to handle alone.

As Sara reached for the phone to make the call, it jangled loudly just as her fingers touched the receiver. She involuntarily jumped in instant alarm and pulled her outstretched arm tightly to her chest in a fist. Her nerves were frayed.

"May I?" Ray asked, and pulled the phone receiver from its cradle. "Hello," he said.

"Yes, yes. . . Ray Ellis. . . Sara Jenkins's boss. . . Oh, no. . . Yes. . . Yes, she's here. . . Yes." As he replied to the caller in short succinct responses, his face grew grave. "I'll bring 'em over there. Be a few minutes. Got t' git ready an' git the place locked up. . . Yes. . . Will do."

The news Ray Ellis had heard would certainly set off a new wave of hysteria so he made a quick decision to minimize what he had been told and simply said, "The police need t' see ya'. Somethin' 'bout yer friend, Elaine. Reckon she's been missin' . . . only for a short while . . . but her folks are kind a' worried an' are wantin' t' gather her friends together t' see what they know 'bout her where'bouts. I'll drive ya' on over t' her folk's place. That's where they're all gatherin'." He deftly took command in the moment by offering gentle guidance. "Git yerself dressed, Sheila, an' Sara, might be good if ya' help her. She needs her mama now."

Hearing herself called Mama choked Sara anew, crushing her spirit with yet another file of memories. Her mama had discarded her long ago like a tattered rag doll but she would not do the same to Sheila. Accompanying her for years had been sadness, anger, and shame, but she was steadfast in the knowledge that she would not abandon her girl as her mama had done her no matter what. If revenge were a part she could play, she would don it like a cape, defying her mama's very essence, finally winning the game of wills that had directed their destructive dance. In absolute opposition to her mama's performance in the past, she would keep Sheila beside her for as long as she needed to be there.

When Sheila had dressed, and both she and Sara were composed, they joined Ray Ellis in the living room. With the apartment securely locked behind them, the trio set off for Elaine's house nearer downtown.

The news was not good. Elaine had left her home in the morning with books in hand prepared for a day in the library. Her time in Chattanooga had put her behind and even in her obvious depressed state she had determined she would catch up. She had always been a stellar student and had been coddled by her teachers and admired by her classmates because she always landed on the top of the heap academically. She had been president of the Beta Club and was adept at keeping others at bay for top honors in her class. The sudden, unexpected pregnancy and the stint in Chattanooga had snatched her energetic, vibrant spirit though. She had had to struggle to retain even a fragment of confidence and self-esteem in a house that was ruled over by a harsh, judgmental grandmother and a stern, aloof grandfather. Under the guise of caring, they had literally imprisoned her in a small bedroom for six months while her pregnancy had run its course. She had been ushered into the house in the cover of night and had not been allowed to leave the premises for any reason. No one in the tight-knit community was to know she was there. Her condition was an embarrassment and her grandmother could not have endured such humiliation if the neighbors knew. Elaine had spent her hours reading alone in her room when she was not ordered to dust the heavy furniture or sweep the hardwood floors or kneed a loaf of bread under her grandmother's watchful eye. Conversations with her grandparents were limited to orders to complete the daily household chores or were quickly-delivered snide and hurtful remarks about the lack of judgment that had placed her in this predicament, a mess that had mortified her family and was likely to ruin her life altogether. As her baby grew inside her, her self-image began to shrink. She would look forlornly into the mirror at her pale face and long blond hair which she often twisted into a knot at the back of her neck or braided into two long thick ropes. She saw a pregnant child when she looked at herself, a pitiful thin urchin face above a heavy, distended middle.

She had suffered fourteen hours of labor mostly alone in her room. Wet with perspiration she had been racked in tight contractions that sputtered across her abdomen landing in an aching knot at the small of her back. She forbade herself to scream or cry though. A local midwife who had been paid handily for her help and her silence about the birth was present when the delivery was imminent. She had pulled the baby from between Elaine's legs, wrapped it in a warm, soft blanket and whisked it from the room. Elaine had not been allowed to see or touch it. She did not even know if her baby had been a boy or a girl. After two weeks, when the bleeding was subsiding, and she could stand without wobbling or speak without crying, she was sent home to Nashville.

And now this. A call to the city librarian had revealed that Elaine had not been in the library at all that morning. Her books had been found in a messy pile just outside the rusting wrought iron gate in front of the proper brick house. They were just fifteen feet from the entryway. Papers that were fluttering in the air outside the fence and into the street had drawn her father's attention and on closer inspection he realized they were Elaine's. Jake Crabtree was instantly wary. His daughter valued her books almost more than anything. She would never have just thrown them away and certainly would not have tossed them into the street. Although he and his wife had come to think of her as a troubled handful, she was their daughter and they loved her. When she had been sent to Chattanooga he had been stern, hurt, and angry, but his parting words to her had been, "I'll love ya' through thick an' thin," and although his single-minded directive seemed to contradict it, it was true. Now, with Elaine not yet home, his anxiety began to grow and his wife was visibly upset as the early afternoon drifted into evening. Elaine was supposed to have been home by noon.

When friends and family were finally assembled, they sat awkwardly on the divan, ottoman, and chairs brought in from the kitchen. Questions and answers revealed that Elaine had not mentioned the name-calling incident to her family; nor had she mentioned the black truck with the two heckling boys inside. Sheila enlightened them. She also told them about the frightening door-pounding episode that had traumatized her earlier that morning. Listening in were Melanie and her mother, Joan and her parents, and Sharon with her boyfriend Joe. Melanie had begun to cry softly and leaned against her mother's shoulder. Joan held her father's hand and stared wide-eyed and speechless. Sharon was smug. "I knew somethin' like this would happen," she said.

"Like what?" the officer in attendance asked.

"I don't know really, but with her reputation now, an' all, I just suspected there'd be trouble."

Sheila shot Sharon a glance that oozed disgust. How could she be so heartless? Didn't she see Elaine's parents here, distraught and pale with concern?

"We're not necessarily expectin' trouble, young lady," he said. "We're simply lookin' at the situation an' hopin' some a' ya' have an idea where Elaine might be. Sheila, here has given us somethin' t' go on, an' I thank her for that."

The officer then added, "I'd like Miss Jenkins an' her mother here t' go on int' the dinin' room an' sketch out a written report 'bout what happened t' ya' yesterday an' this mornin'. Reckon ya' can do that?"

"Yes Sir. I can. Mother?" Sheila reached for her mother's hand and the two exited the living room together. Ray Ellis followed them with his eyes.

The somber living room became eerily quiet then. Only Melanie's sniffles broke the silence. In the dining room Sheila and her mother sat side by side intently studying the official statement form before them. Sheila wrote as her mother looked on, whispering from time to time in her ear. The atmosphere that had been created in the moment distressed Ray Ellis, who stood stoically by the dining room entrance. The scene conjured unwelcome remembrances of the funeral visitation he had endured when his wife had passed five years earlier. The stark, forced silence of that time had been broken only by muffled sobs and hushed whispers and the memory still haunted him. He had had to fight the urge to run away from the delicate sounds of music and muted artificial lights into the freshness of the day, but he had remained and suffered until the bitter end when his mate of twenty years had been carried away and interred at the memorial plot they had selected months earlier when they learned she would not survive the uterine cancer that had swollen her abdomen, cramped her digestive system, and made her double over in pain. Unsolicited thoughts of her had cruelly entered his mind earlier that day as well when he had looked with concern at Sara and her daughter. It was as though his wife had been there quietly chastising him for finally focusing his attention on another woman. He felt a hint of guilt which he stifled quickly when he turned to look at the beautiful woman behind him, cast in golden hues from the lamps around the room. When Sara suddenly looked up and caught his eyes, she actually smiled. It was a small smile, but for Ray Ellis, it was the world.

There was a sound then. It was a loud, startling thump on the front door. All eyes riveted in that direction and in a split second the officer authoritatively ordered, "Don't move! Stay put!" He was at the door then, gun drawn. In a matter of seconds he heard lumbering footsteps, the slamming of the door to a vehicle, and the screeching of tires. He opened the door and his eyes focused first on a truck, a black truck, skidding sideways down the street. It straightened itself and screeched away into the dusk that had closed in on the daylight. His eyes dropped then to a form at his feet. It was a girl. Her body was bent slightly forward, her head against the door jamb. A purple bruise had formed on her cheek and her mouth was agape taking in the cool air as she breathed shallowly. Her eyes which had been closed began to flutter as she fought to regain consciousness. She looked up at the foreign face of the officer above her and fell faint again as he reached to support her.

Jake Crabtree was there immediately, collecting his daughter into his arms and cradling her to him as he would have held an infant. Her mother reached in to support her, touching her face tenderly. Elaine was carried carefully into her bedroom, where her mother pulled down the comforter and blankets and her father placed her gently on the cool sheets where she slept completely unaware of the assembly that collectively sighed in relief but processed her reappearance very differently.

Melanie had dissolved into her mother's arms in hysteria, Joan and her parents appeared stunned, and Sharon responded with her usual venom, "Well, what'd anybody expect? I'm sure not surprised 'bout somethin' like this happenin'. Elaine's been settin' herself up for problems, mopin' 'round, wearin' her depression like a badge on her arm, an' lookin' like a sight t' behold. Seems t' me she was askin' for it."

"Askin' for what in particular?" Joe asked.

"Oh, I don't know. Trouble, I guess," she replied. "It doesn't take a genius t' see a person like she really is."

"I guess you're right 'bout that," Joe said quietly, taking his arm from around Sharon and clutching his hands together between his knees. His head hung to his chest, and his shoulders were thrust forward as though he carried the weight of the world there. He knew he wasn't a genius, but he was smart enough to understand some things.

From her place at the dining room table, Shelia clutched her mother's arm and stared toward the bedroom door, aching to be beside her friend but knowing astutely she would not be allowed entrance to the room where Elaine's father was now whispering to the police officer and her mother was weeping at Elaine's side. Sara's arm was around her daughter's shoulder, but her mind had taken her abruptly to another time. She was suddenly back in Cam's Corner, tucked in her own bed with Mama by her side, grieving the murder of her best friend, Addie. She restrained the urge to cry yet again today, but while she didn't know details of Elaine's worrisome experience, she couldn't help but settle her thoughts on the cyclical nature of life and how close her daughter may have come to reliving her own adolescent anguish. She pulled Sheila closer. When Ray Ellis moved in to sit beside her and when he slid his arm around her, she did not resist. It was an alien comfort that had been absent for far too long.

Chapter Thirteen

The black truck was located three days later next to an abandoned quarry near Smyrna. It had been set on fire and the scorched carcass sat on twisted rims that had sunk into the muddy ground around it. The license plate was missing and the inside of the vehicle was so charred not one shred of evidence could be obtained. The front seat was nothing but a mass of rusty burnt coiled springs and whatever else had been left inside was sodden ash, the result of intense heat and recent downpours of heavy rain. The vehicle identification number, however, although dulled by the fire could still be read and with help from investigators, the ownership of the truck was traced to a man named Fred Ferris whose address was in Chattanooga.

"Why ol' Fred Ferris been dead fer more 'an ten years," the aging county coroner assured investigators. "His place been boarded up ever since he was found hangin' by a noose in his barn, hangin' right over his ol' black truck. Killed hisself. Didn't have no family t' speak of. Only had a wife an' a dimwitted son he didn't want no part of. Both a' 'em left him, middle a' the night, whilst he was rollin' in his own vomit. Couldn't get away from the whiskey, ol'

Fred. Loved it more 'an anythin' else in his life. Cost him though. Wife wouldn't even come back t' pay her respects. Still owns the property but ain't been back t' deal with it. Believe she's off down in Arkansas with her folks. Ain't seen hide nor hair a' her fer years."

Jake Crabtree and his wife were informed that the investigation had hit a dead end. "There just isn't any way t' find out who was drivin'. Only thing we got t' go on is your daughter's recollections an' she doesn't remember much. Prob'ly was knocked unconscious from the beginnin', but ya' can be real grateful she wasn't bothered by those hoodlums whoever they were. Doc issued the report. She wasn't molested; just scared near t' death. Ya' have t' be real grateful 'bout that."

"Ya' didn't find nothin' else?" Jake asked.

"Just who owned the truck, but reckon the ol' fella's been dead for a good long time. Fella from down 'round Chattanooga. Name a' Fred Ferris."

"Knew him."

"What?"

"Said I knew him. Lived down the road from my folks growin' up. Was a hateful ol' sot, I remember. Mean t' his wife an' boy. Always drunk, but I remember he had a black truck. Used t' drive it t' town on a Saturday evenin'. Come home swervin' down the road come Sunday mornin'. Parked it the rest a' the time in the barn out back. Never seen him drive it on a week day."

"Reckon we need t' have a word with your folks then?" the officer asked and stated at the same time.

Jake Crabtree was silent. And then he was seething. He instinctively grasped an unnerving awareness. His folks knew something he was almost certain and the realization gnawed acidly in his gut.

"Yeah. We do. I do," he said flatly, betraying the fury that was building inside him. His anger was not only focused on his folks, but on himself as well. How could he have acted with such a lack of conscience? But he had thought he was right. Hadn't he sent Elaine to his parents' where she would at least be safe and away from the inevitable gossip that always gripped a community when a family fell on hard times? That's what he had told himself. He was protecting her and he was protecting his wife. He had sorted everything out in his mind. She could have the baby in Chattanooga where no one knew her and then she would come home where few people had been apprised of her misfortune. Everything would return to normal. He had trusted his folks to attend to his girl even under the ugly circumstances. He had trusted them. After the baby's birth and Elaine's arrival back in Nashville however, it was apparent that she had returned a changed girl. He repeatedly assured himself that her faraway gazes and sustained silences were only temporary. She would be herself in time. His hopes never left his side. At this very moment though, he felt nothing but bitter remorse. Had he failed his family that miserably?

 The next morning with Elaine and his wife secure at home, Jake and the investigating officer drove to Chattanooga. He had not informed his folks he was coming and desperately hoped a surprise visit would set his mother on her heels and would aggravate his father who did not like his daily routine disturbed. He had grown up in a household where schedules and order were the word. He needed to surprise them and place a stranglehold on their sense of propriety and decorum. Years of living under their control hopefully would come in handy and would assist him in disrupting their habitual existence. If he could do just that, maybe, just maybe he would attain what he needed – conclusive answers to the myriad questions that clawed at him mercilessly.

 "Why Jake, whatever brought ya' here?" The elder Mrs. Crabtree's surprise was evident just as Jake had hoped.

"Need t' get a few questions answered, Mother," Jake said, watching his father step to the door behind his wife. How he understood it was a mystery even to him, but in that instant Jake recognized the truth, not of course the details, but the truth - that his very own parents, Elaine's grandparents, were privy to the particulars he needed to know so badly. For in that moment, his mother's face blanched, and his father's body took on the stance of a bulldog. His thick shoulders widened as he lifted his chest and pulled his elbows outward to maximize his bulk. In front of him, his wife stood pale and stiff. Her hands found each other and she began to clasp them, release them, clasp, release until finally she looked down on them willingly them to stop. Jake burned inside realizing that they quite likely had been distant participants in the abduction and abuse aimed at his daughter. He knew. He knew.

"What's the meanin' a' this?" his father started. "Ya' jist kain't barge in here uninvited, Jake. Ya' don't live under this here roof no more. Ain't we done enough fer ya'? We sheltered yer pregnant girl here fer months an' now ya' come here wantin' answers t' questions? What questions ya' reckon ya' got a right t' ask a' the folks that raised ya'? An' who the hell ya' got backin' ya' up there?"

Jake's childhood came alive inside him as he watched his father transform into a barking bully, the one who had managed his early life like a drill sergeant.

The investigating officer produced his badge silencing the tirade. "We need t' ask ya' some questions, Mr. Crabtree, Mrs. Crabtree. Shouldn't take too long."

With that, the couple stepped backwards into the dim hallway and gestured for Jake and the plain-clothed officer to enter. Manners were ignored, or forgotten, because they were not invited to sit. So they stood, and the officer asked the first question.

"What d' ya' know 'bout a fella named Fred Ferris?" the officer stated directly. He was interested, of course, in the answer, but equally attuned to the couple's body language that in itself spoke volumes.

"Fred? Why he's been gone . . ." Mr. Crabtree's attempt to answer was interrupted by his wife whose slight stature belied the gumption she could generate.

"Ah, Jake, yer girl needed a warnin'," she said. "She left here mad as the dickens, not talkin' an' downright hateful. Ain't never seen such behavior after us puttin' her up an' takin' real good care a' her." In her attempt to defend herself, his mother had caved. She was not capable of understanding that her own feeble defense was her indictment. Jake was not done though.

"Ya took good care a' her? Ya' didn't take good care a' her, Mother. She's . . ."

The elder Mr. Crabtree interrupted, "Now don't ya' go talkin' t' yer mother that way, Jake. Don't care whose badge yer hidin' behind." He was red in the face and had puffed up once again like a banty rooster.

"Ya' sent her home a broken girl, Mother. An' I reckon there's more ya' got t' tell us."

"Let me, Jake," the officer stepped in. "This emotion isn't goin' t' get us answers. All a' ya'll need t' stop this banterin' an' be quiet. Now I'm goin' t' do the talkin'. I got more 'an a few questions t' ask. We're goin' t' need a place t' sit down for a spell an' get t' the bottom a' this." He was in control.

With rights delivered and notebook in hand, the officer began and like a magician, he unraveled the sordid story. The two self-righteous old people who now sat silently before him had carried their smug and pompous attitudes farther than he could have imagined. "Yer girl needed a lesson," they had said. "Spoilt. Jist rotten inside. A no-good embarrassment t' the fam'ly. Kain't understand how Jake let it happen. Her whorin' 'round like she was doin'. Got t' the point I couldn't stand lookin' at her. Jist let herself go. Looked like heck when she was here. Didn't do no work t' speak of. Jist lazy. Readin' all the time. If she's an example a' what's happenin' t' young folks these days, I reckon we're in fer some real hard times."

When the interview ended he called the local authorities and the Crabtrees were led away for booking at the county jail, where at Jake's request, they were later released and sent home. He would not press charges against them. Jake had his own reasons, he guessed, for easing their plight and although the officer disagreed vehemently he would not meddle. The young hoodlums who had perpetrated the actual kidnapping had been paid in cold cash to take the black truck from Fred Ferris's dilapidated barn and had been given explicit instructions. The Crabtrees explained the orders they had given to "scare the daylights" out of Elaine.

"Teach her a lesson or two 'bout keepin' off a' the streets, 'bout keepin' her legs together, 'bout behavin' herself like she should a' did in the first place." The young thugs were instructed, "Scare her, but don't ya' hurt her, an' don't ya' touch her in no improper way. She ain't a clean girl no more but ya' ain't t' touch her in a nasty way." If the boys did that and were found out, they'd be chased down and turned in "fer cert'in" they were threatened. Otherwise, they'd be "off the hook an' nobody'd know nothin'." They both would earn some cash to buy some beer or some women in town and the Crabtrees assured, "We'll be done with ya' then." Mr. and Mrs. Crabtree had never asked the ruffians their names and had not wanted that knowledge to weigh on their warped consciences. They did give a feeble, nebulous description of the boys, but their contradictions created such a vague rendering that the two were never found.

When Jake left Chattanooga that day, he knew he would never set foot in his parents' place again. They had ruled, not raised Jake Crabtree in their prime and had nearly taken his precious daughter in their old age. All ties had been cut. Jake had had enough.

Leaving Chattanooga behind, gave Jake new direction forward. He had made some unfortunate mistakes and misguided decisions and he wasn't sure his family was ever apt to forgive him. He didn't have a choice though. He'd never been one to wallow in the past. He had always just wanted to put it behind him. "Forgettin' ain't what I'm expectin'," he said to himself, "but dwellin' ain't somethin' I reckon I'm goin' t' do neither. I jist got t' step on up and make things right."

Jake's first act was to say he was sorry to his family and mean it. He did. His second was to give his heartfelt thanks to Sara Jenkins and her daughter for their courage and friendship. He did that too. His third act was to figure out how to forgive himself for being a stupid man, for this was his perspective, a view reflected every day in the mirror and a perception that mired his conscience in muddy regret. He would spend the rest of his life working on that one.

Chapter Fourteen

"Time heals all wounds, Sheila." Sara Jenkins told her daughter, grasping on to one of her mama's tired, old principles, hoping it would satisfy. "My mama would a' told ya' that God works in mysterious ways. Heard that more times 'an I could count. That never set real well with me, but she said it umpteen times while I was growin' up. Or she'd say, 'When God closes one door, he opens another one.' An', well, I reckon there might be some truth t' that, but, Sheila, I don't have answers fer ya'. I jist know that I'm a real lucky woman 'cause I got ya' safe with me an' those hoodlums won't be comin' back this direction, more 'n likely."

"God forbid! I sure hope not!" Sheila answered widening her eyes..

"Bad things are goin' t' happen sometimes. Jist the way it is, but there's the good too. Ya' jist got t' keep on marchin' forward. Nobody's goin' t' do it fer ya'." Sara was reminding herself as much as her daughter.

"I know, but it's hard sometimes t' keep from gettin' depressed when bad things happen. Not really depressed, I guess, but sad. Ya' know, feelin' sorry for yourself. I've been feelin' a little sorry for myself, but I feel sorrier for Elaine. She's a good person. One mistake darn near came t' makin' a mess a' her life. Hope she doesn't have t' keep payin' for it."

"I know, honey. I hope not either. Ya' jist keep bein' her friend, but the rest is up t' her. Ya' know, ya' jist got t' make yer own road. Handle the bad when it happens an' when somethin' good comes along, take ahold a' it an' be thankful fer yer good fortune."

"Are you talkin' 'bout Ray Ellis?" Sheila teased.

"Well, I reckon' I might be, Miss Sheila Jenkins! An' what of it?"

"I think it's a real good thing, Ma. He's a nice ol' fella an' I want ya' t' be happy."

"Well, he's not that old!" Sara could feel the rosy blush climb to her neck and cheeks, but she smiled contentedly. "He's likely the nicest man I've been with in a long, long time. Ya' know, it's funny, 'cause I've known him fer years, but I never thought a' him other 'an my boss. That's all he ever was t' me, but now . . ." Sara stopped in mid-sentence.

"But what?" Sheila teased again.

"Oh you! Ya' better behave yerself or I'll have t' get the switch t' yer fanny." Sara laughed.

The two had been lingering over the kitchen table after their supper. Sara had cooked up some hominy grits, spinach, and corned beef hash. Sheila loved fried hominy more than ice cream and would have eaten it every day if she could. "Nothin' better, 'specially fried up in bacon fat, an' with a biscuit on the side," she'd said more times than Sara could count. Sara had learned to cook as a girl and was always eager to mix up a batch of biscuits or drop dumplings, or bake a fresh custard pie. She made her own bread from time to time and would praise it happily when it rose properly. "Why, look at ya'," she'd say, "Yer goin' t' be delicious."

More than cooking or anything else though, Sara adored these evenings when she and Sheila remained at the kitchen table, leaning on their elbows, their hands gesturing in synchronization with the rhythms of their discourse. They discussed future plans, reworked worn-out gossip, or raved about the news. "Reckon we're goin' t' solve the problems a' the world right here 'round this table!" Sara would laugh.

She was laughing more these days. She and Sheila had mended their relationship and were close again after the discouraging months of derision that had turned them both into tense and annoyed adversaries. The near catastrophe concerning Elaine unquestionably had ended on a more hopeful note than anyone had expected at first and for that she was relieved beyond belief. And of course, there was the new friendship with Ray Ellis. She had always possessed a lively vitality, but in recent weeks she literally bubbled with unrestrained energy.

At the J. J. Newberry store, she and Ray retained their professionalism. Sara saw to that. She smiled politely when they met in the mornings in the office to confer about the various components of keeping the store operating smoothly. Shipments were coming in, merchandise was going out, employees were hired or fired or sick or late, and customers meandered down the aisles looking for items they needed and other things they just wanted. Folks gossiped at the lunch counter and swarmed the sales tables. Bargain hunters tossed odds and ends here and there making a mess of the neatly stacked clothes and linens and filling Sara with contempt. How could people be so sloppy? Her stockers restacked and straightened and her sales girls smiled and doggedly assisted. Sara was comfortably controlled as she directed the workers, but at lunch or on break when she ventured back to the office and Ray, she was much less restrained. She had to will her heart not to pound in her chest, and when she saw Ray looking at her she thought her heart had actually skipped a beat. She was like a school girl.

Away from the store, she and Ray began to build on their friendship, keeping it simple, satisfying, and fun. They went to movies sharing tubs of buttery popcorn that greased their hands and lips. They played Gin Rummy or Scrabble on the kitchen table with Sheila or alone together when she was off with her friends. He brought Sara roses, and tulips, and thick bunches of white and yellow daisies; and he brought chocolate covered cherries that oozed a thick, sweet syrup when the crisp chocolate was cracked. They talked. And they talked more, often into the late night when they would lapse into silence and simply sit side by side until a need for sleep begged him home. They walked in the public park in the early evening dusk on weekdays or in the brilliant sun on Sunday afternoons, often leaving the paved paths and venturing into the brush where the trails were narrow and flanked by brambles and weeds that brushed against their legs. When Ray reached for her hand, she did not resist. His hands were rough and calloused and she liked the feel of them. He had never shied from hard work either at his store or at home. When his wife had died years before, he had razed the house where they had lived and built a new one – a big house nearer the shallow pond that was the focal point of his property outside of town. He had hired workers to manage the construction, but he had made sure to pound a few nails and saw a few boards himself. He had helped pour concrete and had pulled electrical wires through studs, and he had drilled, painted, and patched. He had designed this dream house for himself and had assumed he would live out his days there alone, looking from the wide veranda that circled the house on all sides to the pussy willows that lined his pond to the South, or to the deep green cedar woods to the East, or to the wide grassy meadows that extended North and West. His imaginings were changing, however, as he saw more of Sara Mae Jenkins. When he was not with her physically, he saw her in his mind. What had begun as admiration and affection for her had evolved into more. Ray Ellis was in love for the second time in his life and he needed to tell her.

Sara knew already. How could she not know? He had found her at a time when she had not been looking to be found, but she understood without a doubt that she had stumbled upon someone very special. She was not a naïve adolescent; nor was she an impassioned young woman who carried love and luck recklessly with one hand and fate clasped awkwardly in the other. She was a woman who was finally ready. He did not need to tell her. She knew.

Sara Mae Jenkins and Ray Ellis were married in a brief civil ceremony at the court house in Nashville, Tennessee. Four other people were in attendance – Sheila, Elaine, and Jake and Mary Crabtree. After the judge officially named them husband and wife, the two kissed. The first was a quick kiss on the mouth, the second was a peck on Sara's cheek, and the third was a full, moist kiss that pulled Sara to her toes. Rays arms had encircled her and at that moment she never wanted him to release her. Shelia and Elaine clasped arms and smiled. Jake and Mary Crabtree looked first, and then he found her hand, remembering.

Sara and Sheila packed up their belongings and moved in with Ray to the big house not too far from town. It was perfect. Sara and Ray were ecstatic, and Sheila was overjoyed. Even Sunny adapted to the move. She loved lying in the morning sun on top of the fence railing that was connected to the veranda, or Sheila would watch her scamper to the pond to lap up the cool water or stealthily sneak towards the woods like a tiny lion. She brought mouse parts, usually a mangled head or skinny tail, to the door step as gifts to the family. As disgusting as these presents were to Sara and

Sheila, Sunny purred contentedly as she deposited them on the door mat. Everyone seemed to settle in to a normalcy that was comfortable and satisfying.

"Is it wrong t' be this happy?" Sara wondered and then slapped at her subconscious for even conjuring such a thought. Why did it seem so much easier sometimes to buck up and face the bad than to simply accept the good? She wondered at the dichotomy of her thinking.

❧

The next three years sped by and while life offered small changes, routine was the rule. Ray and Sara continued to manage the J. J. Newberry store together during the day and at night settled into their cozy home to learn and appreciate more about each other. Ray loved to sleep late into the mornings when he could and Sara was often up to see the sunrise. She would slip out onto the veranda and sip a cup of hot creamy coffee on cool summer mornings, the air caressing her skin like velvet. She would listen to the crickets and frogs simmer their songs after their long and busy night while the lone red rooster would boldly cackle into the dawn and the flock of chickens and their brood of chicks would dart here and there bobbing their little heads and pecking at the ground for a tiny morsel. Sunny would watch them lazily from her perch on the railing, swishing her fluffy orange tail back and forth in mock anticipation having learned early on that the chickens were impervious to her intimidation. A swift peck or two on the nose by a hen protecting her babies was all it had taken to keep Sunny in her place as a contented observer. In the dead of winter Sara would stand by the wide window in the dining nook and stare out at the frosty mornings. She would gaze past the barren branches of the majestic maples into the dark green cedar woods beyond or even farther out at gray skies that were often streaked with softer lines of white or pale pink beckoning the sun to offer its warmth. Close up on the window panes she would admire the ice crystals that had formed over night, each one uniquely different, sparkling intricacies that made her marvel at their creation. Sunny would be there too, rubbing around her ankles, securing her scent on her slippers and skin. And when she was satisfied, Sara would climb back into bed and into Ray's welcoming arms for cuddling or love making. There was never a plan but always the pleasure of security and warmth.

Sheila also settled into the new setting with ease. Ray made it easy. Showing her to her large new bedroom, he said, "It's yers, honey. Ya' can do what ya' want with it. Make it yer own, now." And Sheila did just that. She painted it eggshell white and accented it with a pale, pale green. Yellow rosebud wall paper adorned two of the walls and her bed was piled high with pillows edged in satin and lace. From the soft comfort of her bed she could look out onto two stunning views. One was the thick cedar woods, a haven for blue jays, cardinals, sparrows, hawks, and sometimes a flock of wild turkeys. Squirrels abounded there as well, as did myriad critters such as skunks, rabbits, and raccoons making the scene almost pulse with activity; the other view was an open meadow that was home to the field mice that Sunny loved to torment and capture. It stayed green throughout the spring and summer and lay barren and brown in the winter unless, of course, it snowed. Then the white drifts would pile against the fence posts or flakes would swirl haphazardly in the cold wind coating the grass with a frozen white canopy. The room was a comforting place that she kept neat as a pin with her precious books stacked carefully in the bookcase and her stuffed animals piled on her bed or in the large wicker chair that stood in the corner. It was the place she studied, had heart to hearts with her mother, dreamed and daydreamed, and where she welcomed her friends. She had developed a gregarious disposition that gained her many acquaintances but throughout the years, her closest companions had remained Elaine, Joan, Melanie, and yes, even Sharon. She soared through high school, standing second only to Elaine Crabtree who had retained her place as top scholar at graduation. Sheila had stood beside her friend, defending her in the face of students who assumed she deserved permanent punishment, or who were curious gossips, and in return, Elaine became Sheila's tutor, helping her with the math classes that confused her and the chemistry class that she detested. The resulting partnership was a blessing to them both, but even more amazing was that all five girls fell into a friendship that would last a lifetime.

Not everything ran smoothly of course and the girls had their share of snits and squabbles, hurt feelings and misunderstandings, usually caused by their interests in the boys who were either on the fringes of their activities or smack dab in the middle. Elaine kept her distance from the boys at school for a long time until she met David in her biology class. They were lab partners and learned first to appreciate each other's intelligence and then more. A quick brush of hand against hand at the microscope led to long looks and shy smiles. Before they knew what had happened they were a couple, holding hands in the hallway, sharing lunch in the cafeteria, or leaning into each other at their lockers.

"Ya'll need t' put a little space in your togetherness," Sharon would say smugly and then stroll over to Billy who had become her steady when Elaine no longer was. Sharon made no attempt to hide the fact that she and Billy had been intimate for quite some time. He had bought her a promise ring and they were going to get married in June just after graduation. Billy had no intention of going to college. He would help run his daddy's business and would likely inherit it outright in time. The business sold tractors, plows, cultivators, and other smaller farming implements to the folks who traveled into Nashville for supplies and equipment needed to support their rural lifestyles. Sharon would be set with Billy. She would not need college either. She would have babies to take care of and a home to set up just right. It was all planned.

Sheila was a little sad to see Sharon give in to Billy and give up on her education. She was smart and her parents had money to send her to any college she chose but she had her mind made up and had no intention of changing it. Her head was usually buried in magazines about fashion, weddings, and homemaking. Sharon was convinced her dreams were right at her fingertips.

Melanie would stay in Nashville as well. Her folks were poor and could never have afforded the cost of college tuition. They were proud people though. They scrimped and saved every penny so that Melanie had the clothes she needed and an allowance that would permit her to keep up with her friends. Melanie did not let them down, either. She secured a Saturday job at the J. J. Newberry store and spent Sundays at home. Her innate shyness hampered her social life though. While the other girls were partying and experimenting with alcohol and sex, she stayed true to the promise she had made years before.

"Oh, I'll prob'ly get married someday," she said one late spring day at the cafeteria lunch table, "but I'm savin' myself for the right time."

"Ya' don't know what you're missin'," Sharon taunted.

"I think I can wait, Sharon," she defended herself. "You're goin' t' be worn out before ya' even hit the altar."

Sheila watched Sharon bristle defensively. "Why, Melanie, ya' got no right t' say such a thing. You're just green, an' green with envy too, 'cause I got a future. What d' you have?"

"I've got what I need. I've got my integrity an' my pride," Melanie said, pointing her chin upward defiantly.

"Well ya' can sleep with your integrity an' pride then, Miss Priss," Sharon said. "You're goin' t' be pretty darn cold with only them by your side."

"I'll take my chances," Melanie said simply, ending the bickering at least for a time.

It was a conversation that remained in Sheila's mind for some time. Who was right? And wasn't everybody having sex these days? Sharon and Billy were for sure, and she supposed Elaine and David were too. How could they not be? Not a minute went by when they weren't looking at each other google-eyed or touching each other here and there. Joan didn't have a boyfriend, but she'd gone all the way with two boys already.

"It didn't amount t' much," Joan had told the girls. "First time it was uncomfortable t' say the least, but even after that it was nothin' t' write home 'bout. Bein' in the back seat in a car up at the lookout wasn't nothin' special. I want more than that. I want the romance."

"Well, girls, I got both," Sharon said self-importantly. "An' what 'bout you, Sheila?"

"My life is my business," Sheila retorted, a glint of anger flashing in her dark eyes. "It's not yours."

"Well, ya' can lie 'bout it if ya' want," Sharon said, "but you're not pullin' the wool over my eyes. I've heard a few a' Billy's friends talkin'."

Sheila closed her eyes then, willing Sharon to shut up or just disappear completely. And then she said exactly what she was thinking, "Shut up, Sharon, or go on away, ya' hear? Ya' make me want t' puke."

Sheila, like Joan, had succumbed to the pressure of her dates a few times too. She had felt scared and ashamed at first, knowing that her mother would be so disappointed in her lack of restraint, but the next time with a little Southern Comfort mixed into her Coca Cola to lower her resistance, it was better. Guilt was not an emotion that plagued her. That was overshadowed by her need to please. "Ya' might as well," Tommy had said. "Once ya' do it ya'll be sorry ya' didn't do it earlier." His logic had been lost on Sheila, but she had given in anyway. Still, she wondered at her thinking sometimes. She always seemed to put the other person's desires first and left herself as a second thought. The boys she had been with had quickly moved on to other ventures and she had been left feeling empty and used. She wasn't her own best ally sometimes, misjudging people and stepping into seamy situations she later regretted. She unfortunately was not quick to realize her subconscious pattern of behavior however and this self-inflicted wounding behavior would follow her for a long time.

Chapter Fifteen

The summer after the girls' graduation sped by quickly. The focus of June had been Sharon's wedding to Billy that took place at the Mission Baptist Church to a bursting crowd of over five hundred people, many of whom Sharon had never met personally. She was aglow in a massive white satin and lace wedding gown with a train that fell behind her like a limp sail. The sleeves of the dress pouffed at the shoulders and then tucked sharply at the crook of her arm into long white gloves that buttoned from elbow to wrist. The front of the dress dipped deeply displaying Sharon's large breasts and revealing cleavage that shocked more than a few of the ladies who were stalwarts of the church.

When Sara saw the bride for the first time on that Saturday, she gasped audibly and then whispered into Ray's ear, "I hate t' be catty, honey, but she looks like she jist stepped out a' *Gone with the Wind*!"

"Thank ya' God she wasn't in charge a' yer weddin'!" he replied squeezing her arm lovingly.

Sharon had four flower girls, two ring bearers, and twelve bride's maids all dressed in frilly lace dresses the pastel colors of the rainbow. Sheila, Joan, Elaine, and Melanie were among them. The others had been selected based on Sharon's appraisal of their popularity or their family's monetary worth. It was a gaudy affair that mercifully was over quickly on a day that was hot, humid, and threatening rain.

The country club reception, however, lasted well into the night. A traditional Southern barbeque, a country song singing band complete with banjo soloist, and a full bar enthused the crowd and annihilated a good many souls who found the food too delicious, the music too invigorating, and the abundance of alcohol too tempting. Poor Billy was among them. By ten o'clock he had passed out in the dirt, leaning against the front mag wheel of his prized pickup. Sharon did not fare much better and was carried out by her father to the family's Cadillac. Her dress had been torn, her hair had fallen from its fashionable French twist, and her shoes were missing completely. The new beginning that Sharon had crafted in her mind now lay buried with the day and in the murky shadows of the night Sheila could not help but wonder about the future of her friend.

Sheila, Sara, and Ray watched the absurd, closing scene unfold with mixed feelings of giddy disgust and sincere sadness. They walked to Ray's car arm in arm, anxious to put the day behind them. It was fitting that as the trio reached the car to drive home the rain began to fall in heavy droplets. By the time they were at their house it had increased to a fury. Torrents of rain bombarded Nashville for four days, leaving the city streets flooded and floating with debris. With unnerving predictability, the weather unhinged memories that took Sara back to the days following her friend Addie's murder so many years before when rains of equal intensity had inundated the tiny town of Cam's Corner. Her musings launched her into an unwelcome gloominess that lasted for days. "In how many ways can a spirit die?" she wondered. Addie's had been snuffed out at a time when she was just beginning to blossom. She had been given no choice. But Sharon? What was apt to happen to her? Where did choice lie in her life? What would happen to her spirit? Had it already been dampened with the rain? Had she already chosen foolishly? The questions were unsettling to Sara as she ruminated on her own life. She had made decisions that had hurt and choices that had healed. She worried about Sheila. She was smart, she was pretty, and she was kind, much, much too kind. She hoped her propensity to please others at all costs would not become a burden.

July and August pressed on, creeping up to the day when Sara and Ray would have to say good-bye to Sheila who would be attending the University of Tennessee. Although she would not be far away, Sara dreaded the day when Sheila would leave. It was a selfish feeling that intellectually she wanted to push aside, but emotionally unbalanced her. The mother and daughter duo had been compromised a bit when Sara married Ray, but with Ray's knack for concession and acceptance and his inherent joy in indulging Sara and Sheila, the three had become a close family. Sara was afraid of the hole Sheila's absence would leave in their home and in her heart. She would have to buck up and face the music yet again. With that thought tumbling into her mind she recalled her own mama's repeated warning when any dilemma had been at hand. "Yer goin' t' have t' face the music, Sara Mae," Mama had repeated over the years. Sara had absorbed that cautionary counsel and knew it as a fact.

In early September when the heat smothered the whole of Tennessee, Sheila said a tearful good-bye to her Mother and Ray on the western veranda of the big house on the outskirts of Nashville and settled into a small dormitory room at the University of Tennessee in Knoxville. Despite the small living space, however, she suddenly felt as though the whole world had cracked down the middle, opening like a plump seed pod and scattering an offering of new adventures and experiences before her. She felt excited and alive with only an inkling of apprehension diminishing her spirits. She would miss her family but welcomed the newness of the tiny room that she hoped would become a comforting retreat for the next few years. In this place she would study and sleep, laugh and cry, and confide in new acquaintances and old friends. Elaine and Joan were nearby, Elaine at the University of Tennessee as well, and Joan at Tusculum College. Their friendships would remain intact.

Sara and Ray remained close from afar, sending newsy letters and care packages filled with cookies or fudge, soaps and toothpaste, or the odd photo of Sunny or the house or each other. Sheila relished these offerings but moreover felt deeply indebted to Ray whose love for her mother and for her as well provided the tuition and allowance she needed to get by. She had no intention of letting him down and set it to mind that she would make her folks proud.

School wasn't always easy though. The classes were often challenging and the relationships she made both pleased and plagued her. She was a dorm girl, not affluent enough to pledge a sorority that for many of the girls was a must. More than a few budding friendships were quickly severed when girls moved off to keep company with the fraternal groups that were exclusive and elite.

"You're not pledgin' Sheila?" "You're sure goin' t' miss out." "Doesn't it bother ya' t' have t' stay in the dorm?" "I feel s' bad for ya'." "Well pledgin' is the most important part a' college, Sheila. You're missin' the best part." "How are ya' goin' t' meet the best boys if you're not in a sorority?" "Guess we won't be seein' much a' ya' now." "I feel real bad for ya'." She was bombarded with snide remarks from privileged girls that snipped into her self image.

She found her own way though, shoving her pride aside and focusing on her studies. She found a job shelving books in the library and the small salary helped buy a few frivolous items she could not otherwise have afforded. She was friendly with the director and her innate instinct to please and willingness to tackle the tedious job of organizing and categorizing secured her comfortable position. She had always loved her own books and during slack times would simply walk the aisles perusing the titles and touching the spines gingerly. For some reason in the obligatory quiet of the place she felt alive and scholarly as though she were absorbing the knowledge locked inside the volumes through an odd, anomalous osmosis. The library was also a place where she could study in a quiet concealed corner away from the bustle of the commons or noise and chaos that abounded in the dorm. She was content there.

The library was a stark contrast to the dormitory where in the second year at the university, Sheila was assigned a new roommate, Connie Sue Collins, a country girl who in the expanded world of college life was spreading her proverbial wings in every which direction. She caked her face in foundation and rouge and liberally spread red lipstick over her pouty lips giving her the appearance of a small clown or a budding prostitute. Sheila couldn't decide which. Connie's long hair was died ink black and cascaded over her shoulders in limp ringlets. Sheila's mother would have called her a "coal yard blond" and she'd have been right. It was all Sheila could do to be civil to the girl who chewed gum incessantly, snapping the small bubbles she created with gusto and who winked her heavily mascaraed black eyes brazenly when she spoke to anyone, stranger or acquaintance. She dressed in short skirts that exposed her plump naked knees or capri pants that were too tight edging into the crack of her ample bottom. If she was aware of a discomfort, she didn't seem bothered. She'd swing her way down the hallway to the common living room where a continuous string of boys was waiting for her. Sheila had never seen her study and when classes were in session, Connie was usually snuggled sound asleep in the twin bed that faced Sheila's. It was fortunate for Sheila that Connie's stay at the university was cut short after the first semester when she began complaining of sore breasts and nausea. She smelled of alcohol nightly when she arrived at the dorm room door just under the wire of the mandated curfew, so Sheila assumed the morning nausea was the result of too much whiskey or a few too many beers. She was only partially wrong. Connie's short-lived academic education ended as abruptly as it had begun but in her wanton way she thought she had attained just what she had come for – a boy and a baby. She was indisputably pregnant. Unfortunately the boy disappeared quickly and she wandered home carrying a baby that was born months later in the tiny house on her family's farm. Sheila did not hear from her again.

When the room became her own for the rest of the year, Sheila sighed in relief. She didn't particularly like acknowledging the simple hateful truth before her. The fact was, however, that she relished the departure of Connie Sue Collins. She couldn't help herself. She had felt only a tinge of pity for the girl, but she was quickly able to dispose of that sentiment and began enjoying her privacy. Connie was only one of many characters Sheila encountered during her days at the university, but she would always linger as one of the most memorable.

In due time, Sheila began to venture from her room and from her library hideaway into the mainstream of university life. For over a year wariness and loneliness had stifled the extroverted personality that once had been her forte, but with the emergence of spring something happened. It was as though her identity had morphed once again and she resolutely reclaimed her outgoing manner. She acquired new friends and garnered more than a few invitations from men on campus. From time to time Sheila would meet Elaine for lunch or a quick chat in the wide expanse in front of the commons. It was a beautiful place open in the middle and filled with bright sunshine even in the winter when the sky was clear. Around the periphery were evergreens of various shapes and sizes as well as tall elms and maples whose limbs had been stripped naked by the relentless winter winds. Tiny green buds were beginning to emerge, miniscule tips on bare branches that teemed with anxious birds searching for nesting spots. Sheila felt happy and content being there with her old friend, although when the girls were together their conversations often led to memories of Nashville and times past. It was then that Sheila would feel a pang of uncomfortable homesickness. They loved to reminisce, laughing as they recalled their adventures and mishaps, and they filled each other in on the latest gossip from home. Elaine knew for a fact that Billy and Sharon had moved into a brand new double-wide trailer that had been placed in a vacant field behind his parents' house. And, Sharon was pregnant, ready to deliver any day. Sheila could only assume Sharon was living the life she wanted but the thought of home being a trailer plopped in the middle of an empty field with Billy and a baby made her shake her head in repulsion.

"I just can't imagine settlin' for that," Sheila said sadly.

"Me neither," Elaine agreed. "Makes me feel real lucky."

Melanie, Sheila shared, had progressed in her job at the J. J. Newberry store and likely would assume Sara's position as assistant manager in a year or two. She fit right in and adored Sara, calling her "my second mom". Sara had confided to Sheila about Melanie. She was such a hard worker, quick to learn and happy to help, but she was sometimes a sullen girl.

"It's real hard t' git that girl t' smile sometimes," Sara had mentioned. "I reckon she misses her friends an' smart as she is, she's not likely t' git the schoolin' she needs. I try real hard t' keep her hoppin' at the store an' ever' once in awhile I can wring a grin out a' her, but I worry 'bout her sometimes. Seems she needs more in her life than trottin' over t' the J. J. Newberry store ever' day. Says her mom's been real sick an' her daddy's back t' his horseplay. I was real sad t' hear that."

Sheila was too. Melanie's life had been rough from the beginning and she truly wished better for her friend. Of all the girls, Melanie was the one who had held on to her principles and likely would until the day she died. Sheila could picture her even at this moment trudging home from work to a house that was unkempt and stale, smelling of camphor and alcohol as her mother sought a bogus remedy for her illness. The welfare doctors had diagnosed her with liver cancer too late for treatment. She had only months to live. Melanie chose not to burden anyone else with the news, so alone she cared for her mother and watched as her father's anger at the life he considered a rotten mess selfishly turn a deceptive direction. He would be gone for days, leaving the two women alone. Melanie did what she could to preserve her mother's dignity in her final days. She bathed her gently with warm soapy sponges and combed her thinning hair, knotting it into a bun at the back of her neck. She patted her emaciated hand, fluffed her pillow and said, "It's goin' t' be okay, now. Just rest a bit. Think 'bout a good time when ya' had the world by the tail! Remember your happiest day." She would close the bedroom door then, wander into the kitchen, and numbly prepare soups or stews that lasted for days and provided sustenance for her mom when she was at work. She watched her mother's skin dry into a paper-thin yellow-grey hide that stretched over a skinny frame. Her face became a skeleton mask with eyes sunken deep into eye sockets that were flamed with deep purple and red. It was no wonder Melanie didn't smile. She was the sole observer of her mother's decline and her heart cracked a bit more with every passing day. It would be several months before the end came.

⁂

On the other side of Melanie's world, metaphorically speaking, Elaine and Sheila embarked on new adventures that carried them into some awkward and seedy situations, and introduced them to a flock of new faces, a few they wanted to forget, and a handful they simply wanted.

At times their old high school friend, Joan, would come from her college nearby to join them. Joan had gained a tremendous amount of weight, probably seventy pounds or more, since beginning college but she seemed content with her appearance. An enormous roll of gelatinous fat hung over her waist and jiggled when she walked or laughed. In comparison to her spherical stomach, her generous breasts seemed diminutive. She was wide in the bottom too, and as Sheila glanced furtively at Joan's doughy butt strangled in a pair of too-tight denim jeans she was strangely reminded of her mother. Sara had always been reluctant to admit it, but she had an abhorrent dislike for grossly fat people. "It's a flaw in my personality. I know it," she had said from time to time, but Sheila knew if her mother saw Joan's voluminous figure, she'd ogle at the change and say something akin to, "Why, my word, she's as big as the broad side of a barn! What on God's Earth has gotten int' that girl?" Joan still brushed her golden hair into a pony tail but now it was tied with a bright flowered scarf and lay at the nape of her neck instead of high near the crown of her head where she perkily had worn it in high school. Regardless of her girth, Joan's face retained a simple prettiness. The added pounds had broadened her face making her dimples more pronounced than ever. Whenever she flashed a smile or simply talked excitedly her dimples would move in and out at such a rate Sheila couldn't take her eyes off of them. She was entranced by Joan's body's natural way of communicating.

Despite her weight issue, and perhaps because of it, Joan had found the love of her life, an economics major named Dwayne who had worked his way through college waiting tables at a local Italian restaurant that Joan frequented regularly. Dwayne was a big fellow himself, at least six feet four and weighing well over two hundred pounds. Beside him Joan seemed the perfect plump match and the way he hovered over her protectively and looked at her longingly anyone could tell that that was his sentiment exactly. He was a jolly young man whose droopy eyes were heavily lined with long straight brown eyelashes that belied his intelligence and drive. He would go places in life and contentedly would take Joan with him. Theirs was a bond that all the girls would come to envy.

In their final years at the university the girls had to fight hard to retain their academic level-headedness. The world was bigger than they had thought possible growing up. They were lured and enticed by friends and boyfriends to skip classes for more attractive opportunities. Parties miraculously developed at the drop of a hat at any time of day or night. Girls would sway provocatively to loud music and with eager hands grabbing their hips, young men would grind their bodies forward into them. Beer cans were stacked into pyramids as high as the ceiling, beer kegs were pumped dry, marijuana was rolled expertly into thin white joints, hashish was mashed into short fat pipes, and the thick essence of incense wafted its way around bodies that glistened with perspiration or sprawled on Goodwill couches and dirty mattresses shoved in corners. Spontaneous sex became the rule for many. It was a new world. While the war in Vietnam was escalating and young men were dying for a convoluted cause, students at home were resisting and rebelling. Free love was the rage and "Peace Now" was the slogan. As the movement swelled even in Tennessee away from more notable metropolitan areas such as New York, Los Angeles, and San Francisco, pretenses dropped away and folks frittered away their time strumming guitars and debating causes for the war and ways to end it. Small demonstrations and feeble protest marches were common around the campus and were embraced by activists and political science majors, tolerated by faculty and students who were just trying to get by, and detested by some who staunchly believed that such issues were out of the proverbial hands of idealistic scholars and should be left to the politicians and the military machine.

Amid the constant upheaval Sheila struggled to hold on to her promise to make her mother and Ray proud. Keeping her focus on classes that were difficult and demanding took its toll and when she was home in early winter to attend Melanie's mom's funeral, Sara was appalled at Sheila's appearance. She was as thin as a rake and her cheeks had grown pale with the absence of make-up that had once been an unstated requirement for Sheila and her friends. Her hair had lost its natural silky luster and hung down her back in a dark, thick unruly mass. She had abandoned the traditional skirts and slacks that the sorority girls still dressed in daily as a matter of principle, if not fashion, and wore tight bell-bottomed jeans with colorful paisley peasant tops or a sweater that was too big and would cling to her body like a loose cape.

"It's what people are wearin' these days," she told her anxious mother. "An' I'm fine. Just tryin' t' keep up with my classes an' I am. Ya' know my grades. Still on the Dean's List."

She was right about that, but seeing the abrupt change in Sheila's appearance shocked Sara. Her innate propensity for neatness found the new look offensive and inappropriate.

"Yer never goin' t' git a job lookin' like ya' jist crawled out from under a rock!" Sara said with unusual harshness that surprised even her.

"Well, I do have a job. At the library," was the retort. "Nobody there worries 'bout what I'm wearin'!"

"Well ya' kain't go pay yer respects t' Melanie's mama lookin' like ya' do."

It was a useless debate, Sara could see, but she knew inside that when Sheila returned to the university she would cling to the apprehension and uneasy misgivings that knotted her gut. She had made her mistakes in life and worked hard not to judge, but she was worried now, and rightly so.

Chapter Sixteen

The service for Melanie's dead mother was somber and brief. The pastor of the Mission Baptist church offered his services for free and the poor woman's body was interred in a wooden casket in the welfare section of the cemetery at the edge of the city. Melanie was numb with grief. She did not cry during the memorial service, but when the plain wooden box thumped onto the moist soil next to the grave site, she shuddered visibly and sobbed mournfully. The day was as bleak as the moment with a mass of thick gray clouds covering the sky and a brisk breeze shuffling dry brown leaves around the graves that appeared indiscriminately marked with tiny headstones or handmade crosses. It was a miserable, paltry resting place that mirrored what had been the woman's dismal existence for years and as she was lowered into the ground, not a dry eye could be seen among the watchers there. Stifled sobs, muffled sniffles, and nervous coughs filled the air and played there like a sad, insignificant symphony. Ray, Sara, and Sheila huddled together, each apart in their own thoughts. Unwelcome memories of his first wife's memorial crowded Ray's mind while Sara was immersed in the distant recollections first of the despicable death of her friend Addie and then of her own mother's pitiful and painful burial. Sheila, who to the knowledge of most of the people around her had never suffered a significant loss, clung to her mother's arm, keenly aware of her warmth and struggling to deny an uneasy unshared truth. An anxious fear rose inside her. She could not bear the thought of ever losing her mother.

Elaine and Joan had moved to Melanie's side and held her hands. Joan's chubby fingers caressed her shoulders gently until the heaving stopped. Across from the gaping hole, some distance away stood Melanie's beleaguered father, shabby, unshaven, and alone. Far to his left were Sharon and Billy with their bundled sleeping baby in tow. Sharon's face was gaunt, serious, and sad. Sheila couldn't help but wonder if her grief was the result of multi-layered heartbreak intensified by this poignant moment. It would stand to reason. Sharon was clearly pregnant again and stood next to her husband who for this solemn occasion had not had the decency to discard the wad of tobacco that was evident beneath a bulging lower lip.

After overall-clad cemetery workers had hastily covered the grave with dark loose soil, Melanie knelt and placed a single pink rose in the center of the mound. She stood then, looked with hollow eyes in the direction of Ray and Sara, and nodded. In unison the group of friends silently wandered away from the site to their vehicles which were parked in a line at the edge of the thin gravel road that wound through the graveyard. One by one the cars twisted their way to the main road and out of town to Ray and Sara's house for an informal gathering. It was the first time the five high school friends had been together since Sharon's wedding and as different as each one had grown from the others in looks, lifestyles, and circumstances, the remarkable bond of friendship remained in tact. The tacit essence of it filled the room and the girls grasped and hugged each other first a bit awkwardly and then genuinely. In the midst of the quiet turmoil of the day, a swelling of acceptance and relief swirled around them like a warm and gentle, refreshing wave that offered phenomenal comfort to them all. Sara and Ray held hands in the kitchen and watched the lovely scene play out before them.

When the sky could no longer offer a speck of light, and when the copious assortment of hors d'oeuvres had been consumed, an awesome quiet ensued touching every person with a strange but welcoming contentment that left them silenced and spellbound for measured moments. For hours that afternoon past escapades and experiences had been recollected and shared while dreams of the future had been offered and batted around the room a few times, but amazingly as though the clock of time had wizened them with wisdom, they did not judge; they did not criticize. Not even Sharon who perhaps for the first time understood what it was like to be in another's view master. And now, with no words spoken, they all knew it was time, time to part yet again for an extent of time not one young woman could have forseen. With the tears dried and the laughter gone each one of them seemed satisfied that she could say good-bye. Elaine, Joan, Melanie, and Sharon went their separate ways into the night, leaving Sheila alone and together with her folks in the security of their home.

Sheila turned back into the house and immediately began gathering dishes and straightening tables and chairs. She stacked empty plates and dirty silverware in the sink for rinsing and wiped the counter clean. Her flurry of activity was accompanied by silence however. She didn't feel she could voice another word until she suddenly stopped still. In the bustle of her movements she had brushed her Mother's arm a bit too roughly and she moved quickly to mollify the moment with a sweet cuddling embrace.

"Sorry, Ma. Didn't mean t' hurt ya'," she said and the words lingered in the room like dust particles floating between them, not settling, not going away.

Sara had been staring at her daughter and recognized herself in what she saw. She had watched Sara's frenzy and understood the signs. For more times than she could count her mama's voice popped into her head, *"Git busy, Sara. It'll take yer mind off a' yer troubles."*

"Do we need t' talk a little bit?" she asked her daughter tentatively.

Sheila didn't say a word, at least not at that instant. She couldn't, for a thick lump had formed in her throat and tears streamed down her face. Sara had never seen her look so forlorn and her heart felt full to the bursting point both with trepidation and with tenderness. She had her daughter back. She glanced at Ray who stood in the shadows and then watched him retreat into the back of the house. He would give them the time they needed. It was in his nature to give.

When Sheila could talk, she did, and Sara listened to a story she wished later she had never heard for it exasperated and hurt her. It drew up records from a locked file in her brain and she was incensed both at the memory and at the feelings that crawled cruelly up inside her. She grew angry as Sheila's tale unfolded and was more than miffed at her daughter's lack of restraint and absolute failure to use common sense. Her own mama would have called it stupidity, plain and simple. Her own mama would have cast her out. Sara finally had a concept of her mother's thinking so many years before when she had ushered Sara from her house forever. She could almost understand the angst her mama must have felt but she would not emulate it. An appreciation for her feelings and actions did not warrant a replication of them. Sara had been emancipated reluctantly, and the alien autonomy she had found at the time had left her alone and frightened. She would never forget the stark despondency she had felt then. Remnants of the experience had ridden on her shoulders for a lifetime. "I'm not my mama," she told herself. "I will not do t' my daughter what she did t' me."

So she listened and the story was told.

They had been at the Commons. Sheila and Elaine had gone there for coffee and a break from a study session at the library. It had been an extraordinarily quiet afternoon there and the warmth and coziness of their corner table helped release the tension that had been building with upcoming mid-terms in the offing. Shelia was scoffing at one of Elaine's elaborate tales of sleeping with her roommate Kathy's boyfriend the night before.

"He just came int' my bed while I was asleep an' started rubbin' my body an' coverin' me with kisses," she said.

"I'm not Kathy," she had told him.

"Ya' think I don't know that, Lainy? Kathy's not around right now, but you are." He had taken to calling her Lainy of late and Elaine was smartly suspicious of his intentions.

They had intercourse three times that night. "The boy was insatiable," she said. "Couldn't get him off a' me. Figure he finally wore himself out, 'cause he crawled out a' my room 'bout daylight. Left me in a sticky mess, I mean t' tell ya'."

"God forbid, Elaine. Don't ya' feel a little bit bad 'bout it?"

"Well, if Kathy knew, I would, but she doesn't have a clue."

"I wouldn't count on that! She's apt t' know somethin' 'specially if he's goin' t' be hangin' 'round callin' ya' Lainy," Sheila told her, shaking her head in annoyed awe at her friend's exploits, and then she added, "Be careful, Elaine. Ya' worry me sometimes." Sheila knew she was judging, but she wondered about Elaine's sporadic self-destructive behavior. It seemed she had an uncanny way of putting herself in situations where she was used or abused. It had happened more times than she could count.

Lost in their conversation, the girls didn't see at first a motley group of students enter the room. Sheila knew some of them from her classes, but a few faces were new to her.

"Hey, we're gettin' together a party, out on the edge a' town," one of the girls told them. "It'll be fun. Music, beer, boys. Ya'll want t' come? Take your mind off your troubles!"

They had gone.

The party took place in a large sprawling brick house that was situated on a two acre lot in one of the more affluent neighborhoods of Knoxville. It belonged to the parents of one of the boys whose folks were off to England, France, and Italy. Whether they knew their home was being invaded by a rowdy bunch of students no one really knew or cared for that matter. With selfish insolence and blatant audacity the partiers made the place their own. The owners' son was the worst offender, opening the liquor cabinet and kitchen to all. He turned on folksy rock music that bawled into every corner, showed eager couples to empty bedrooms, and dumped five dime bags of marijuana onto the polished surface of the dining room table. "Ya'll can have whatever ya' want t' eat, drink, or smoke," he hollered. Sheila couldn't help but think he was holding a grudge and a big one too against his parents. She imagined they were too strict, too pretentious, or too powerful when they were present, but in their absence their boy was in charge.

Sheila and Elaine made themselves comfortable on a thick overstuffed leather sofa in a living room that looked more like a study, with bookcases that lined two walls from floor to ceiling. Crammed on the shelves were volumes of books, some leather-bound, all hardbacked, pushed together tightly or lying horizontally to form book ends. Set cautiously in spaces between the books were pristine porcelain vases, bronzed statues, and silver-rimmed frames preserving sepia photographs of people from long ago. The carpet was a deep rich forest green with a classic intricate Asian rug placed on top. It was a stunning room, beauty lying in every corner. It would become ironically evident later however that this loveliest of places would become home to an ugly scene that would shatter a life and scar a few more.

Like many others, Sheila was lulled into a complacent state by the music, a few beers, and tokes from joints that had been passed *through the room unceasingly. When the afternoon had disappeared and the darkest of nights leaned against the windows, the lights were dimmed, the music lowered, and connections made. Elaine had somehow found Kathy's boyfriend again and they were quick to find a corner on the dining room floor to carry on where they had left off the night before. Elaine's recent risky behavior was worrisome to Sheila. She seemed to lap up the attention she had been receiving like a puppy hungry for affection, and she bragged about her boldness in talking dirty and saucily into the necks and ears of her lovers. She found powerful pleasure in taking the lead in her sexual encounters stroking men's egos with her words or her tongue. It was as though she had transformed into a devilish diva, captivated by her own charms and intent on whipping up excitement.*

Sheila sat alone for some time listening to the sounds of sex and distant dialogues. She thought about finding a way to exit, but the beers and pot had their hold on her. She felt like a weighted doll so heavy at the bottom that she could not move so she sat and sat, closing her eyes until he was there. Adam, the boy in charge, took charge of her. Without saying a word he pushed her roughly back onto the couch knocking her head against the heavy wooden end table that butted up to the leather arm of the sofa. She squealed in pain, but he immediately covered her mouth with his thick fleshy fingers and held them there firmly. She squirmed in instant fear. It was hard to breathe and in her panic she heard the blood rush to her ears, leaving a hollow pulsing echo. She had been with other boys, but none had ever forced himself on her. This was new and her mind was awhirl searching for options, questioning, resisting. But he had her. On his knees beside her he tugged at her jeans until they lay in a heap on the floor and then he was on her. He straddled her legs and while he still held her mouth with one hand, he searched between her legs with the other, jamming his fingers into her vagina until it hurt. She twisted under his grasp, but he was too heavy, too big, and too powerful. Finally his hand left her and he gripped his thick erect penis and shoved it violently into her. It took him a long time to finish, and while he pummeled her she froze under him. She could not move and she closed her eyes tightly willing him to vanish or wishing she could. How had she gotten here? How had this happened? What had she done wrong? And then he was gone, as quickly as he had come. He left without uttering one word. Afraid to move, she lay on her back for some minutes until her courage returned. She dressed quickly in the darkness and then stumbled to the heavy front door where she pushed herself out onto the stone steps that led to a broad circular driveway. She had no way home. It was dark and it was cold and she hurt inside and out. With no choice, she re-entered the house and tiptoed into the dining room where Elaine was passed out alone under the table. With strength she had never imagined she had and definitely had never employed, she pulled her friend from under the table to the corner of the room and huddled there with her arms around her until the morning light edged its way into the windows.

"We have t' get out a' here," was all she said.

Elaine did not resist. They crept to the front door, pushed it open, and walked into the cool of the morning leaving a silent house behind them.

"We walked all the way back t' the university together that mornin', holdin' hands like little girls," Sheila told her mother. "An' the next day we heard the news. He was dead."

"Who? Who was dead?" Sara asked, confused.

"Adam. The boy who raped me. He was dead. They found him with a needle still stickin' in his vein. He was lyin' on the leather sofa, just sprawled there, they said, with no shirt an' his jeans unzipped 'round his hips. He was cold when they found him. It was heroin they said."

"Heroin?" Sara mouthed the word rather than speaking it for drugs were something talked about in the news or found in dark city alleyways. They were foreign to her and her thoughts went unspoken, "How did heroin get t' Tennessee an' t' a party where Sheila was?"

"Me an' Elaine, Elaine an' I, "Sheila corrected herself subconsciously, "didn't talk 'bout that night again, not for a couple a' months. We were scared 'cause there was an investigation an' the police were lookin' t' talk t' anybody they could find who'd been at that party. We stayed quiet 'cause it was a night we didn't want t' remember, an' we were scared. Me 'specially. But we had t' talk about it later 'cause there's more."

Sara was afraid to even speak.

"I got pregnant, Ma. From that night, I got pregnant."

Sara could not move. A jumble of emotions she could not define had enveloped her and she began to shiver inside. She had to will herself to hear more, for the rapid palpitation of her heart had silenced her other senses.

"It's gone though. Ma, I had t' get rid a' it. I found a place that did abortions, an' I went. Elaine went with me. No one knows, just Elaine, an' now you. I don't cry 'bout it any more, but I did. I did a lot. I'm sorry Ma. I know I'm a disappointment an' ya' prob'ly hate me, but I couldn't have kept it. Not with what happened. I'm sorry Ma. Please don't hate me."

Sara was still for a moment longer and then she found her voice. "Sheila Masie Jenkins, I will never hate ya'. An' yeah, I'm sad, an' angry, an' upset, but more sad than anything else, not s' much at you, as the story, the situation, the boy, the baby, ever'thing. I don't reckon I understand the world I brought ya' int'. I must be gettin' t' be an ol' woman, cause yer world's too big fer me. I would never in a million years have wanted this fer ya', honey. An' my heart's achin'."

Sara looked at Sheila then and understood the disheveled look, the gaunt face, the clothing that spoke to Sara of self loathing.

"I've lost my words right now," Sara said. "I'm havin' trouble digestin' what ya've told me, but I will tell ya' one thing. I love ya', honey. Through thick an' thin, I love ya' more than tongue can tell. Kain't put it no other way. It's the way it was told t' me an' it's the way I got t' tell ya' too."

The two looked at each other in the dim light for some seconds, both numb with the revelation. They had been sitting side by side facing each other, facing the truth, and putting their bond to an incredible test that would leave them both deep in reflection for many days. When Sara took Sheila's hand it was the signal Sheila needed. Her head leaned to her mother's shoulder, her long hair cascading over the side of her face and Sara began to comb it with her fingers as she had done so many times before. They sat silently together, mother and daughter, frozen in the warmth of the affection that was as solid and impenetrable as ever.

Chapter Seventeen

When Sheila returned to the university she was more than relieved that the disclosure of the sickening story was behind her. She had not intended to add angst to her mother's life by telling her, but the unforeseen impromptu moment had presented itself. It had not been her plan ever to tell another soul, but now that she had, she felt ever so slightly absolved, not from the horrible memory, for that would last, but in the telling she had relived it, and in the telling she had diminished the weight of it just a bit, and because of the telling her mother had given her the gift of understanding and unconditional love once more. On the cold, frosty morning when she departed from her mother's house, she wanted desperately to leave a part of herself there, safe, secure, and sheltered from harm, but that was not to be for she already had opened the pages of the next chapter of her life.

She had not been completely forthcoming with her mother and with guilt plaguing her silently and mercilessly she was trapped in her own web of unwitting deception. What she carefully had not mentioned was the development of a lengthy liaison between herself and her philosophy teacher, a man more than twice her age.

"Ya' have more potential than any other student in the class," he had told her. "Ya' can go places. Ya' just have t' know the right people an' play their game. You're a natural leader, Sheila, an' a natural beauty too, I might add." He had looked at her adoringly and with words that had flattered her, Sheila fell into a hornet's net.

First a compliment, then a slow sultry stare, and a touch on the arm that lingered a bit too long, led to a request and then a demand. "Would ya' stay after class for just a minute, Sheila?" His soft, lilting accent drew her in with a mysterious invisible force she could not resist.

"Well..."

"Ya' need t' stay for just a moment. I need t' speak with ya'."

When the other students had filed out the door of the classroom that was tucked into the third floor corner of the humanities building, the professor had firmly pushed the door closed and turned to her. She had not refused his advances. He was handsome, sophisticated, and intelligent beyond belief, and he had picked her. They met in clandestine places, never in public, but Sheila didn't mind. He had his position as a respected faculty member to uphold and she didn't want to jeopardize that. After all, he had sent her flowers repeatedly, all with cards signed with scrawled initials that no one but she could have deciphered. The secretiveness became part of the intrigue for her and when they were together, she would fall into his arms surrendering to him completely. When she was asked to meet him after dark at a motel outside of town, or when he had picked her up before dawn at the corner a block from her dormitory, or when he hustled her into his office for a student conference and closed the door to the hallway, she was not offended. She thought it sweet that he wanted to protect her from the gossip of others. He warned her that no one would have been able to accept a love like theirs; people wouldn't be ready for it, and she believed him. She knew he wanted her just for himself and she had a profound respect for the creative ways he contrived to accommodate their furtive encounters. She did work for him, too, researching alone for long hours in the library, typing his nearly indecipherable notes for lectures, or reading mundane essays written by freshmen who had no concept of what philosophy was and who spilled out their dreary, drawn-out thoughts for pages. Sheila hated reading those papers and would often grow numb with boredom, but she did it anyway, for him. He praised her time and again.

"You're a Godsend, Sheila. Don't know what I ever did without ya' in my life. You're such a beauty an' I just love havin' ya' near me," he had whispered into her hair.

She adored the man. For four long months she thought of nothing else. She would awake in the morning and could see him so clearly he might almost have been there. His handsome chiseled jaw, striking amber eyes, and thick, silver-streaked dark hair combined to create a refined and erudite look that magnetized her. In her mind's eye she reconstructed moments spent together – an hour-long tryst in a small motel room, with lights dimmed low, the curtains drawn tight, and the television news blaring over their noises; a hasty lunch at the Tip Top truck stop, followed by heated sex in the tiny, seldom used women's room; or hours just spent in his office pouring over papers, sipping cold coffee, and eventually clawing at each other's clothing behind the locked door, careful to be quiet, careful to hide from the constant parade of students and professors who had classes to attend. She watched him from her seat in the class he taught to her, a class exploring the ideas of Kant, Descartes, and Schopenhauer among others. She intentionally pulled her long brown hair over the sides of her face to hide the blush that flourished there when he looked in her direction. She bent over her desk making herself small and quickly wrote copious, sloppy notes in an attempt to occupy the mind that would not cease its chatter. On her papers she read long, convoluted comments that he had scribbled in the margins, comments that spoke more to their relationship than to the contents; she was left confused then and even embittered that he had not taken her academic efforts more seriously. It was an oddly strange new insight that fell fleetingly over her but stubbornly inched into her consciousness nonetheless.

And then, it was over.

On a breezy spring morning on the day her final paper was to be delivered to his office, she found him conspicuously absent. His desk had been cleared of his mess, the coffee cup she had hand picked for him lay atop an overflowing trash can, broken. His favorite poster of quotations by famous philosophers was missing, and in his squeaky leather chair sat the skinny, red-haired, freckle-faced assistant professor, his intern, who had shadowed his classes for the semester.

"Where's our esteemed professor?" she asked, omitting his name in an attempt to slyly mask her bewilderment.

"Oh, didn't ya' know? Thought he told most a' his students. He's gone. Left late last night. Took his wife an' kids t' Europe for the summer."

She was undone. No she had not been told. No she had not known. No. No. She could not believe her stupidity. She had been duped by his charms and blinded by her own lust and childlike need for acknowledgement and approval. He was a mature man, wasn't he? He had wanted her, hadn't he? She had believed him. He lived alone in the plush new apartment complex near campus, he had told her. He had never taken her there, but she knew, didn't she? She was overcome with an intense rage and a miserable sadness, forceful emotions that pulsed through her and caused her to stagger slightly. She grabbed the door jamb for support, instantly grasping the idiocy of her recent reckless conduct.

She stared into the pale blue eyes of the assistant professor and was momentarily mesmerized by the odd effect the light played on them reminding her of an early morning cobalt sky seen through an ice-covered window pane. They were eerie eyes that looked intently back at her.

"Are ya' all right?" he asked.

"Yeah. Yes," she mumbled. "Here." She handed him the thick packet that was her final project, and looked for the last time into the tiny space where her deluded promise of a brighter future and her broken dreams now lay. She had been ruthlessly rejected and the questions that seethed inside her would go forever unanswered.

Sheila wandered the campus that day aimlessly, deadened by the pain of his deception. Eventually she found her way back to her little room where she lay atop the bed fully clothed in a tight fetal ball for hours. The tears did not come for many hours and when they did, they were not so much for him as for her. She was infuriated and as she recalled their times in sordid places and in squalid surroundings, her fury grew. She had been an insignificant speck of life for him and she had allowed him to play her like a spinning top and toss her about like a tattered toy. She understood now. He had never respected her. He had never admired her intelligence, her beauty. He had used her for his own pleasure and she had naively let him. She hated herself. A dismal cloud of desolation would weigh upon her for a long, long time.

In the week following the departure of her professor, Sheila descended into a miserable state. She didn't eat, bathe, or sleep. She sat mostly in the midst of the rumpled blankets on her bed, picking at her toes and fingernails until they bled. She didn't cry. She sat. And she thought, and then thought more until there was nothing, just the silent beating of her heart. Elaine came and was shooed away, but she came back, and back again until finally Sheila let her stay.

"Sheila, ya' have t' get movin' now. Ya' have t' take a shower now, right now. Come on, Sheila. I need ya' t' do this for me. I need ya' t' let me help ya' like ya' helped me once." Elaine pleaded with her and would not leave her side. "I brought us a picnic, Sheila. Just like the old days. We're goin' t' the park. We're goin' t' have a picnic in the park."

And finally, she did move. She had listened and she moved. In an almost trance-like state she showered, she dressed, she even applied a touch of make-up, and then the two young women walked into the sunlight and across the glistening pavement of the street to the city park that was filled with laughing children climbing monkey bars, swinging on swings as high as their little pumping legs would take them, digging in the sand box, and playing tag. Sheila watched them silently from a mound covered in freshly-mown grass as green and soft as an emerald carpet. Elaine spread a red and white table cloth beside her and began to empty the contents of her hemp bag onto it. She had brought sliced apples and grapes, flimsy slivers of Swiss cheese, and fresh wheat bread sliced as thin as a pencil; she had iced tea in a thermos, fat coconut macaroons, and four wide chunks of chocolate fudge. It was a feast.

Sheila began slowly initially, touching the treats first with her eyes, and then gingerly picking up morsels that made her mouth water. She watched the children before her, and then turned to Elaine who was patiently watching her. Shelia smiled then, a whimsical little smile that made Elaine grasp her hands in delight. Her friend was back.

They talked for hours in the park until parents began tugging their reluctant children home and the sun began its gradual descent behind the lush evergreens. When quiet had settled over the place, they made their way to the commons where at their customary quiet corner table they talked more, sipping cokes and dipping potato chips into catsup just as they had done at the Buttercup Diner in high school. Sheila told her story and Elaine heard her. Elaine didn't have to judge her, for Sheila already had concluded that she was an idiot. She was her own worst critic, chastising herself much too cruelly in Elaine's opinion and she said just that.

"Ya' made a mistake. Yeah, but so what? Ya' made a mistake, but ya' aren't the mistake. Ya' just made it! Didn't ya' learn that much from me? God, Sheila, let yourself off the hook. Take it as a lesson, an' a huge one, I might add," she chortled teasingly, "but try t' learn from it. Ya' got yourself in a mess, a big mess, an' I don't doubt an excitin' one, but the jerk's not here any more. Don't know why we girls get int' such ridiculous fixes sometimes, but seems we do. Put it behind ya'. You're not goin' t' forget the son of a bitch, but ya' can put him behind ya'. Think about stompin' his ass with a high heel shoe or somethin'. Think about somethin' real heinous that ya'd really never do, just to get it behind ya', an' then move on."

Elaine's animated advice made Sheila smile and she wanted desperately to believe her, but she simply said, "Thanks, Elaine. I can't thank ya' enough for not givin' up on me."

"Ya' never gave up on me, did ya'? When ever'body else wanted to, ya' didn't. I won't forget that either, but I do have one thing more. For God's sake, don't tell anybody else!"

She paused and then added, "That's the only advice I'm goin' t' give ya'. Oh yeah, one more thing. Ya' have an assignment ya' prob'ly forgot about. We have t' get crackin' an' find a quotation for our philosophy class, the one that skinny, emaciated intern's goin' t' be tryin' t' teach."

It was the only class the two had had together their entire four years of college. Thinking back on the semester, Elaine couldn't help wondering how she had been so blind to the affair that had taken place right under her nose and to lighten the moment she said as much. "Don't know how ya' pulled it off, Sheila, with me bein' right there in the lecture hall with ya' both. I suppose if I'm goin' t' get int' medical research I'm goin' t' need t' hone my ability t' focus an' pay attention t' what's goin' on 'round me, don't ya' think?" She laughed at her own feeble assertion.

Sheila answered her with a silent nod of amused exasperation. She had a way of getting to the heart of the matter.

The closing philosophy class was presided over by the young rusty-haired assistant professor whose disquieting blue eyes blinked nervously as he perused the disparate group of students who were astute enough to assume that with their professor away, the assistant's input likely would have an impact on the final grades. They had been asked to select one quotation or passage from their studies that represented their experiences in the class or at the university overall. Many would be departing in a few days for directions as diverse as they were. Sheila and Elaine would be among them. Before they left, however, there was the annoying matter of attending the last class. The students would be discussing the quotations and passages in a roundtable configuration in order to fill out the last required hours of the course and their verbal participation was a requirement.

With no limitations stipulated in regard to the source of the quotation or passage, the students were free to say whatever they wanted. A quotation was but a quotation; one could have made up a saying on the spot, and in fact, more than a few indolent folks did just that. Sheila and Elaine, however, took the somewhat asinine assignment a bit more seriously. It was, after all, a philosophy class and notable sayings had been verbalized all semester. Sheila's selection was easy because for some reason it had occurred to her in the middle of one of the solitary nights when she had suffered in her silent room. She recalled it not because of the silly task that had been assigned; she remembered it because at that moment she had felt so childlike, vulnerable, and alone. Isaac Newton had spoken the words many years in the past, but they amazingly had come to her as she shivered sadly in the cold dark by herself. *"I am only a child playing on the beach, while vast oceans of truth lie undiscovered before me."* How applicable his words were for her. She had been so foolish and although she was an adult, she knew she had much more to learn. How many times had her mother told her that there was a difference between being intelligent and being smart? How many times had she listened but not heard? Sheila would read Newton's words because for her they were explicitly true, as agonizing as it was to admit.

And Elaine? Elaine had little trouble finding a suitable quotation either. Hours of conversation with Sheila had left her with a bitter view of the man who had been their instructor so she searched for just the perfect words that would have put him in his place if only he'd been present to be slapped with the veracity of them. John Locke expressed her sentiments exactly: *"I have always thought the actions of men the best interpreters of their thoughts."* It was simple enough. Remembering that saying was significant to her, for she believed it pertained to all of mankind, men and women. One could have unraveled the meaning behind the words either positively or negatively, she imagined, but she would protect the idea and hold it close. It was a must, for her years at the university, and even before, had made her keenly wary of the unpredictable ways of the world.

Part Three

Chapter Eighteen

When Sheila left the University of Tennessee, she never returned, and like her mother so many years before, she did not look back. It was over and done and she relished the thought of no more late nights studying, no more projects and papers, no more bullshit! If college had done one thing for her, it had given her a much more colorful vocabulary if not a defined and refined one.

"Sheila Masie Jenkins, I wouldn't have that in my hands much less in my mouth," Sara had said forcefully and somewhat piously when Sheila's first words upon arriving in the house were, "Shit, Ma, I'm so glad t' be home!"

"Oh, sorry, Ma! Just habit."

"A habit ya'd better lose in this house, young lady. Ya' better understand that in no uncert'in terms!"

"Yes, Mam. I'm sorry. Just forgot where I was."

"Well, ya' better remember 'cause Ray'll be home in jist a minute or two an' he needs t' talk with ya' 'bout somethin'," Sara said seriously.

"About what?" Sheila asked, concerned.

"You'll see. Now go unpack yer things."

Her mother's command crawled under Sheila's skin a little bit, irritating her. After all, she was an adult now, but she bit her lip and did as she was told. Her room had remained virtually the same since she had left it four years prior. She had been home for short visits but now, before she moved on to her next venture in a month or two, she would reclaim her adolescent domain and happily so. It was a sweet room, one she had decorated with excitement and care years before, and it still looked pretty to her, though a bit childish with the stuffed animals still piled high in the wicker chair and the lacey pillows plumped up next to the headboard of the bed. "Need t' do a little adjustment, I guess," she said to herself while her mother stood at the doorway watching.

"Ya' haven't changed anything, Mother. Why not?" she asked.

"Oh, keepin' it the same was like havin' ya' still 'round, I guess. I'm jist a sappy ol' Mother, I reckon. Used t' come in here once in awhile an' jist sit, an' I'd think 'bout ya', hopin' ya' were fine. Hopin' ya' weren't havin' troubles, an' jist thinkin' about the nice times we use t' have." Sara smiled then and turned toward the hallway, for the front door had been opened. Ray was home.

When she saw Ray again, Sheila threw her arms around him, planting a firm kiss on his prickly cheek where a day's stubble had grown out. He had begun to age, with thinning light brown hair that had grayed at the temples but his bright hazel eyes still twinkled with youthful good humor. He wore his rimless glasses near the tip of his nose looking over them more often than through them, and he chewed on a toothpick as he had done around the house for years. Sara had tried to break him of the habit, telling him he looked like a real hillbilly, but changing his ways was not that easy. Now she just looked the other way.

"Welcome home, honey," he said, squeezing Sheila to him.

She hugged back content to be in the arms of the man who had become like a father to her and she loved him because he was generous, caring, and because he loved her mother.

"Mother said ya' needed t' talk t' me," she said.

"Indeed I do, young lady," he answered. "Yer in a heap 'a trouble."

Sheila was momentarily startled and then saw him wink at Sara who stood behind her watching the reunion.

"Come with me. We need t' have a little talk," he said and grabbed her hand, leading her out of the front door, and down the shallow wooden steps that jutted from the wide veranda to the paved circular driveway. Parked there was a bright red Volkswagen. "Guess now that yer goin' t' be travelin' 'round the county doin' all that social work ya' been educated t' do, yer goin' t' need some transportation. So here ya' go, honey. It's yers. Congratulations on yer graduation!"

"Really, Ray? For me?" Sheila was a little girl again, jumping up and down in delight.

"Figure ya' earned it," he said. "Not real enthused with these foreign cars. Should prob'ly have bought American, but heard these were reliable an' the mileage is good. Looks like a sow bug t' me, all rounded int' a ball, but reckon it'll git ya' where ya need t' go." Ray was playing down the gift, but underneath his feigned distaste, he was more than pleased. To him, as trite as it might sound, giving was the greatest gift of all, and he did have the means and moreover the desire to keep his girls happy. Sara had moved beside him and had wrapped her arm through his, leaning into him, the top of her head just reaching his shoulder. Her broad smile matched his.

Besides the present, Sheila was given a choice. She could stay at the house for as long as she wanted, or Ray and Sara would fund an apartment for her until she was on her feet financially. In time she would move away again, but for the summer she was content to live at home with the two people she loved most. She would not begin her job until the fall, so she spent the summer rejuvenating her bond with her mother.

Mornings were the best times for them. Though she had always cherished her silent morning reveries, Sara was delighted to have her daughter's company. They were different women, and yet they were similar in many ways. On quiet mornings, they communicated without talking, silently sipping warm coffee as they sat in the two oversized rocking chairs that were positioned on the East side of the veranda facing a certain sunrise. The days of summer warmed quickly, and they relished the relative cool the mornings offered. They watched the sky lighten to a pale blue-gray until the sun pushed its way over the dense woods into the sky turning it into a brilliant cerulean canopy where lazy fluffy clouds would drift about with the wind's capricious currents. Sheila would pull her legs up close to her chest hugging them close willing her chair to cease its rocking, while Sara leaned back, head against the wooden slats of the chair and gazed at the scene before her, her legs outstretched and her bare foot tapping the porch lightly to keep the rocking chair locked into its rhythm. Sunny, who had grown old and thin, stretched her stiffening back legs behind her and ambled over to the straw basket Sara had provided for her. She could no longer jump easily to her railing perch, so she was content to hunker down into the soft blankets that filled the basket. From there she contentedly looked with weepy eyes at the women before her. She was no longer the hunter, though one could imagine she still remembered the thrill of the chase, because in her sleep, her tiny paws quivered and padded the air as though she still was running through the meadow. Before the end of the year she would be gone.

Sara was delighted that her summer garden was the best ever. She and Sheila planted rows of seeds that soon produced such a bounty of vegetables that they fed not only themselves, but their neighbors as well. Sara, like her mama so many years before, loved to dig in the dirt and found weeding her garden a private pleasure. She donned her straw hat, and wearing a thin flowered sundress or soft cotton pedal pushers and a sleeveless blouse, she knelt or sat among her plants pulling to her heart's content. Often she shed her gardening gloves, and with bare fingers she pulled tiny weedy sprouts from the ground and filled her bucket to the brim. At other times she struggled with a stubborn dandelion root as wide as a thick carrot, pulling until it almost knocked her backwards when the soil finally released it. In a large round basket she placed rich red tomatoes, green, red, and yellow peppers, and squashes of various colors, sizes, and shapes. She pulled fat radishes from the dirt disturbing the wiggling earth worms that frantically dug their way back into the dark moist soil, and she stripped ears of sweet corn from stalks that seemed to grow inches a day toward the sun. Her fingers grew filthy, with dirt hiding under her fingernails and in the crevices that lined her fingers. It took minutes of scrubbing to make her hands presentable again. Sheila helped Sara to tend the garden, but her strength lay more in the preparation of the bounty than in the gathering of it. She loved to cook, and to the delight of Sara and Ray, prepared scrumptious meals that added more than a few pounds to their maturing bodies that summer.

In the evenings Ray often joined Sara and Sheila and together the three walked to the edge of the small pond that was a haven for frogs that sang their songs in horrific chords all afternoon long and into the night. The crickets added their scratchy melody while buzzing fire flies flitted amidst the tall pussy willows with tiny lights flashing on and off in a feeble attempt to illuminate the scene. Occasionally a skinny garter snake slithered past their feet to the water's edge, or slid swiftly and silently into a tiny hole hidden in the weeds. It was a beautiful place marred only by the mosquitoes that loved to lunch on Sara and Sheila's arms and legs. Ray seemed immune to them, laughingly telling the women that he wasn't sweet enough for the pests.

On warm afternoons they strolled to the west edge of the property where blackberry bushes grew wild, their long prickly branches wrapping in and out of each other to form a shapeless tangle. When the fruit was ripe they picked and picked until their fingers were black with the sweet juice and their arms were covered in bloodied pricks from the thorns that sought to protect the plants from their plundering. Ray ate more blackberries than he plopped into the waiting buckets and his lips and chin turned purple from the juice.

"Yer a sight t' b'hold, Ray Ellis," Sara would scold him. "Yer not gittin' near me with those lips!" After that, without fail, Ray scooted to her side, pulled her to him, and kissed her with dramatic passion. Sheila laughed at their antics and secretly hoped someday to be that much in love.

At home Sara and Sheila attempted to make jam which always seemed to turn into syrup as it had done years before when Sheila was a little girl. "Never quite got the knack fer makin' jam, I guess," Sara said, pouring the thick liquid into mason jars. "Guess we got enough syrup fer a lifetime."

And so the summer passed. It was the sweetest summer of their lives and they were in love, all three of them, with the precious life they had been given.

Sheila's job as a social worker came as naturally to her as breathing. She had been hired by the city of Nashville to work with families with children, families that had been affected by poverty, crime, the new wave of drugs that had infiltrated the city, domestic violence, and worst of all to Sheila, child abuse. She was given ten cases to begin with and with eager anticipation she located on a map the homes she would be visiting. In her new little red Volkswagen she quickly learned the streets of Nashville like the back of her hand. In the course of the next few years, she would learn much more.

Her profession humbled her, for she realized at once that hers had been a privileged life unlike the lives of some of the individuals she would be counseling. She and her mother had not always had a great deal of money, especially when she was small, but they had always had enough to get by and when Ray entered their lives, they were fortunate indeed. Her mother had loved, pampered, and respected her even when she knew she had disappointed her. In the realm of her childhood, and even until now, she recognized that she had been lucky, very, very lucky. At moments when she reflected on her past, she realized that the dark moments, the bad choices, the floundering decisions had been unquestionably created by her own doing. She knew right from wrong. She did. Sara had pounded it into her as a child, but she had not always practiced what she had learned. She had not always practiced what now she would, in essence, be preaching. She found herself in a very real and very troublesome quandary about her qualifications. In the context of her budding career worrisome doubts began to pick at her conscience and she remembered some of her poor choices and her lack of ethical conduct. In the past she had compromised her principles and the realization of that tugged at her. She couldn't help wondering, "Am I worthy of this job? I haven't been the perfect person."

But then she remembered Elaine, who was now attending graduate school and studying medicine at the University of Kentucky. Elaine would have said, *"Put it behind ya'. Let yourself off the hook. Learn from it."* Sheila remembered her saying, *"Ya' made a mistake. You're not the mistake."* It was strange that at the very moment she needed it, Elaine's advice resurfaced and calmed her misgivings. It was as though her friend, Elaine, was beside her, and the notion made her feel pleasantly eerie.

Chapter Nineteen

On the first of October, with the summer over, Sheila made the decision to move into the city. She would be nearer to her office and to the families she was helping. She also would be closer to the social action that the city offered. Her mother and Ray were understanding and supportive, actually helping her find the perfect two-bedroom apartment in a modern complex near downtown, but on the morning when Sheila's car was loaded to the brim with all of her belongings, Sara broke down. It had been a charmed summer and she hadn't wanted it to end, so she cried, and she did so with honest sorrow for she knew Sheila would not be back. She would visit, of course, but as though she were a fortune teller, Sara pictured the next few years of Sheila's life. She would work hard, be successful in her career, meet a stunningly handsome man, get married, move into a beautiful home of her own, and have babies.

So why was she crying?

"Ma! I'm just down the road. Ya' didn't cry this much when I went off t' the university," Sheila said, unnerved by her mother's reaction. "An', look, with me out a' your way, ya' can fix up my old room. Make it a study or a sewin' room. Make it your own!"

"I know. I know. Like I tol' ya' before, I'm jist a sappy ol' woman, Sheila. I'm jist goin' t' miss seein' ya' ever' day. Got used t' havin' ya' back with us this summer an', well, damn it, I liked it! Don't worry, I'll be fine in a minute or two."

"Mother! Ya' said 'damn it'!" Sheila teased.

"Well, it jist seemed t' fit!"

"I couldn't agree with ya' more!" she giggled and after a brief pause, she added quietly, "I love ya', Ma."

"I love ya' too, honey."

"More than tongue can tell?" Sheila asked, looking for a smile.

"Of course, honey, more than tongue can tell," Sara said, hugging her girl mightily.

Sheila gave Ray a rub on the back and caressed his arm gently. "Take care a' things, Ray."

"Ya' know I will, honey."

"Bye, then. See ya' real soon." And she was off.

When she arrived at her apartment, she unpacked her car and carried her belongings into the upstairs unit. She was amazed to find it took countless trips to empty the little Volkswagen, and she was perspiring profusely when she eventually was finished. She could feel droplets of sweat sliding down her back and her face was warm and flushed. She had tied her long brown hair into a pony tail to allow the air to cool her neck, but the heavy humidly offered little relief. Sighing to herself she mumbled under her breath, "God, I got a lot a' shit." When she finally stepped over the threshold into the dim light of the small living room, however, she felt content. "So this'll be home for awhile," she told herself, knowing instantly she would enjoy her new independence. What she didn't know was that from behind a curtained window in the group of apartments across a wide expanse of neatly groomed grass someone had been observing her.

"She sure is somethin'," the watcher was thinking. "I'll be gettin' acquainted with that girl real soon." James Madison Jackson was his full name, and with powerful intent, he would ingratiate himself into Sheila's life, sweeping her off her feet, into his arms, and onto an emotional roller coaster that would leave her reeling.

Ray and Sara had helped Sheila furnish her new little home with a small flowered divan in shades of green, gold, and orange, a solid olive green arm chair, a tall skinny pole lamp with four lights that turned in different directions, an ordinary, functional rectangular wooden coffee table, and a five-foot tall, yellow-painted step ladder with wide rungs that would serve as bookshelves. In the bedroom a slightly marred wooden chest of drawers stood against the wall, and a double bed mattress, box springs, and bed frame had been placed in the corner under a small window that looked out onto the parking lot below. Sara had provided a passel of linens and a bright colorful bed spread, an old toaster, a waffle iron, a new set of stoneware dishes the color of desert sand, some well-used pans for cooking, and some silverware garnered from the J. J. Newberry store. It was a start.

Sheila spent the first evening in her apartment unpacking and straightening, wiping the counters and stove of the already clean kitchen, making the bed, stacking books on the ladder shelves, and looking out of each of the windows, securing her bearings. From her bedroom window she had a view of the parking lot where her car was parked neatly under the flimsy-looking metal roof of an open carport. The empty second bedroom offered an identical view. From the kitchen she could see the busy street below with two narrow lanes of continuous traffic stopping and going in both directions, and from the living room, she could see the lawn which was dotted around the edges with trimmed boxwoods and low-lying junipers. The area looked plain to Sheila who would have appreciated at least one or two mature trees to offer shade. Instead, tied firmly to thick poles were several spindly maple trees that were known to be very slow growing. It would be a hot place under the summer sun.

It took only days for Sheila to slip into a routine that suited her. She enjoyed keeping a precise order in her own personal everyday activities for it balanced the unstructured chaos she often observed in the lives of those she served, people whose lives were so turned upside down she knew they wouldn't recognize normalcy if it was offered up on a platter. Households around her were often disorderly places where turmoil was the norm and commotion was the rule. She worked with confused and unruly teenagers who slipped bags of marijuana into the pockets of their jeans and skipped school, small dirty children who were dressed in tattered clothing and whose hair and appearance were in constant disarray. She knew they were hungry. Their hollow eyes told her so and she worked with local schools officials who saw to it that they were given a warm breakfast and adequate lunch. Beyond that, no one knew the quality of their care, for often the mothers worked well into the night cleaning office buildings, scrubbing floors on their knees, and wiping public bathroom sinks or toilets with smelly cleansers. The fathers would find menial work at local construction sites or in busy warehouses, but they would often spend their pitiful paychecks on beer or whiskey at the local taverns, ignoring the fact that hungry children were at home alone. Their wives would offer retaliation by leaving their houses filthy and unkempt until the husbands would rant and rave about the mess. Fights would ensue and women, or sometimes even the men, would endure slaps or scratches on their faces, or arms wrenched out of place, and the children would hide under beds and in closets away from the fray.

On one particularly hot and stuffy October afternoon, Sheila received a call from a hysterical woman who lived in a rundown two bedroom apartment across town with her four small children. She was unemployed, living on the welfare checks that barely made ends meet. Her husband was usually absent but would return from time to time to push her into bed for an hour and then verbally accost her for being a poor lover and terrible mother. This day had been no different from many others before it for the woman, but when Sheila arrived on her doorstep she was met with a monster, for the woman's face had been battered purple, one eye completely swollen shut and a deep bloody gash over the other. She was missing two teeth and her lip was puffed wide like an indigo sausage. She had wrapped her arm in a thin rag that covered a deep red contusion under which a broken bone distinctly protruded under her skin. Her four children who ranged in age from two to eight sat huddled together in a row on the sofa. The oldest, a girl, had protectively placed her arms around the others who all silently stared wide-eyed at Sheila who had gently guided their mother to a straight-backed cane chair. The woman sat with her head hung down, looking at her own skinny hands that lay limp in her lap. Her thinning hair had been pulled back into a knot at the back of her neck and was held with a thick rubber band. The apartment was a mess with clothes and a few broken toys strewn about the floor. Dirty dishes were piled in the kitchen sink and scattered about on a small metal table. A profuse smell of urine permeated the thick humid air. Sheila had no choice. She called the police who arrived quickly. Two somber-faced officers efficiently took the report, curtly spoke to the injured woman, and then to the frightened children. The woman was ushered into an ambulance and the children were separated in twos and placed in protective custody. This had not been the first time and they complied without crying. They knew they would return to this place in a few days. Nothing would change.

In November when she arrived at her office she was met by a man whose age she could not determine. He was dressed in coveralls over which he wore an ancient leather jacket, the mottled sleeves scratched and faded. It had probably been beautiful once, but now it sagged from the man's shoulders like a primordial elephant hide lending an aged look to him overall. He had most likely been handsome at one time, she imagined, but now his cheeks and neck were covered in a scraggly beard and his skin was weathered brown with deep wrinkles on his forehead and under his eyes which were strikingly blue and looked at her now with a distinct yearning, a call for help. He obviously had been crying. His sixteen year old daughter who had been a runaway for two weeks had reappeared that morning, trying quietly to crawl into her bed unnoticed, but he had heard. She was instantly asleep and when he went to her, she stirred briefly, mumbling something incoherent about home before she drifted into sleep again. He had watched her for a long moment. She was pale and fragile, a child who wanted so badly to grow up. Without the heavy make-up she usually wore, she looked like his little girl again and he was sad, because she smelled of smoke and whiskey and sex. He had no clue where she had been. Losing women had been the story of his life he had said. His first wife had been killed in a car accident, and his second had left him two months after the birth of their daughter. He had never seen her again. He had done his best, he said, to raise the little girl, but she was on her own too much. He needed some guidance. He was afraid.

December brought three reports from school officials of suspected child abuse – bruises on an arm and neck, a cigarette burn on the back of a tiny hand, broken glasses and a deep cut under one eye. It brought frantic calls from parents whose kids were out until all hours, creeping in at dawn, passing out in the doorway, or blatantly having intercourse in the shadows on the front porch. It brought warnings from unknown sources alerting Sheila and her cohorts that a neighbor had left his or her child or children alone for three days or four days or forever. It brought a call from a teenage boy whose mother had passed out in the bathroom and could not be revived and from a ten-year old girl whose grandpa was cold and dead in his wheel chair in front of a blaring television. It brought calls from foster parents who could not control a wayward teenager or could not comfort a baby born to a drug addicted mother. It brought call, after call after call. Sheila had been left shaking inside at times as adrenaline took its hold on her when she felt frightened or intimidated or sad. But by January, she began to relax. Although demoralized by more than a few despicable situations she had learned to restrain her immediate reactions and even hide her emotions so she could do what she had been trained to do. Giving and helping were as much a part of her being as the skin that held her, but as time wore on, she was beginning to develop a harder shell at least in regard to her profession. In other areas of her life she was less disciplined and controlled.

The rash of emergencies and seemingly constant crises delivered to Sheila in the first few months of her job brought her more than enough to occupy her mind, but the season also delivered, right on her doorstep, another dilemma – James Madison Jackson. On the day he had watched her move into her apartment in October James had marked her as his next conquest, and he was quite sure she would not resist him. He was, after all, good-looking, intelligent, and well on his way to being wealthy. With a law degree under his belt and a position at one of the most prestigious law firms in Nashville, he was set. His parents had provided him with presidential names and he aimed to hold the standard.

In a sweet and gentlemanly manner he wooed Sheila aggressively and effectively. First, by designed chance, he met her in the apartment complex parking lot on a beautiful autumn evening, pulling his new Ford Mustang so close to her little Volkswagen that she couldn't open the door. She had no option but to talk to him.

"Hey there," she said, "Think you're a little bit too close. Don't think I can get out a' my car."

"Why that's a shame," he said. "Guess you'll just have t' talk t' me for a minute now won't ya'?"

Sheila rolled her eyes, but smiled anyway. He was nice to look at. That was certain.

"My name's James," he said politely. "Saw ya' movin' in a while back, but haven't had a chance t' meet ya'. I live in the other building just across the yard from ya'."

"Sheila. Sheila Jenkins," she offered in reply.

"What do ya' do, Sheila Jenkins?" he asked, charming her immediately by addressing her with her full name and grinning a smile that caused his deep brown eyes to crinkle closed.

"Social work. Work for the city a' Nashville. Was hired after I graduated from the university." Was she telling him too much?

"Tennessee?" he asked.

"Yeah, University a' Tennessee, down in Knoxville," she added. "An' what do you do?"

"Law. Benson Law Firm hired me on beginnin' a' the summer. It's been a real nice opportunity."

"I reckon it is," she said, instantly wishing she could abandon just a bit of the southern vernacular that was so engrained and then she added, "Sounds nice, sounds like a real wonderful profession."

"I think it will be," he replied and then with the same quick spontaneity as when he had swiftly and smoothly maneuvered his car in beside hers in the parking lot, he said, "Can I take ya' t' dinner, Sheila Jenkins? Think I won't be able t' sleep tonight 'less I spend a little more time with ya'."

Sheila laughed then, and it felt good to do so. Her days had been so serious of late that she had wondered if laughter had deserted her completely.

"Well, I'm not goin' anywhere 'til a certain person named James moves his car, so I can get out a' mine!"

His eyes crinkled again and he started his car, backing out quickly and then expertly redirecting it into the middle of the space. Before she could gather her belongings, he was there beside her window, looking down at her and opening the car door. He was tall, very tall. So was she, but she had to look up to James. "Well?" he asked again. "Ya' goin' t' say yes?"

"I know ya' as James. That's all. Maybe I should know your whole name if I'm goin' t' have dinner with ya'."

"So ya' will then? Good," he said, happy he had won his case. "My name's James Jackson, James Madison Jackson t' be exact," he said, and then added jokingly, "My parents want me t' be president."

That conversation began it all.

James was more than attentive during the first year they were together. Every Friday evening he brought her flowers: plain white daisies wrapped in yellow tissue, brilliant red roses kissed with baby's breath, or bouquets of colorful mixed flowers. "T' perk up your weekend," he'd say. They had dinner every Saturday night, lingering over their dessert and sipping port, wine or coffee swirling with whipped cream. A few times they dined at an expensive downtown restaurant he had selected, sometimes he suggested they simply walk to the small cozy diner around the corner, or more often, Sheila would cook, turning out a gourmet meal that James said was second to none. Sitting comfortably on the sofa, James would watch her whip up their supper, calling out like a country bumpkin, "Where's my food, woman?" And although he was teasing, the reality was that he relished being waited on by Sheila. He knew he could become very used to this. It didn't take long either for them to find that they were as compatible in bed as out of it, and they spent many sultry hours exploring each other in the darkened bedroom. Sheila gave herself to James completely and although she was not always sexually fulfilled entirely, he was.

On Sundays they would drive in his sleek black Mustang to the countryside and explore sites they had never seen before. He would spread out a map on the hood of his car and point, "We're headin' here t'day," or "I want t' see what this area's like." Sheila would silently nod in agreement with his decisions. She just wanted to be with him. They would walk hand-in-hand along manicured park trails, or find a rock on which to perch near a lazy stream. They talked and talked, usually about his cases and his ambitions, until their thoughts were spent and then he would kiss her so sweetly she would have the urge to nibble on his lips, but she would pull back and look again at the crinkled eyes hiding in his smiling face.

Sheila introduced James to her mother and to Ray who both were instantly charmed by his fine, smooth manners and gift of gab, as Sara called it. He would talk Ray's arm off about hunting and fishing, football and basketball, automobiles, politics, or the weather. It didn't matter. James knew he could chitchat with anyone and when the moment was right he would wink at Sara behind Ray's back. "Now James Jackson, ya' better behave yerself," she'd scold, but she loved the attention and he enjoyed hearing her amused and artificial protest. "My mama would a' called him a looker fer cert'in," she told Sheila when James was out of earshot, "An' I reckon he'd be a darn good catch!"

"Oh, Mother, we're not there yet," she had responded repeatedly over the course of a few months, but the fact of the matter was, the catch was close at hand. James would soon broadcast that he had snagged the girl who was going to be his wife. Sheila and her mother planned the wedding between job obligations and times protectively set aside by James for his bride and himself alone. Sara had wanted a late summer evening wedding outside near the pond by the house. She had envisioned a simple affair with only friends and family gathered there to share the moment. James had insisted it be at the largest Methodist church in Nashville. His whole firm would be invited, as would their families. He had an image to project and with his lovely bride secured, the setting for the marriage was most important. The wedding would be in October, he said, because that's the month he had first seen her. Although he was not sentimental in the slightest way, he knew how to ply and nudge until he got his way. Not wanting to disappoint him or start their married life out on the wrong foot, Sheila acquiesced.

Ray and Sara generously supported James's decision, but the fact that the wedding would be financed by them bothered Sheila and she bristled inside more than a few times when James's arrogant demands imposed on her folks. She loved him though, and when he said, "I want your weddin' day t' be perfect, Sheila Jenkins," she believed him, burying with his words the uneasiness that began to dwell inside her. Her mother and Ray appeared to take their obligatory responsibility in stride although they seemed less enthralled with James as the wedding neared. Sheila wondered if behind closed doors they weren't annoyed and aggravated to have been relegated to the role of providers with little consideration given to their input. Eventually to alleviate the burgeoning costs, Sheila secretly took her entire savings and slipped it confidentially to Sara who took it without a word.

The wedding would be a stunning event, for James wanted it no other way and in the background his family egged him on with ostentatious orders and pretentious plans of their own. Long stretch limousines, dark tuxedos complete with tails, a flowing white satin beaded wedding dress for the bride and demure dresses the subtle colors of burgundy and creamy white for the bride's attendants were ordered. An adorable flower girl dressed in pink and white and a ring bearer donning a tiny tux would complete the wedding party. Pink roses secured with satin and velvet ribbons would drape the ends of the pews on each row of every aisle in the church and dominate every table at the sit down reception supper. A string ensemble was hired to provide the appropriate music for the ceremony and a jazz band was employed for reception dancing. And, of course, champagne and other inviting liquid refreshments would be offered liberally, and one would assume, consumed without restraint. Not one detail was missed.

Despite the monetary imposition, Sara was caught up in the excitement of the planning and buoyed Sheila's spirits when she was overwhelmed with the details. Fortunately Shelia's choice for her maid of honor and other attendants was honored. Elaine, Melanie, Joan, and Sharon would stand beside her on the day she became James's wife and although their friendship had remained loosely in tact at best over the years, the wedding would be a chance for another reunion, this time occurring on a happier occasion than the one following Melanie's mother's funeral.

What they could not foresee however, is that although they would joyfully be together during the morning and for the actual wedding ceremony, at the evening's end each would drift away from the lavish event a bit disillusioned about the fate of the union.

October in Tennessee could be breathlessly hot and humid or it could be very, very cold with arctic air sliding down through Illinois, Indiana, and Kentucky to the countryside below covering it with a thin layer of frost that warned of winter. On the day of the wedding, however, it was neither. It was balmy and mildly humid but with an oppressive tenor to the air that lay over the city of Nashville. In the early morning Sheila had heard vague rumblings of thunder in the distance, but the sky had remained a remarkably deep blue with dark dense clouds visible only in the remote northwestern sky. It reminded Sheila of tornado weather, but it wasn't the season for that. Tornados happened in the spring usually, or in the early summer and surely would not happen on this day.

The ceremony had been scheduled for the late afternoon in order for James and his associates from the law firm to play a round of golf and down a drink or two afterwards at the country club. Sheila would not see him until the moment Ray walked her down the aisle. She had stayed with her mother the night before, and on that morning only the female members of the wedding party were invited to join her. All of them would dress there and at three o'clock in the afternoon they would be whisked by limousine to the church. James had forcefully overseen the timing of the event assuring the wedding party that his logic and control would be appreciated when a flawless day prevailed.

While James was golfing, Sheila was panicking.

"For somebody havin' the biggest weddin' a' the century, ya' don't look real happy, Sheila," Sharon said.

"I'm happy. I am. I am happy," she said three times consecutively as if to convince herself. "I'm just worried. What if somethin' goes wrong? James'll have a hissy fit."

"Well it's your day as much as his, remember," Sharon added. Though her sarcasm had somewhat moderated over the years, she still told it like it was. "Ya' need t' put a smile on that face. Right now ya' look like ya' just met up with some kind a' varmint in your kitchen!"

"Good grief," Elaine chimed in. "Where in the hell do ya' get these harebrained images, Sharon?"

"Only tryin' t' lighten up the mood 'round here, that's all!" Sharon defended herself.

Sheila watched the two women interact and was abruptly and rather unexpectedly taken aback by the change in roles they had assumed with the passing of the years. Sharon had always been the one to throw her judgments like tainted darts at other folks as she had done when Elaine had endured her teenage pregnancy years ago, but now Elaine had the upper hand. She was educated, independent, and well on her way to being a doctor. Sharon had softened her sarcasm but Sheila suspected she had hardened inside for the dimpled smiles were few and far between. Too many years of dealing with Billy's belligerent behavior and diapering the three children they had produced in quick succession had taken away her saucy spark. She was still a pretty girl, perhaps even more so than she had been in high school, for the haughtiness had lessened. She still had her say when she felt she could, but more often than not, she was silent, especially in the presence of her too often inebriated husband. Her marriage clearly had not been the fairy tale Sharon had envisioned, although anyone who knew her doubted she would admit it. Now, however, Sheila wondered if this day, her wedding day, was conjuring memories and more than a few regrets for her friend.

"I reckon I need t' start on this hair a' mine," Sharon said. "It's a sight!" She was right. Over night her bouncy brown curls had transformed into a mass of frizzy fluff that lay tangled on the back of her head and neck.

"You're goin' t' have t' wet it down an' comb it out," Melanie said gently, still hesitant to give even the slightest hint of advice. The years had not been kind to Melanie either. Sara liked to excuse her appearance, citing the years of poverty and grief over her mother's horrific illness and untimely death as the culprits that had made her age before her time. She was still thin and willowy, but her once shimmering light brown hair was already streaked with gray and lay flat against her head, cut bluntly at the shoulders. To Sara's knowledge she had never had a man in her life after her mother had died, but she had moved from the rundown house of her parent's and now lived in a small, quaint cottage in a quiet Nashville suburb. She still worked at the J. J. Newberry store, and efficiently directed the bustling business just as Sara had done. Ray thought the world of her and kept her content with hefty raises and unexpected bonuses in order to retain her at the reins of his store.

"Well, I reckon ya' need a little work on that mess a' yours, too, Miss Melanie!" Sharon snapped showing a bit of the old fire and creating an uncomfortable silence.

Joan, who had been calmly munching on a fat chocolate doughnut, fortunately broke in with her usual good humor, "Well, I guess we all better get crackin'. Poor James is goin' t' break down in tears if we show up at his weddin' lookin' like we all just came in from out a' the rain!" Unknown to her, an unsightly blob of thick chocolate had stuck to the corner of her mouth giving her a piggish appearance.

"Good grief, Joan. Look at ya'," Elaine said, brushing her thick blond hair that had grown nearly to her waist. She was conscious of her beauty, and was determined to keep herself healthy, thin, and well-groomed. Her world at the University of Kentucky was a hotbed of horny young interns who would lavish her with compliments and then take her to bed. She was disgusted looking now at Joan's chubby face and arms, not because she disliked her in any way. In fact, she adored Joan and admired her for her tenacity. She had a stick-to-it-ness that few people possessed. She had held true to her college sweetheart, Dwayne, and they had married quietly in the evening shadows of a chapel near Tusculum College with only their parents as witnesses. Dwayne worked now in a bank in the heart of Nashville, his economics background, imposing size, and booming voice, being attributes that had him solidly in line for management. Joan had become a kindergarten teacher, her sweet smile and soft, plump body a pleasant welcoming form for frightened children who often were attending school for the first time.

"I love ya', Joan," Elaine continued, "But ya' need t' get int' that gorgeous dress James an' Sheila's picked out for ya'. Ya' worry me sometimes." And it was true. Elaine wished Joan could lose some of the flabby fat for her health if for no other reason.

"Yes, Mam, doctor," Joan chuckled, letting the admonishment slide over her like a puff of warm air. "I'll get myself int' it, an' I'm goin' t' be gorgeous. Why Dwayne's goin' t' want t' marry me all over again!"

The playful conversation continued throughout the morning and into the early afternoon and by then Sheila was a bundle of nerves. When she finally retreated to her old childhood bedroom with Sara, the other women knew it was time. They primped and teased and combed until all were satisfied with the mirror's reflection. With mascara, shadow, blush, and lipstick lavishly applied to perfection, they slid on their burgundy dresses and stood in an awkward circle staring at each other. And then it happened. A snicker from Joan opened the doors and the four fell into gales of laughter. It was a sweet and sudden release of emotion that astonished them all, and then the absurd inapt hilarity ended just as quickly as it had begun.

"We look beautiful," Sharon said candidly, "All a' us."

"Why, Sharon, I think you're right again," Melanie said, looking down at herself and gently brushing the front of the burgundy satin.

"Thank ya', God, we're not goin' t' disappoint ol' James after all," Joan said, not relinquishing her obvious distaste for the man's pomposity.

"Be nice, honey," Elaine said. "James deserves his day too." She didn't know why she was defending him, because she actually agreed with Joan. The arrogance James projected had not been lost on her either.

At that moment the door of Sheila's old bedroom opened and Sara stepped out looking incredible in a long, stylish beige dress that accentuated her still slim figure. Her face was glowing and she beamed her beautiful smile as she announced, "Ladies, the bride."

Sheila had never looked more beautiful. The exquisite bridal gown was adorned with beaded pearls and intricate tightly embroidered lace over pure white satin forming the upper bodice and then flowing down a narrow train that extended for three feet behind her. The neckline dipped alluringly and the slender capped sleeves sat delicately at her shoulders and accentuated Sheila's well-defined tanned arms. The white satin skirt of the gown was slender and touched the ground with perfect delicacy. Her long dark hair had been curled and was clipped with tiny white rosettes that also secured the veil that James had insisted she wear. Satin pumps added inches to Sheila's height and when she glided into the room her friends couldn't take their eyes off her statuesque image.

"Oh, Sheila, you're a vision, honey, a perfect vision," Sharon said, and although her throat tightened with an unexpected and unexplainable sadness, she meant it.

When the shiny white limousine arrived at the front steps of the veranda at the exact moment it had been expected, the women were more than ready. They were anxious actually to get on with the day, for the long morning had been oddly exhausting. While their reunion had been anticipated and even welcomed, unknown to the others, it had left each woman toying with the curious realization that their lives had moved in surprisingly different directions. An unexplainable bond of friendship held them together and yet fate and choice had determined distinctly diverse paths for them all. It was ironic that while they would not have chanced to articulate the feelings they had, they secretly all felt the same, and as they left the house that afternoon a pall of uneasiness set over them.

The driver, accustomed to his role, expertly helped the women into the vehicle making sure that dresses were not crumpled and hair not mussed. He held their hands until they were seated securely, and then he said, "I reckon yer all ready fer the big day. Hope the clouds yonder keep their distance fer a spell." When he closed the door the women could hear muffled thunder in the distance. Sheila touched her mother's hand gently then. Sensing her need for reassurance, Sara cradled her daughter's hands in her own.

"That darned ol' weather'd better keep its distance," Sara said softly, recognizing the worry that settled in her stomach.

"You're right about that," Elaine added. "It will. Why the sky's still blue overhead. I think if a storm comes in, it'll be t'morrow." She had no idea how prophetic her seemingly innocuous statement was.

Chapter Twenty

When Sheila stepped onto the wide carpeted aisle of the church that day she held Ray's arm so tightly he stopped for a second and reached around to pat her shoulder reassuringly.

"Yer beautiful, honey," he whispered. "Smile yer beautiful smile, now." He was a happy man that afternoon for Sheila had made sure he knew he was the father she had never had. He was honored to escort his wife's daughter as though she were his own.

"Thank ya' Ray," she responded, tearing slightly. "Thank ya' for comin' int' my life."

"I'm honored, honey, t' give ya' away," he said into her ear, "But don't forget t' keep a little piece a' yerself."

She looked at him, confused by his words, but she smiled and they began their trek down the aisle to James whose eyes were riveted on them.

The wedding seemed to be over before it began and later as Sheila would remember the event, it came in snippets – the walk with Ray that seemed an eternity, the joining of hands, the minister's words of hope and promise, the rings, the I do's, the removing of the veil, the kiss that lingered a bit too long, and then the smiles and the hasty exit. The church had been packed, the sea of faces joyful, and the heads bobbing for a better angle with which to see the striking couple better. She recalled the flowers and the long ribbons that trailed from them at the end of each pew. She could actually see the streaming ribbons fluttering in the tiny breeze that was created as she and James brushed by them. It was that minute detail that would last the longest in her memory. She wasn't sure why her eyes had fallen to them as she and James left the church. Perhaps it had been an inadvertent action that hid the emotions that her eyes would not have been able to hide, for at that very instant she was unsure about James for the first time. She loved him, but she wasn't sure if it was too little or too much. The promise of the happiness she had dreamed of lay before her as though on the precarious edge of a deep precipice.

Sheila endured the wedding reception receiving line shaking the hands of people she had never seen before. Friends and associates of James they were, so she smiled until her face felt frozen. She received hugs and squeezes and too many kisses from old men who smelled of cigar smoke or whiskey and by overly made-up women with bouffant hairdos and heavy perfume that preceded them by yards. *"Yer jist such a sweet couple,"* they would say, *"a downright charmin' couple." "An' I reckon yer goin' t' have little ones b'fore ya' know it." "Such a lovely weddin', wasn't it, sugah?" "Reckon yer goin' t' remember this day fer a long, long spell now."* Sheila's voice left her mute in the face of such comments and she felt the smile transform into a smirk.

Younger men shook her hand lightly and guffawed to James that he was a lucky old buck while their wives or dates would flash a disdainful look at Sheila and then smile demurely at James. Little girls wearing frilly dresses puffed out with crinolines and too-tight patent leather shoes would hold Sheila's hand and look up at her as though she were a princess. By the time the last person had passed by her, she felt light-headed and silently wished for sleep.

The evening was a whirl as the wedding ceremony had been. She remembered picking at her supper, sipping champagne from a crystal glass, hearing a toast from the best man, followed by a flurry of unsolicited toasts from men who were drunk and crude; she remembered being pulled to her feet for her first dance with James as his wife. He had held her close and looked over her shoulder at the line of women who enviously stared at Sheila in his arms. She danced then with Ray, and with James's father, also a James, and with a few other souls who passed her from one to the next as if she were a package on an assembly line. When she could escape, she did, finding her mother leaning close to Ray at a corner table. They had retreated too from the frenetic confusion of the dance floor. Sheila did not have to say a word. She just sat for a time enjoying their quiet company and understanding that they must have felt as ill at ease with the garish gathering as she did. James was in his element though, chatting with his associates, their wives, and even their children. He had danced with Sara, his mother, and all of Sheila's attendants. His eyes had disappeared into deep crinkles as he smiled time and time again. He was having the time of his life.

When it was time, the crowd ushered the newlyweds to the waiting Mustang that had been decorated tackily with off-color remarks scrawled in white shoe polish on the windows. Behind the car, tied with heavy string were tin cans and empty beer cans that would clatter noisily on the pavement when the car finally departed. James and Sheila would spend their first night together in their new house, a modest red brick affair that was located in one of the new subdivisions sprouting up on the outskirts of town. Their house sat amid a cluster of modern, brand new structures that all looked similar and that stood naked of adornments on barren lots at the mercy of the elements. The couple had their work cut out for them. James had put a down payment on the place before he had even shown it to Sheila and had carried her over the threshold three weeks before they were married. "This is goin' t' be our little home, Sheila Jenkins," he had said, "an' when ya' become Mrs. Jackson, we're goin' t' fix up the yard, get ourselves a dog an' a cat, an' have us some children. You'll be able t' stay home in no time an' take care of the place."

Sheila had let him talk but in the back of her mind she had thought, "I do have a job, James, an' it's one I like," but the words had lodged there and were unspoken. They had dragged their furniture from their apartments in town and furnished the house as best they could. James's folks had bought them a new Frigidaire and a range the color of burnt gold. The also had given them their first living room set, a traditional arrangement that Sheila thought would have looked better at an old folks home, but she had thanked them profusely and told herself it would make do. It was a start.

The day after the wedding they were to set out for Gatlinburg, Tennessee for a five day honeymoon. James had secured a quaint chalet with spectacular views of the Smoky Mountains. At this time of year the trees would be a masterpiece of color as the winter chill bit into the landscape changing leaves from green to gold, red, orange, yellow, and rusty shades of brown. Sheila could hardly wait to get there.

Over night, however, while James slept soundly, sporadically piercing the night with his snores, Sheila lay awake listening to a heavy rain that pelted the roof of the house mercilessly. Sheets of water smacked against the window panes in a repetitious rhythm that accompanied the thunder's resonating echo. The growling sound was no longer far away, but above them making its presence known with booming force. Lightning lit the sky, with brilliant flashes bringing details from the darkness. Without a sound, she slid from bed and stood at the window watching the spectacle play out before her. Lightning bolts quivered across the black sky in majestic arcs that splintered brightly sending branches of silver in myriad directions. Thunder would follow then, cracking loud and close, shaking the windows and doors dauntingly. The cacophony of nature's tumult was awesome and frightening. The relentless wind whistled and howled throwing God only knows what against the windows and then whisking it off again into the blackness. Sheila saw a limp lawn chair flip into the air and then land smack down into a deep puddle. A child's tricycle rolled over and twisted violently into the sloppy mud of the adjacent yard that was vacant of any landscaping. A huge barren stick blasted toward the window where Sheila stood, and slammed against the glass sticking there. The shock of its force made her step back hastily and almost involuntarily. Feeling vulnerable and alone, she snuggled back into bed and willed sleep to come to her. When finally it did, she was awaked by James who had sobered enough to want her and while he heaved and moaned on top of her, she lay still. He didn't seem to notice her lack of passion and when he was done, he rolled on his back, stretching his limbs and sighing deeply. Oblivious to the continuing clatter of thunder and rain, almost instantly he was asleep again. She looked at his handsome face in the gloomy morning light for a moment or two and then she turned away curling into a fetal position and she lay there motionless as hot tears rolled down her cheeks onto the sheet that had cooled in the night air.

"Sheila, what are ya' thinkin'? I'm not drivin' all the way t' Gatlinburg in this weather. It's floodin' ever'where. Ya' need t' get your head on straight! I thought I'd married a girl who had a little more common sense than you're showing me." James forceful words stung Sheila. He had never talked to her in that tone before.

"I just asked if we were still goin'. That's all. Didn't mean t' get ya' all upset."

"Well use the good brain God gave ya', Sheila. It's just logical that we can't go now. We're goin' t' have t' hole up here for awhile," he said. "But I'll make it worth your while, sugah baby!"

"Sugah baby? What has gotten int' ya' t'day, James? You're like a different person," she said seriously, ignoring his innuendo. "I'll get your breakfast. You're prob'ly starvin'."

The first conversation on the first day of their marriage established a disconcerting and perplexing pattern that unfortunately many more of their exchanges emulated in the months that followed. James was a perfectly sweet and doting husband at times, but it was as though his good humor and bad behavior came and went in a circular motion, leaving Sheila off balance and unsure. She found herself dreading the mornings because she didn't know what mood he would be in and it was his frame of mind that set the tone of the day.

Sheila strangely found solace in her job, a job that sometimes in the past had been taxing and stressful. More and more, however she would welcome the challenges her profession offered and it kept her very, very busy. She was an industrious, diligent worker who became adept at resolving crises that were perpetually presenting themselves. She quickly found that when she was involved in helping solve the problems that confronted other families she was able to push aside, at least for a time, her own confusing anxieties. The days would fly by. She was, nonetheless, unable to escape completely the reality of her own circumstances and suffered silently as a result. Obscure and indecipherable dreams dominated her sleep, or sleep evaded her altogether. Then she would force herself to lie perfectly still and stare into the night not wanting to toss and turn and wake her sleeping husband. Sometimes she would get up and wander into the kitchen and gaze blankly into the refrigerator, or she would sit in her rocking chair, the one Sara had given her, and look out the window slowly pulling images from the inky shadows outside the window until her eyelids grew heavy. She would often doze there until the pale morning light begged her to start another day. If James missed her presence in bed, he did not let her know. In four months she had lost ten pounds and she was plagued by unwanted rosy blemishes that appeared at will on her cheeks and nose. Food was unappealing though it was a focus for her as she prepared sumptuous suppers for James night after night. Her mind was never silent. Ceaseless chatter dominated her thoughts as she became more and more mystified by the dreadful demeanor James demonstrated in her presence regularly. As loving as he was at moments, it was as though he would transform into another person at the drop of a hat. From a state of seeming contentment, he would suddenly become harsh, judgmental, and condescending. "Sheila, do somethin' with your hair, would ya'. Ya' look like a floozy." "Read the newspaper once in awhile. Ya' might learn somethin' an' be able t' hold a decent conversation." "What in God's Earth prompted ya' t' buy that lamp? It's God awful. Now get it out a' here." "Sheila, I think the least ya' can do is have dinner ready when I get home, for Christ's sake!" "Are ya' takin' care a' yourself, Sheila? You're lookin' a little bit shabby. You're not goin' t' the country club social lookin' like that. Do I have t' go alone?" On and on the comments continued wearing heavily on Sheila. She was becoming run down and so tired that she secretly worried about her health.

Fortunately the winter had passed quickly and Tennessee was enjoying an early spring that year. The warm sun beamed its radiance on Nashville drawing little miracles out of the ground – crocus, daffodils, irises, freesias – and the trees were alive with the twitter of tiny finches and sparrows. Fat breasted robins would step delicately across the warming soil and pluck juicy earthworms, pulling and pulling until they sprang out of the ground in a twisting fury, while vigilant Blue Jays or portly Blackbirds would incessantly squawk at their industry from a distance. It was the time of year when Sheila loved to drive out to visit her mother and Ray where the beauty of the season seemed to be multiplied ten-fold.

On one particular April morning, feeling dazed by dreams that had tormented her night, Sheila couldn't seem to arrive there fast enough. She loved the place. Sara would prepare something simple and delicious and she would bask in the warmth of her mother's company. On this day, however, in the midst of their lunch, Sara gingerly commented on Sheila's appearance. Besides the dark circles under her eyes, Sara had noticed the sloping shoulders and crossed arms, an unusual posture that made Sheila look as though she was closing in on herself, making herself smaller.

"Are things all right with James an' you?" Sara asked. "Ya' look a little tired, honey."

"Yeah, they are. Well, usually. He's pretty cranky sometimes though."

"What da' ya' mean, cranky?" Sara was concerned.

"Oh, he just says things that make me feel kind a' blue. Says I don't look good enough. Says I'm not smart. Sometimes I get real down in the dumps 'cause of it."

Sara bristled when she heard. "Why Sheila Masie Jenkins, yer as smart as a whip an' cute as a button. What in the world is wrong with that man?"

She did not even notice her inadvertent omission of Jackson, Sheila's married name.

"I don't know, Ma, but sometimes I want t' be at work instead of at home. Sometimes I just don't want t' be near him 'cause he whips me like a dog with what he says. An' ya' know what bothers me s' much is that I should know better than t' let him. It's my job. I know my job better 'en I know myself sometimes an' when people act like jack asses, like James does now an' then, I try real hard t' stop it."

Sara could feel herself tensing, eager to respond, but she remained silent and let Sheila continue.

"I see it ever' day, Ma. Folks hurtin' other folks. People bein' treated unfair. People hurtin' real bad. I can help them, but when it comes t' James, I just can't seem t' stand up for myself. Seems I've lost all my oomph, at least 'round him. I don't like him much these days, t' tell ya' the truth an' I'm fed up with myself for puttin' up with his shit, but I just don't have the energy t' fight it." Sheila wished instantly that she could retract some of what she had just said, but the words had poured out of her like raging water, the heat of her emotion having melted the icy restraints that bound her. The last thing she wanted was to worry her mother but the release felt warm and liberating.

"Good grief, Sheila. Yer jist too good t' James. He don't likely appreciate ya' an' what ya' do. An' ya' been there fer James, cookin' an' cleanin' that house a' his. Why it looks jist like a little doll house. Pretty as a picture, it is. Do ya' reckon ya' done spoilt James? Ya' always did wear yer heart on yer sleeve. Why, when ya' were jist a little bit ya' used t' come home with birds with broken wings or butterflies that couldn't fly. Ya'd cry over a crippled dog an' want me t' take home ever' little kitten we'd see that was offered up in a basket or box somewhere. Ya'd never even kill a spider. Made me gather 'em up on a paper an' shoo 'em outside. Ya've always been so good t' ever'body, all yer friends, 'specially Elaine when she was goin' through a bad patch. An' now yer out an' 'bout town helpin' all kinds a' folks ya' don't even know. Don't seem right t' me that anybody'd treat ya' unkind an' t' think James is doin' that makes me s' mad I could jist spit!"

"Oh, Ma, I believe maybe he's under some pressure at his job, tryin' t' look good an' make his mark. He's been workin' real hard, stayin' at work late sometimes. Oh, he'll bring me a batch a' flowers from time t' time, 'cause he's feeling guilty I guess."

"Guilty?"

"Well, I think he feels bad when he's real late or comes home grouchy. He can be real ornery when he gets in 'til he gets some food under his belt. So he'll bring in some flowers or a little somethin' t' say he's sorry, I guess."

"Does he ever say he's sorry?"

"No. For heaven's sake, Ma, he'd never do that. Don't think he has it in him t' actually say the words. That doesn't fit with his personality. Ya' know James, Mother. He doesn't like bein' wrong 'bout anything, an' he sure isn't goin' t' admit t' somethin' he's done wrong no matter whether he should or not."

"Well, 'scuse me fer givin' ya' a word a' advice that I reckon ya' prob'ly don't want anyways, but ya' need t' speak up fer yerself, Sheila," her mother admonished.

"I know I do, an' I will. I will. It's just lately I've been s' tired. Havin' crazy dreams like flyin' on a roller coaster over an ocean, an' there's no end t' it. Or I'm on a big cargo boat goin' down a channel out t' sea. Don't know where the boat's goin', just on its way somewhere with me on it. Or I'm swimmin' in a swimmin' pool s' big it's amazin', an' I just swim an' swim. Don't ever get out. Pool's outside a big ol' mansion, white columns, an' green gardens as neat as a pin."

Sara listened. It was all she could do, but worry crept over her and her convoluted thoughts swirled in dizzying circles almost making her nauseous.

"I had a dream the other night 'bout walkin' 'long side a canal an' the banks were all sandy an' collapsin'. Some little ragtag boy was tryin' t' sail a boat in the water. It was a teensy toy sailboat an' the water was real murky an' dirty. I told him t' get back 'cause I was afraid he'd fall in. Don't remember if he listened t' me or not. Guess I woke up 'fore I found out if he fell in or got away. Aren't those crazy dreams, Ma? Don't have any idea if they mean somethin' or not."

"Well, folks say dreams mean somethin'," Sara offered.

"They're pretty interestin' t' me. All in color. Lots a' action. Sometimes I just want t' go back t' sleep an' get back int' the story. Ya' know, find out what's next. An' I remember 'em. Fact is, I've been writin' 'em down, 'cause they interest me s' much."

"Well, I've had a few dreams myself, but what yer describin' takes the cake. I always figured when yer dreamin' yer jist workin' out yer demons or sortin' out yer hopes an' aspirations."

Sheila giggled then, the little girl giggle Sara had heard for years. "Maybe I'll tell 'em t' James. That'll really send him reelin'!" The dark eyes flashed their golden spark and Sara was relieved to see Sheila's spirit that had been absent of late, rekindled just a bit if only for an instant.

Sara smiled and then asked one more question, one that had been nagging her although she recognized it was not really her business. "Is he good t' ya otherwise, Sheila? Are ya' gettin' along, ya' know, in the bedroom?"

"Yeah, Ma. We're good there, I guess. James is always ready for that. I'm keepin' him happy in that way, I guess. When he's hateful though, my heart's not quite s' in t' it.

But, we're okay. Fact is, I think he's wantin' children. Says I'll have t' quit my job though. Wants me home if it comes t' that."

"An' what d' ya' want yerself?" Sara asked.

"Don't know if it's time yet. I like workin', but then again, I think maybe a baby might perk up our lives some."

"Well, ya'll are goin' t' have t' think 'bout that real hard. Startin' a family's a big decision. I reckon I kain't wait t' be a grandma though. Think I want t' be called Grandma Sara."

"Good grief, Ma. Guess James just got your vote!"

Sara blushed. "I'm sorry, Sheila. Like I been tellin' ya', I believe I'm turnin' int' a sappy ol' woman, but I remember ya' when ya' were a little thing an' ya' made me happy as could be. Jist wanted t' look at ya'. Could a' spent my whole day jist lookin', ya' were so sweet."

"I love ya', Ma. Thanks for listenin' t' my woes."

"I'm always here fer ya', honey. Always."

Chapter Twenty-One

Sara didn't realize it then, but she would get her wish and would also be held to her promise. On Christmas day, eight months after their springtime chat, Sheila and James presented Sara and Ray with a tiny box wrapped in shiny silver paper and a bright blue bow.

"Not much of a gift, this year," James said slyly, "but we're watchin' our pennies."

"Open it, honey" Ray said to Sara taking in the scene. Always the observer, he watched his wife gently pick at the present, not wanting to tear the ribbon or the paper. It was her habit to keep things neat and tidy. While he would have ripped the box open in seconds, she took her time. Sheila looked on, with a slight grin toying at the corners of mouth. James was serious and consciously so. When finally the tiny box lay free of its wrapping, Sara opened it. Inside were two teeny blue booties. That was the announcement. James and Sara's baby would be born in June.

"We're lookin' t' have a boy," James said self-assuredly.

"Well, 'course we don't know for sure," Sheila said timidly, "but that's what James wants. A boy, first. Guess we could find out, but we're wantin' it t' be a surprise."

James shot her a hateful look that did not go unnoticed by Ray. It troubled Ray deeply and he aimed not to forget it. A loathing glance like his at the moment when such a pristine announcement had been made was incongruous to say the least. He looked at Sheila whose face had taken on that of a stricken, injured child, and then at Sara who had not noticed and was blathering with joy.

"Ah, honey, this is s' wonderful. S' excitin'. My goodness, how life's goin' t' change 'round here with a little one t' cuddle up an' love." Sara was ecstatic and her mind was an immediate whirlwind, thinking of all that needed to be done to prepare for her first grandbaby's birth.

"Well, ya' have a good while t' wait, Mother." Sheila said in an unemotional tone that belied the trembling she felt inside. She bit her lip to stop the tears that threatened to expose her feelings and then, like clockwork, she busied herself, first rushing to the car where all the other presents lay waiting, shuffling them into the house in great shopping bags, and then flitting about the room playing Santa Claus. She lost herself in the pleasure of watching the others leaving her own gifts unopened until Sara chastised her gently.

"Sheila Masie, yer turn! At least open this one."

It was a bright green package tied with a minute red ribbon so tiny Sheila might have missed it had Sara not have plucked it from one of the lower branches of the tree and handed it to her. Inside, lying in a bed of soft white cotton was a lovely gold locket, the same antique locket that Sara's mama had left her in her Will. It had been polished until it sparkled and when opened Sheila found two little photographs, one of Sara and one of herself. She held it gently for a moment and then began to cry. "Oh, Ma," she said, "Your mama's locket."

"I want ya' t' have it, honey, an' some day it'll pass on down t' yer little girl. That's the way I hope it'll be."

"It will be, Mother. I'll make sure of it."

The men looked at the two women's interchange, Ray with a gentle grin and James with a cold stare.

The rest of the Christmas day passed in a blur of vapid conversation and meaningless discussions about topics no one would remember after that afternoon. Sara had prepared a feast of turkey, corn bread stuffing, gravy floating with woo woos, as her mama would have called them, baked yams still in the skin, fluffy mashed potatoes, and her favorite green bean casserole, the recipe having been passed down from her mama's mama. She served cut-out Christmas tree cookies covered with too-sweet colored icing, pecan, mincemeat, and pumpkin pies, thick chocolate fudge packed with walnuts, and dates filled with creamy powdered sugar icing and pecans. And there was a fruit cake that had been jammed with candied fruits, walnuts, raisins, and soaked in rum. To drink she served hot custard, sweet apple cider, and chilled Chardonnay wine. When the meal was over, the men slouched on the overstuffed divan and dozed while Sara and Sheila cleaned the kitchen. It was a traditional and customary Christmas day, save for an undercurrent of hostility that no one could have denied existed and that lay festering in James's core.

In the months that followed, while Sheila's body blossomed, James struggled to maintain his civility. A bitterly cold January and February mirrored the relationship between the two. Sheila had wanted to work until the spring, but in early March, James put his foot down.

"I won't have ya' traipsing all over the city in your condition. Ya' need t' quit your job, an' now, Sheila."

"I'm fine, James. I have clients who need my help."

"Sheila, I'm sayin' one last time, ya' need t' give up your job. I'm insistin' on this now an' I won't have ya' disputin' what I say," he snapped. "I've got more important issues t' think about than worrin' 'bout you."

His words stung.

They called for a heart-to-heart, but this time, instead of bothering her mother, Sheila called Elaine who was still at the University of Kentucky deep in her medical school studies, and then she called Sharon, who now lived nearby in a new brick house not too far from Sheila's. She had finally graduated from the double-wide trailer and was wrapped up completely in decorating her house and picking up after her children who were holy terrors.

"Tell him t' get his head out a' his ass!" Elaine had said. "Who in the hell made him God?"

"Well, I can't quite put it that way, Elaine."

"I could, if I were you. Ya' have a career, Sheila. Ya' don't have t' give it up just 'cause you're havin' a kid, for Christ's sake! Ya' just need t' stop workin' when ya' have the baby an' then ya' can go back, unless ya' want t' give up your entire self for that pompous son of a bitch." She couldn't hide her disdain for the man any longer. "Is that what ya' want, Sheila?"

"I don't know, Elaine. I love my job an' I'm good at it, but I'm not sure this is worth the battle. He's goin' t' keep harpin' on me, an' then pesterin' some more. He can be s' hateful sometimes."

"What are ya' goin' t' do all day at home? Just sit? I couldn't take that myself, but then, I'm not you, Sheila. You're goin' t' have t' stand up an' either do what ya' want yourself, or give in t' him. It's your choice, honey. I love ya' no matter what ya' do. But don't give yourself up completely."

"When are ya' comin' home again, Elaine?" Sheila asked then, missing her friend more than ever.

"I'll be back t' visit one a' these days real soon, honey. Got a shitload of studyin' t' do. I'll be in touch. Ya' take care a' yourself now."

From Sharon, the advice was like night and day. "Oh my, Sheila, I reckon I'd jump at the chance t' stay home if I were you. I'll tell ya' the God's honest truth. I haven't worked a day in my life, 'cept t' take care a' the kids, an' that's enough for me. Billy's doin' real good with his daddy's business now an' we got just 'bout all I could want. Billy's gone a good amount 'a time durin' the day, an' lets me handle the kids my own way. When he's home, I'm there for him an' he brings home the bacon so t' speak."

"Ya' ever get tired a' bein' alone? Stayin' home all the time?" Sheila asked.

"No, Mam, I sure don't. Wouldn't change a thing. I love bein' home for Billy. Why we're in hog heaven an' I'm just as happy as can be," she said, perhaps convincing herself more than her friend.

"If I were in your shoes, Sheila," she continued, "I'd quit that stressin' job quick as I could an' get on with life. Why James an' that little baby you're goin' t' have are what's important. Not all those poor people who have more troubles than ya' can shake a stick at!"

Sheila should have just made up her own mind, because her friends' comments confused her even more. Elaine was right. Why give up her career? And Sharon had a point too. Wasn't her family more important than anyone one else's? What convinced her finally was James himself because his demanding pleas became belligerent threats.

"You're goin' t' quit that job or else, Sheila. People at the firm are talkin' 'bout ya' an' judgin' me 'cause I don't have control over ya'. That don't set well with me, so you're goin' t' quit an' stay home. I'm not discussin' this any more." His face had turned red and the veins in his neck pulsed in and out repulsively. Sheila was afraid of him for the first time. She gave in then, thinking naively that when she did so, he would change. He would revert into the sweet charmer she had married.

It was not, unfortunately for her, to be so.

※

On the first day of summer, one day after the date that Sara's mama had died years before, Sheila gave birth to a chubby eight pound baby girl. James was conspicuously absent on the day she was born, miles away on a business trip in Chicago. After a quick and relatively easy labor, the baby was placed in Sheila's arms under the bright lights of the delivery room amid several competent smiling nurses and a sober-faced doctor who stood between Sheila's sprawled out legs with a needle in his latex-gloved hand. He had anesthetized her private area and performed an episiotomy to ease the baby's entry. Now he was expertly stitching her vaginal opening, closing the incision. "You're goin' t' be good as new," he chuckled tacklessly. "You'll be perfect for your husband when the time comes."

"What are ya' goin' t' name your baby girl?" a nurse asked from the side of the room. She was efficiently filling out the birth data on a paper form. James and Sheila had not discussed a name for a girl. If the baby had been a boy, it would have been named James, James Madison Jackson, the third.

"She's goin' t' be Lainy Raye," said Sheila. "Lainy Raye Jackson's her name."

She named her after Elaine and Ray, the two most important people in her life aside from her mother.

Ray took on the dubious task of informing James that his healthy baby girl had been born in his absence. He noted an extended silence on the end of the phone line after he had broken the news that had elated the rest of the family, and then James informed him in a cold, emotionless voice that he would not be returning for a week or two. He was involved in a pressing case, he said, that would keep him in Chicago for some time more. He did not even ask the baby's name.

Ray did not try to convince him to come home. He did not try to convince him that his wife would expect him, that custom would have him cuddling his baby and passing out cigars to his friends and family. He did not try to convince him because in the year before Lainy's birth, he had grown to detest James. James had become increasingly arrogant, having gained attention locally by trying a few notable cases, one which had led to the incarceration of young teen who had been caught stealing from Ray's store. Ray had felt the penalty too harsh, but James had pushed for the maximum sentence, dragging up the boy's horrendous family history, and embarrassing Sheila who had once had them as clients and had not been able to help them sort out their sordid lives. Having his name or photograph in the newspaper meant more to James than even he could ever have imagined. He read news articles over and over and insisted that Sheila cut them out and carefully place them in a scrapbook that highlighted his cases and his accomplishments. James also had made it an objective to be seen at expensive cocktail luncheons in town with local businessmen who recognized James's increasing power and tried to influence him with lavish gifts and other offerings that left him on the golf course too long or that took him on business trips to other cities too often. Ray expected he had been given access to more than a few young escorts for evening events that he would not allow Sheila to attend because of her pregnancy. Ray hated to admit that he harbored such a hostile unforgiving opinion about James but the man's extreme egotistical bearing was an affront to

Ray's more unassuming disposition. In the past year when they were together it was like mixing oil and water, and both Sheila and Sara had begun to make excuses for not arranging family get-togethers to avoid the uncomfortable atmosphere that none of them could deny dominated the gatherings.

When James did finally come home in early July he looked at Lainy as though she were a repugnant rag doll. He chose not to hold her, much less change a diaper or a tiny soft or frilly article of clothing. He resented her cries or babblings and was repulsed by her smells. He would spend enough time with Sheila to take her to bed, eat his supper silently with her, and then excuse himself to his lounge chair to read the newspaper or review his proofs. If the baby cried, Sheila was instructed to shut her up any way she could so that James's comfort and quiet were not disturbed. Sheila put up with his pig-headedness, not because she was afraid of him, and not because she was conditioned to it, but because with the passing of every day she disliked him more and more and willed herself to ignore his obstinacy. She did not hate him, but she knew she did not love him enough either. She numbly existed when he was present and breathed more easily when he was not. She would have given anything not to care at all, but unfortunately that was not the case, and her inability to help herself began to affect her in a harmful, disconcerting manner. Elaine had warned her before the baby was born not to give herself up completely, and just before the wedding, Ray had told her to keep a piece of herself. She had not understood fully what either of them had meant at the moments the loving warnings had been issued but she was afraid as she evaluated her present circumstances that she had disappointed them both, as she had herself. James regarded her only as his dutiful wife – the one who prepared his suppers, kept his house respectably clean and presentable, and spread her legs for him on demand. She saw herself as Lainy's mother, Sara's daughter, a friend to a few, and nothing else. Her former profession as a social worker had given her life a purpose that had filled her with energy and powered her innate sense of organization and compassionate nature. It was gone now, and while she would never have dismissed her motherhood as insignificant or purposeless, it left her with too much time on her hands and too little intellectual stimuli. It was then that an unwanted melancholy and dreary depression edged into her days and remarkably vivid dreams of theatrical proportions invaded her nights.

She began to eat then too, and she ate more and more until in no time at all, she had gained fifty pounds of delicious fat. She actually loved being chubby because James stayed away longer and she had Lainy to herself. She spent more time with Sharon who was more than happy to have Sheila's company, and her old friend adored Lainy. She would plop the baby over her knee and rub her little back watching from above as she would smile a sideways toothless grin and drool onto Sharon's legs. Sharon took it in stride, enjoying having an infant in her arms again. Her three were growing faster than weeds and she fortunately had convinced Billy that the kids they had were plenty. She was taking every precaution not to have another, and although Billy liked to ride her like a truck whenever he could, she was careful of their timing.

"Oh, God, Sheila. Ya'd think we were back in high school the way Billy is these days. Can't seem t' get enough."

"Well, I hate t' say, it Sharon, but sex isn't somethin' that's happenin' in my life these days. James is gone all the time it seems. I've been readin' an' readin' ever' evenin' 'til I get s' sleepy my eyes won't stay open. Sometimes Lainy'll keep me awake nights, but she's sleepin' better an' so am I. Been dreamin' dreams that keep me wantin' t' sleep all day."

As active as she appeared to be chasing Lainy around the house, shopping for groceries at the Kroger store or for nothing in particular at the J. J. Newberry store just so she could gossip for a spell with Melanie, visiting Sara or Sharon, or tending her extensive vegetable garden in the back yard, Sheila still led a sedentary lifestyle that added to the inches around her belly. She cooked, cleaned, or shopped in the morning and then watched soap operas in the afternoon, waiting for a phone call from James alerting her if he'd be home or not. He often offered some explanation or excuse as to why he would be late or why he would not be home at all. On occasion the call came well into the night after supper had been prepared for hours and sat cold and blubbery on the table. As the months passed, periodically James did not call at all. If he did come home he expected his supper ready; if he didn't he disregarded his own insensitivity, saying nothing. He would never have apologized and Sheila learned not to expect it. To onlookers their little family looked typical enough, but Sheila understood that it held very few of the characteristics that defined normalcy. With dysfunction at its core, its unraveling was a certainty, although even Sheila had not come to grips with the veracity of James's duplicitous existence with her. Both she and James were friendly and chatty to their neighbors, attended services at the Methodist church where they had been married on Easter or Mother's Day, Thanksgiving or Christmas Eve; they barbequed with Sharon, Billy and their kids on the rare occasion that James would stand for it, and once a few months after Lainy's birth they had driven off for a five-day vacation to the mountains.

During the days of late summer and early fall Sheila and Sara would meet for lunch or drive to the produce stand outside of town. They bought bushels of fruits and vegetables and laughed with each other over the steaming stove filled with pots of boiling water and liquefying fruits or stewing vegetables while Lainy wiggled and cooed in her bassinette in the corner of the kitchen. Sterilized Mason jars stood in rows like obedient hostages on the tile countertop, their wide mouths ready for filling. Ray sometimes stopped by just to watch the two women work, cuddling the baby and making silly noises that made Lainy smile widely, exposing her bare pink gums, and cause Sara to roll her eyes at his antics. At those times they were happy, all four of them. But when Sheila drove away to her home in town, Sara and Ray vented their frustrations about James who Ray now referred to as "a plain ol' ass" and who Sara called an "ol' so an' so". They routinely and astutely confided to each other their worries about Sheila and Lainy and knew insightfully that they were correct to do so.

"Sheila, what in the hell have ya' been doin' all day?"

James was in one of his moods again, dark, brooding, and angry, a likeness that emulated the first autumn storm that had been threatening all day. He had been gone for a week, again in Chicago, which seemed to have become his home away from home.

"I was at my mother's. Didn't know ya' were comin' in t'night. Ya' didn't call." Sheila said, defending herself and hating the fact that she felt she had to do so. She had left the kitchen in a hurry that day, leaving dirty dishes piled in the sink and several of Lainy's dolls and ABC blocks tossed around the linoleum floor. Her dreams had left her groggy that morning and she had decided that the dishes weren't running away. She'd planned to be home before James anyway, but the canning project had taken longer than she had expected.

"I did call ya', but ya' were gallivantin' 'round God knows where. Christ Almighty, Sheila. Look at ya'!"

"I told ya' I was at my mother's."

Sheila looked down at herself then, suddenly embarrassed at what she saw. She wore a pair of Ray's old overalls with a thin pink blouse under it and although she had worn an apron all afternoon splatters of sticky strawberry and plum juices were stuck to the sides of the legs. She had a habit of wiping her dirty fingers on her hips when she was in the midst of one of her cooking projects, being more intent on the process than on her looks. She reached up to touch her long hair that she had woven into two long braids and found a clump of sticky goo tangled there as well. And she was barefoot. Lainy clung to her leg, a mess herself, with a sticky purple stain around her lips and on her tiny fingers. She wore a soiled pink polka-dot dress and had dirtied her diaper on the ride home adding a less than inviting smell to her appearance. Her hair had not grown enough to take a definitive shape, and it stood out from her head in a wild fluff that looked like soft, dirty straw. She looked up at James with wide brown eyes as though he were a stranger and began to whimper. Sheila protectively gathered her into her arms abruptly and walked directly towards the bedroom.

"I'll get your supper in a minute, after we clean up."

"I don't want your supper. Ya' disgust me. I'll go to the club where I don't have t' look at ya'." He slammed the front door on his way out, but Sheila knew he would be back soon enough, for his opened luggage filled with wrinkled dirty clothes lay on the bed in their bedroom. She knew she would be expected to unpack his things and wash them immediately. Who knew when he'd be leaving again?

When he was gone, Sheila wandered into the bathroom with Lainy and ran a tub of luke warm water. While Lainy sat in the shallow suds, smacking her hands happily against the porcelain tub and squeezing her plastic yellow duck, Sheila stripped off her clothes. When she was naked she did what she had seldom done since Lainy's birth. She looked at her body in the mirror. James was right. She looked disgusting. As she gazed at her now fleshy body that had once been willowy and slim she began to weep. Where her stomach had been firm and flat, a roll of flabby fat had formed. Silent tears ran down her face and she knew she had made a disastrous choice. Rather than speaking her mind, rather than stating her opinions, she had silenced herself. In the face of James's intimidating power, she had submitted, and she had lost herself in both body and spirit.

"What have ya' done?" she said to herself and then she added, "What have I done t' myself, little girl?" looking at the adorable baby who smiled up at her.

"We got t' take hold a' this, an' now," she said out loud. Tenaciousness had always been one of Sheila's assets, and she determined at that moment, that she would find her voice again. She had to, for herself, if not for her little girl.

When James returned later that evening, Lainy was sound asleep. The kitchen was spotless, the toys put away, and Sheila had showered. Comfortable in a mocha-colored satin gown and robe, she sat in bed, leaning against the soft pillows. Her beautiful, long hair had been washed, dried, and brushed until it sparkled even in the dim lamp light. On her lap lay open her latest novel of choice, *Angle of Repose* by Wallace Stegner, but she had not been reading. Not tonight. For at that moment in her fist she held an earring, a woman's small pearl and diamond earring. She had found it stuck in the silky lining of James's suitcase. It was not hers. She held it tightly with an intensity that mimicked the beating of her heart and the sinking feeling in her stomach. Would she have the courage to confront James about her finding? She had emptied his luggage completely, tossing dirty clothes into the new washing machine that had been a gift to her from Ray and Sara when the baby was born.

"Yer goin' t' need this t' help ya' out more 'an anything," Ray had said authoritatively when the machine had been installed, as though he knew a thing about taking care of an infant. She knew Sara had convinced him to purchase it and adored him for his generosity and love.

But when James's clothes were thrown into the gaping machine that night, Sheila felt anything but love. She was enraged. With each item she threw in she added an expletive. *"Ya' ass! Ya' son of a bitch! Ya' bastard! Ya' jerk! Ya' slimy worm!"* On and on, she talked to the clothing as though the items were James himself, hating the fact that she was touching them, hating that they had touched someone else, hating, hating. She was furious at James, but equally angry at herself for being ambivalent, for being stupid, for ignoring the signals that James had been sending her for months. How many nights had he come home late or not at all? How many weeks had he spent in Chicago? Other lawyers at the firm stayed in Nashville. The other lawyers went home to their families. Why was he the one sent out of town? He had said it was because he was the newest member of the firm; he had said he was building his practice; he had said his reputation warranted it; he had said he needed to make the right connections; he had said it was for her and for their family. He had lied. Over and over he had lied.

And this night, he lied once more.

When he walked into the bedroom he looked at her through glassy eyes and muttered, "Ya' look real beautiful there, Sheila. I think I'm goin' t' make love t' ya'."

"No." It was the only word she could manage, but it was a word.

"What d' ya' mean, no?" he slurred.

"I mean, no," she said again. "Ya' can make love t' your girlfriend." There. She had said it, and as she did, she threw the earring at James.

"I want ya' out a' my house."

"Ah, Sheila. These are for you. I got this for you. There's another one somewhere," he said, fumbling in his jacket pocket, his pants pocket, and then patting the bedspread without rhyme or reason with his outspread fingers. He leaned into her then trying to force his lips onto hers. She smelled him. The odor was musky, sweet and sour at the same time. She knew that smell from her own body, from touching herself, from their own love making.

"Who have ya' been with t'night, James?" she asked. "Who this time?"

At the moment the words were issued, his body straightened and tensed. His eyes narrowed and disappeared in the deep sockets on his flushed face. He had been caught, and because of that his arm pulled back and then began its forward motion in her direction. A flat palm landed firmly on her cheek, and she reeled back, knocking her head against the headboard that slammed the wall noisily. She was more startled than scared, but she gathered her book to her chest and through clinched teeth managed to say, "I want ya' t' leave. I want ya' out a' here. Ya' can get your clothes another time. Get. Get while ya' can, James, 'cause if ya' touch me again, or if ya' wake up my baby, there'll be hell t' pay."

She was silent then and she glared at him with a vehement hatred, but her heart was racing so quickly and pounding in her chest so profoundly that she was sure he could hear it. Her words floated in the air between them and he looked at her with a sick grin. His eyes had disappeared again into the face she had once found so alluring, and for the first time in her life she hoped never to see them again.

He turned then, and walked out. When the door had closed and she heard his car crunch on the gravel driveway outside, she finally breathed. She sat for some moments in the still of the night, unable to move, aware only of her heart that continued beating violently in her chest. And then the silence disappeared and she welcomed into her consciousness the gently grating sound of crickets in the grass outside, of a bull frog calling in the distance, of a cooing dove in the darkness, and of Lainy's tiny cry that resonated in the dark and then silenced itself. It was a moment Sheila would remember for a long, long time. It was the moment when she knew she had left at last her silent self behind. She realized she had a journey ahead of her, but she was willing to take it. She would take it, not because she had to do so, but because she chose to do so. It was a horrid, satisfying awakening.

<hr />

When at mid-morning, Sheila finally opened her eyes to an unexpectedly bright sun shining through the white chintz curtains she realized surprisingly that she had slept. She could not recall falling asleep but she knew she had because she had dreamed, and the dream was as vivid in her consciousness as a movie scene, colorful and played out in slow motion. As though readying herself to write a script, she recreated the dream for herself. She did not want to forget it.

I can see her in my big house. It's a rambling, multi-storied house that sits alone on a bluff above an ocean, but I see her only in my private bathroom, a small space; she is there, undressing, gyrating, showing her tiny breasts to the mirror, her shoulders slumped first forward and then eased backwards, her short-cropped, dirty blond hair wet with sweat and sticking to her forehead. She thinks she's sexy, I know. I perceive she has this perception and I'm watching, sitting half naked on the toilet with purpose postponed, in amazement of her assuredness, of her ability to move in a manner, which God only knows why, must have moved him. I'm not able to take my eyes from this woman who slowly removes the items that are her clothing . . . a sleeveless navy blouse, stylish Capri pants, khaki-colored I believe, and held with a wide red vinyl belt. Beneath are panties, cotton, not brief, but small because she is; and she holds a lacey white bra used to cover her minute breasts. Several unsightly hairs are projecting from each and glinting in the light that seeps through the tiny window onto her moist body. I wonder where he is. Not visible to me; to her, he is, because she smiles, a wistful, pleasing smile that knows its job and that has seen its success.

And elsewhere in my house, I hear the noises of others. They're the social workers I know and admire, the anguished mothers who call for my help and my high school friends. I hear Elaine's soothing voice, and Sharon's, yelling happily at her children. I hear Joan's jolly giggle and Melanie's tearful sobs. In my house are former lovers and future ones, maybe. They're gossips and well-wishers and hangers-on, those who somehow gain strength from another's sadness, confusion, and pain. They roam my big house and wait for me to find them. Before I can seek comfort in their being there, they disappear and she, the woman with one pearl and diamond earring, fades away . . .

Sheila suddenly became aware of Lainy's whimper. "How long has she been cryin'?" she said aloud to herself. It was past nine o'clock and Lainy was usually awake by seven. Jumping from the crumpled covers, Sheila practically sprinted to her baby's crib. Lainy lay there red faced and mad as a hornet, as Sara would have described her, her lips puckered into a tiny O that oozed bubbles of spit. Her eyes were wet, her already-long lashes clumped together dramatically as though they belonged on the painted face of a doll. Her hair was spread out wildly in every which direction, an image of electrified fright in the absence of her mother.

"Oh, honey. I'm so sorry! Did Mommy ignore ya'?" Sheila picked up Lainy into her arms and cuddled her, filling the tight wrinkles on her little neck with kisses. The baby stopped crying immediately and began her morning ritual of cooing and babbling. Sheila sighed, relieved that no harm had been done, but she was agitated and irritated with herself. Was this the way she was going to begin the next phase of her life?

When Lainy had been fed and dressed, Sheila sipped black coffee and bit hungrily into a ripe banana. Today was the beginning. Though her dream had left her somewhat groggy, confused, and shaken that morning, she had not forgotten the formidable evening before. She certainly had not forgotten the interaction with James, for her cheek still bore a dark pink shadow, an imprint left from his palm and fingers, but she also remembered her vow to herself. She wanted herself back now. She knew she had lost what she thought she had known so well; she knew she had given the very essence of herself away, but the promise she had made to herself just the evening before had not been an empty one. With renewed spirit flickering in her core, she knew what she needed to do.

She looked around the kitchen and began hefting unwanted items into the garbage can – a loaf of white Wonder bread, a thick slice of chocolate cake that sat appealingly on its plate wrapped in cellophane, an unopened package of apple and brown sugar crunch pastries, a nearly empty half gallon of chocolate milk, a half gallon of French vanilla ice cream, a half-eaten bag of potato chips, and a box of sticky caramels that James had brought home as a peace offering some weeks before. It was a start.

When the phone rang, she jumped, afraid to answer, afraid not to.

"Hello?" she said tentatively.

"Hi, honey." It was Sara. "I know James is there so I won't keep ya' but I want t' bring by a few jars a' the jelly we made yesterday. Got some strawberry, plum, an' blackberry. Looks real good. Can ya' believe, it actually jelled? Don't know what we did right this time! Would it be a bother if I run by? I'll leave Ray here. Love t' see little Lainy fer a minute or two though." She was chattering happily and then stopped noticing the profound silence on the other end of the line. She was instinctively uneasy. "What? What's happenin'?" she asked, her voice filled with concern.

"Oh, Ma, I need ya'. Can I come out there? I need t' be in a place I can talk."

"Ya' come on out right now, honey. Are ya' okay? Can ya' drive? Do I need Ray t' come git ya'?"

"I'm okay, Ma, but I have a lot t' tell ya'. I have s' much t' say, I don't know where I'm goin' t' begin. I'll be there in two shakes." And then she added, "It's over, Ma. James an' me. We're finished."

With the connection severed Sara stood staring vacantly, holding the phone receiver in her hand as though it were a trophy. She was overcome with a sense of joy she would never have fathomed and definitely not expressed to anyone, save Ray. "Ray," she called, "Somethin's happened."

Sheila grabbed Lainy, a few toys, some clothes for the baby, two bottles of formula, and her bag. She ran to her Volkswagen, backed it out quickly and was on the road in seconds. Her timing was perfect, for just ten minutes after she had left, James drove into the driveway. He had sobered and his serious face meant business. His jaw was set firm, his dark eyes narrowed, and his mouth was drawn into an unsmiling arc that made him look older than his years. Anyone who may have looked at him at that moment knew that his appearance displayed the same intent and determined expression that had manipulated his colleagues and countless others, had won many of his cases, and had launched his career. What they may not have known is that the same face and the mind-set that accompanied it had in effect incarcerated his wife and child for months. Now, in his own selfish inimitable way he was reaping what he had sown. Though he would be quick to comprehend the turmoil and anxiety he had created, he would not so easily accept his culpability in the matter. He was so lost in his own self-importance that his ego would not allow that, and yet to his chagrin, the acknowledgment and acceptance of the newly denigrating circumstances he had attained would take time and effort even James was not sure he could muster.

Chapter Twenty-Two

James set forth a superficial struggle to keep his family intact at first but his intent to do so quickly materialized as shallow and halfhearted resulting rapidly in the first significant loss in his life. With apathetic appeals he asked Sheila to stay with him for his career, for his reputation, and for financial reasons, but his halfhearted efforts fell on deaf ears. Sheila was through. She had had enough of James Madison Jackson for a lifetime, and with more support than she knew what to do with, combined with her mantra of "Stay mad. Stay mad," churning in her thoughts day after day she was able to maintain her resolve.

"Thank ya', God," Elaine said when she heard the news. She expressed her feelings with absolute certainty. "It's about time ya' got that asshole out a' your life! I couldn't be happier for ya'."

Sharon had been less sure. "Well, I think maybe ya' ought t' try an' work things out. Maybe give him another chance? Ah, shucks, Sheila, I'm goin' t' miss your company in the neighborhood an' I hate t' see ya' havin' t' work again. Won't be good for Lainy. She needs her mama 'round." Sharon had driven to Sara's house and sat on one of the rocking chairs on the veranda watching her children race around the fenced-in meadow like young race horses. She chewed her lip, and looked completely crestfallen, most likely wondering how she'd fare in a similar situation. She would never leave Billy, no matter what. God only knew he wasn't perfect but he was steady enough and she knew what she needed to do to keep him home. She stared at Sheila sullenly and muttered, "Hell, I can't tell ya' what's right, can I? I reckon ya' ought t' do what ya' want t' do. It's not what I'd do, but I can't change nothin' 'bout this situation. It just makes me sad, that's all." Her acquiescence surprised even her because her own self-interested intent had been to convince Sheila to reconcile with James no matter what anyone else said.

Joan was aligned with Elaine on the matter. "Never did like the son of a gun," she said. "Always thought ya' deserved better. He was s' stuck on himself he didn't give ya' the time a' day as though his custom was the rule. An' the way he treated little Lainy, ignorin' her like he did, why I was afraid he might scar her for life." Joan was the elementary teacher who saw every child as a unique little being made to be nurtured and primed for the future. She was out to save every one of them.

Melanie kept her opinion on the matter to herself, but she did suggest an attorney, her friend, a woman named Charlotte Owens, who in no time had set the divorce process in motion.

Ray was happier than a pig wallowing in warm mud. He had watched Sheila suffer silently and had wanted more than anything to help, but he was in the odd position of being Sara's husband, not really Sheila's father. He had made it a point to be careful, not wanting to interfere in matters that were too personal, too daunting, and too private. He had provided where he could, but had been astute enough to stand back when he knew it was best.

And Sara? Sara was happy too, not because she wanted her daughter's life to be more difficult, as it was likely to be now that she would be raising Lainy mostly by herself. She had been in the same position years before and knew the challenges, but Sheila would cope just fine. She knew her daughter well enough to know that. James had made it clear he wanted nothing to do with the baby. He would give Sheila full custody. That in itself was a blessing to Sara because in her mind James would have done more harm than good when it came to Lainy; furthermore, James's parents had him on such a pedestal that they would not fight to see her either. If she wasn't worth James's time, she certainly wasn't worth theirs.

Sara tried to soften the situation, by telling Sheila, "I know it's common t' say, but the apple don't fall far from the tree. It's the truth. An' I remember my own mama used t' tell me over an' over, 'Sara Mae, ya' need to remember that two stones hewn from the same rock are likely t' be purty much jist like each other.' Then she'd say, 'Remember that, 'cause recognizin' it'll come in handy sooner or later. It'll help ya' with yer judgment a' folks.' My mama was always full of advice."

Sara's faraway look made her appear sad momentarily, but she was not. On the contrary, she was thinking of her mama with rare warmth. After all these years Mama's worn out sayings still rang true and bolstered her judgment of Sheila's current state of affairs. From early on James and his pretentious parents had rubbed Sara the wrong way and she was content to know that neither he nor they would ever set foot inside her door again.

After the initial flurry of explanations, consolations, advice, and congratulations, Sheila took control. In two months the house in the subdivision had been sold to an eager couple with three scruffy little children under the age of five, Sheila had regained her job as a social worker for the city, she had found a comfortable little cottage close to Melanie's to live, she had hired Sharon, who was more than enthusiastic about it, to babysit Lainy when Sara could not, and she had lost twenty pounds. She felt exhilarated about the new course her life was taking as the days flew by, but at night she was still plagued by dreams that she could not yet comprehend. That would take much more time.

Part Four

Chapter Twenty-Three

On Lainy Raye's third birthday, all hell broke loose. After a morning of bright sunshine, the day began to darken rapidly, thick sinister clouds tumbling over one another like rolling ocean waves in the black and purple sky. The air grew more ominously heavy and humid as the minutes ticked by and every person at Ray and Sara's house stood in awe of nature's swift and fickle fury. Nashville's weather had always been a meteorologist's dream with climate extremes that never failed to excite even the most staunch and resolute forecasters. Today would be one to remember for all of them.

Sharon and Billy were at the house doting happily on their uncontrollable children, as were Joan and Dwayne who clung to each other like fat monkeys, always patting and grooming each other, the touches becoming caresses when their arms eventually intertwined completely. Also there were Melanie and Charlotte whose close relationship was a secret to everyone except their close group of friends, present company included. Even Sharon, who could be as abrasive as a flint when it came to judging others, took their relationship in stride. The fact of the matter was she had never seen two people more suited for one another. When their eyes met, it created an indescribable current that hung in the air like a rich and smothering sweet perfume. It could not be overlooked or disregarded. Elaine was expected any minute with her new boyfriend, a doctor from Lexington who had broken hearts all over the University of Kentucky campus when his eyes had landed on Elaine. He had been smitten from the beginning, and although she had resisted him at first, she eventually had fallen head over heels in love with Dr. Steven Matthews, an internist who practiced in town and lectured at the university.

In the middle of the afternoon when everyone had been fed and the women had settled for a spell on the veranda, rocking gently or leaning warily against the railings watching the sky, Shelia put Lainy down for a nap in her old bedroom. Too much cake, ice cream, and excitement had transformed the normally calm little girl into a cranky, sniveling brat. Even Sheila, who had the patience of a saint couldn't wait for sleep to overtake her. Sharon's boys were still circling the meadow, but had slowed considerably and were gazing upward at the churning charcoal clouds that had nearly turned their bright day into night right before their very eyes.

"Ya'll come on in now," Sharon yelled at them. "Looks like it's goin' t' pour. I don't want ya' gettin' soaked t' the skin!"

It was late afternoon, but the sun should still have been high in the western sky. Instead it had disappeared completely behind the menacing clouds. The contents of the brick barbeque still smoldered in the yard outside. Billy, Ray, and Dwayne stood around the structure, wispy smoke swirling around their heads sporadically before being sucked upwards towards the heavens. The smell of charcoal and sweet hickory still wafted through the air but the wind began to strengthen taking any hint of fragrance with it. The breezy air around the house was whipping the fragile colorful balloons that had been tied to the railing of the veranda into a frenzy of tangled strings and the balls of color slid against each other with annoying screeches that made the children scream and hold their ears.

"It's too late in the season for a twister," Billy said looking upwards into the sky. "Sure looks like it though. Ya'll come in now," he hollered at his sons. "I said, now! This instant!"

The three tow-haired youngsters paid direct attention to their daddy who didn't have to ask twice for them to obey.

"Reckon we all should go inside," Ray said. "Maybe we can catch a forecast on the television. This don't look good, if ya' ask me. Don't reckon I've ever seen it cloud up s' fast before. Looks like the devil!"

Once inside, the group of friends settled on the divan and floor in front of Ray's new Motorola television. It was a new console that made Ray proud as punch to own and show off. "I'm not much fer material goods," he said. "Can take 'em or leave 'em, but I mean t' tell ya' this television here is real nice. Why it gits four channels an' the black an' white's as clear as a picture. Real crisp like."

"Yeah, it's a beauty," Billy commented, coveting it and figuring furtively a way to manage one himself. Why he'd be he envy of the subdivision with that thing in his living room.

Baseball games dominated two of the channels and a minister was preaching on another, but the fourth channel was fortunately focused on the weather. In no uncertain terms the forecaster warned local folks to get inside, and fast. A tornado had set down in the county just west of Nashville and two others had been sighted, wide swirling funnels that had been seen spinning down from the clouds, but had not touched ground. People needed to be ready for the worst. Reverting to his southern accent, the reporter spoke with anxious haste, "Close your windows an' doors. Pull the shades an' get int' the basement soons ya' can," the newscaster said. "If ya' have a cellar a' some kind, climb int' it. Get some water an' stay put 'cause we're predictin' . . ." and then all was static. The picture swirled into jagged lines of grays and charcoals before going completely black.

"Let's go. Basement's this way," Ray ordered. He began pushing his guests forward into the kitchen and towards a closed door behind which a staircase led down to the basement that housed the fat coal furnace and was where Ray stored his tools, old newspapers, magazines, and discarded clothing. It was a damp, black, mold-infested pit. The smell of mildew permeated the cold air there making the children protest the stink and hold their noses. "Go on now," he directed them firmly ignoring their whines. "I'll find a jug a' water an' think I got a transistor radio somewheres 'round here. Ya'll go on down. Sit yerselves in a corner." Outside the rain had begun pelting the house, blowing sideways into the windows while the doors vibrated in place ominously.

"Lainy, Lainy. Got t' get her," Sheila hollered. She ran into the bedroom that had been her own cozy haven years before and collected the little girl into her arms that were tense with fear. She was on the staircase behind the others in seconds.

"Get a flashlight, Ray," she could hear Billy order and then she heard the front door fly open, the wind racking it against the wall. Billy had run out the front door to his truck where he knew his own flashlight was tucked in the glove compartment. As he touched the door of his truck a bolt of lightning lit the sky and thunder crashed instantaneously. "God, that was close!" he said to himself, grabbing the flashlight and bolting back into the house. It took effort to push the door closed behind him and as he was doing so, he noticed headlights bobbling in the rain that was peppering down relentlessly.

"Who in the hell would be out in this?" he thought and then he remembered Elaine. A tiny sports car veritably skidded to within inches of the back of Billy's truck and he saw instantly the look of terror in the faces of Elaine and Steve who tore out of the car and through the door into Billy's broad arms.

"Shit, Billy," Elaine sputtered. "There's more wind an' rain than I've ever seen out there. Scary as hell. Billy, Steve."

"Good t' meet ya', but we got t' get out a' this doorway an' now. Come on. Ever'one's in the basement." Together the two men pushed the door closed, latching it against the raging downpour outside.

Ray was the last person down the stairs. He and Dwayne had found a jug for water and carried the illusive transistor radio that Ray finally had located in the pantry. He grabbed a box of crackers and some cookies for the children, closed the door to the basement, and had just reached the bottom of the stairs when the sound of shattering glass deafened them all. The wind was a whistle then, a loud screeching howl that drew shrieks from the children and cries of alarm from the others.

"God almighty," Ray shuttered. "I reckon we've done been hit."

For twenty minutes the group huddled together in the northwest corner of the basement. They could hear crashes above – splintering wood, metal objects slapping into each other, and glass breaking. In the darkness not one person's limb was not touching at least one other arm or leg, neck or head. The group held each other and then Sara began to hum. She remembered, for some reason, one of her mama's favorite songs, *Rock of Ages, Cleft for Me*. She hummed, sweetly and clearly beneath the fury that was creating havoc above them. No one joined her song, but no one protested either; instead they all grew quiet. Even the children stopped their whimpering, and then, it was over. As intensely as it had begun, it ended. Above them was an overwhelming silence, and when it seemed time, one by one, they stood in the darkness as Ray led the way up the stairs to lightening sky.

They stepped into a kitchen devoid of windows, the bright calico curtains torn into shreds and flapping in empty frames, and yet the cabinets remained firmly closed, the dishes resting neatly on the shelves as though they had just been placed there. The refrigerator door was open and askew on its hinges, the contents strew across the linoleum floor. The kitchen table was gone completely and the chairs were on their sides. One stuck stubbornly in the middle of a window frame devoid of glass. The brick barbecue pit lay in rubble outside, and while the birthday balloons were long gone, a tenacious circle of string was still tied to the railing of the veranda. A railing had become disjointed from the framework of the porch in several places, but still stood stubbornly wobbling in the wimpy breeze. Miraculously, the only room damaged severely was the kitchen. Several windows in other parts of the home had broken glass and the roof had lost many of its shingles, but beyond that the house had fared relatively well. Most importantly, the people who stood there surveying the aftermath of the storm, individuals who were or would be friends for a lifetime, were unharmed, at least physically. Even Sara's newest cat, a white fluff ball named Snowball, had survived. She slinked out from under the veranda, peering wide-eyed at the assembly of shaken humans before her. Sara picked her up and stroked her gently and then she walked to Ray's side welcoming his arms around her.

Only in the days to come did Sheila and her family come to understand the impact the storm of the century would have on them. Nashville had been hit by four separate tornadoes that day, one that created its destructive swath the mile width stretch from the edge of Ray and Sara's property to the outskirts of the city. Had it been centered just yards farther south, the entire house would likely have been destroyed and the lives of those huddled in the basement that day certainly would have been compromised.

The other twisters, touting winds of over one hundred and fifty miles per hour, had battered west and north Nashville for hours, taking more than a few lives with them. Among those who perished was James Madison Jackson who had been caught in the storm just outside of town driving alone in his newest silver Mustang. The angry winds had taken his vehicle, flipped it into the air and carried it for a quarter of a mile across an empty field, tossing it like a toy ball into the center of a tiny pond in a municipal park at the edge of town. James could not have survived. His neck and back were broken, his skull was fractured, and when he was found he lay face up in the front seat of the vehicle, a smirk lined with deep crimson blood dominating his face that otherwise was ashen in color and had bloated to unpleasant proportions from the water in which he floated. Sheila was notified by James's father who was so gripped with grief he could hardly speak. He had felt it only right to notify Sheila and let the little girl know that her daddy was gone. Lainy Raye was not mentioned by name.

Sheila was oddly saddened herself by the news of James's death. She had never wanted James in her life again after their hasty divorce, but he was her daughter's father and now Lainy would never have the chance to know him if for some reason she might have had an inkling to do so in the future as an adult. Sheila recognized a slightly perverse benefit to his untimely death. At least Lainy would be told when the time was right that her father had been killed in a horrible accident that prevented him from ever seeing her. She would never have to know that her father had made it perfectly clear that he wanted nothing to do with her. And in the aftermath of the death Sheila dreamed.

He is wandering around an empty house. It is actually more than empty; it is unfinished. He strolling from room to room, passing through walls like Willy Loman; his eyes are red rimmed and glassy. He looks old, drawn, and unattractive. I don't feel sorry as I watch him stumble about in search of some illusion. A sad face is not easy to forget, however.

The unexpected passing of James led to Sheila's own wonderings about her true father, the soldier who had disappeared into a war zone before her birth. Sara had mentioned him only a time or two, and for no particular reason Sheila had never been overly interested in knowing more about him. She had adored learning about their star-crossed love story, but it was the romance that had captured her imagination, nothing more. After all she had a mother who was better than two parents could ever be and she had Ray, who had nurtured her from the time she was a young adolescent and who had been her support and her friend for many years since. She respected him and could not have wished for a better father-figure. Yet, the unnerving events created by the recent horrifying storms upended her complacent notions about her father and set off a whirlwind of its own in Sheila's mind.

"Where was he?" she wondered. "What did he do? Where did he live? Did he have children of his own? Did she have half-siblings she did not know existed? What was her heritage?"

These were unsettling questions that persisted well into the next year. She was not quite sure how to go about seeking answers to them or resolving the unexpected invasion of them in her mind anyway. For the time being they would have to remain unanswered for presently more pressing matters took precedent.

In the weeks that followed the tornados Sheila worked harder than she had in years. First, she had to help Ray and her mother. Their kitchen was in tatters and the rest of the house, although livable, needed many repairs, and even though they assured her in no uncertain terms that they were fine and would soon be on their feet, for Sheila assisting them was instinctive. Since they temporarily had no place to cook, she took supper to them every night and packed picnic lunches for them every day. She'd fill a basket with sandwiches, boiled eggs, apples, grapes, oranges, crackers, cheese, and drinks, delivering it to their doorstep before work. In the evenings she would carry covered dishes filled with fried chicken or roast beef, ham or pork chops, potato salad or mashed potatoes and gravy, heavy homemade wheat breads, apple, peach, or cherry pies, and myriad other goodies that had Sara and Ray eating better than they ever had in their lives. And they were eternally grateful, for although their house would be repaired as good as new, the process for the two had taken its toll. Ray especially tired more easily than he liked of late and worried about Sara who still had nightmares about the storm. As with all else, it would take time.

Sheila was up late every night cooking, tending to Lainy, and thinking about the multitude of problems that had cascaded onto the lives of many of her clients, for one of the tornadoes had ripped through one of the most poverty stricken areas of the city taking with it what little the inhabitants had had in the first place. Many were faced with homelessness as well as the loss of family and friends. Shelters had been set up, but the marginal living conditions there were crowded and temporary. Those who chose not to live in the government-provided accommodations existed in squalid conditions in small spaces that had been damaged and were often unsafe. Childen were exposed to the cold, to danger, and to the wrath of their parents whose anger and worry boiled over in unfortunate and reprehensible ways that made the youngsters cower in corners or run away. Depression became the rule for many and crime in the area escalated as desperate men and frantic women fought for any morsel free or otherwise. Sheila's colleagues along with folks such as Sharon and Joan organized food drives, clothing drives, and set up free counseling stations in neighborhoods that were still picking up the pieces of their lives, literally and figuratively. The community, the churches, even the politicians did not let them down.

The children in Joan's elementary class were among those who lived in the most affected neighborhoods and they acted out their fears and despair in her class and on the street, leading to arguments, fights, petty thefts, and more than a few confrontations with the police and eventually the courts. Joan tirelessly tended to their emotional tantrums and poignant problems making it her mission to see that the administrators and other teachers did the same. It was one of the rare occasions when the educational community came together as one, setting aside petty agendas and focusing on the children's needs beyond the classroom.

Elaine and Steve took three weeks away from their offices and studies to tend to victims of the catastrophe. Having survived the ordeal firsthand they had gained a perspective about their own existence and mortality that others who had not been a part of the disaster could never have grasped. With altruistic commitment they worked side by side to aid the victims and were able to convince several of their colleagues to join their efforts. With the help of donations from local agencies and the Red Cross, they stitched cuts, bandaged abrasions and contusions, and set a few broken bones for folks who had no other source of medical care whatsoever. Sheila, Sharon, Joan, and Melanie opened their houses to the medical workers who volunteered their services and within the allotted weeks a friendship united all of them. In time, however, when a minute sense of normalcy began to settle into the city, the volunteers returned home leaving only the memories of their selfless efforts behind.

The repairs on Ray's house were completed rapidly with help from neighbors and local contractors who offered time and discounted supplies to the victims of the storm. Ray worked doggedly from morning until night determined to repair the damage to his home as well as to his psyche and that of his wife. He was not for a moment afraid to admit that he had been terrified that afternoon in the cellar of his house. The fear of losing what he loved most had shaken him to the core, for in his soul, he knew Sara Mae was the woman he had wanted all his life, and he thanked the good Lord every day that she returned his love. Perhaps it was not with the same intense passion and fervor, but her affection had been given to him honestly and appreciatively. She loved him. There was no doubt about it. They had established a wonderful life together with seldom a harsh word between them and a gift for compromise that made their lifestyle as smooth and bright as the surface of his pond on still sunshiny day.

Fortunately Sara's nightmares had subsided, but Ray still had been awakened several times by her whimpers in the middle of the night, tiny cries she had no idea she was making. The moans were so sad and mournful that Ray couldn't help wondering if the crisis had dredged up some deep-seated memories that had lain dormant for years. Loss or fear of loss could linger endlessly, he knew, and he was well aware that Sara had had her share when she was just a girl. She had told him about more than a few, and he had watched her mouth tighten and her face fall when she mentioned Addie, her childhood friend, or her mama, and even her papa who she'd never heard from again after her mama's burial. "Wonder where he went off to?" she'd muse. "Reckon he's dead an' gone by now too." Ray was reminded of quicksand that could pull a living thing into its clutches little by little the more one fought against the force, and he worried secretly that the horrendous loss of life in and around Nashville, including that of her former son-in-law, would act as a catalyst pulling Sara away from him and into depression or worse.

When he finally alerted her to the nighttime sobbing and his fears about her health, she listened intently, and then amazingly, she smiled. "Mama would a' said, 'This too shall pass'," she said. "My mama said s' many crazy things, I didn't half know from time t' time what she was talkin' 'bout."

Ray looked at her with head cocked sideways then, showing his confusion until she added, "Don't ya' worry, honey. I'm goin' t' be fine. This too's goin' t' pass. We'll be fine. I think sometimes ya' just have t' work out things in yer dreams an' I think that's what I've been doin'. That's what I'm always tellin' Shelia, anyways, so I reckon I better take my own advice as God's honest truth. Do ya' think I'm right?" She looked at him sweetly, not wanting an answer, and added, "An' one more thing, jist so ya' know. Yeah, that darn ol' twister scared me half t' death. Don't know what I would a' done if I'd lost ya', or Sheila, or Lainy Raye, or any a' the folks down there with us. We were more 'n lucky, I reckon."

"We were," Ray said emphatically. "We cert'inly were."

And finally after the frenzy of the weeks following the tragic storms, their lives took on a normal routine. Neither of them knew for how long, however.

Chapter Twenty-Four

Although two years had passed since her divorce, the recent death of James Jackson had rekindled memories that stubbornly plagued Sheila. She had lost another thirty pounds without even trying and selfishly relished her newly defined body. She would lie in bed and feel her flat abdomen, her slim legs and the hip bones jutting upward through now tight skin. It felt good. She was relieved to have at least regained the slender figure that had been one of her assets.

While her body was in shape though, her mind was not. She was still bothered by tormenting inexplicable dreams from time to time. They came to her unexpectedly when she had fallen asleep, overly tired after a day at work or an afternoon with her family. Often the weather predisposed her to them, especially if it was dark and stormy. Many times she awoke from her sleep and lay in bed sweaty and spent. She attempted to analyze her dreams and even tried to reason with them. "What in the hell was that about?" she'd say out loud to herself. She sat in bed for long minutes frequently recalling as much as she could, even writing down her thoughts in a tattered little cloth covered diary that she kept hidden under her pillow. In time she found it logical that her subconscious in some way linked James and storms together, an incongruous parallel perhaps, but the consistent connection of the two in regard to past incidents was profound enough not to be ignored. The remaining content of the dreams, however, was a mystery.

They are in my big house overlooking an ocean. They are the boys from college – Joe and Adam, or is it Pat and Gary? Who knows? The names don't matter. They are there, aimlessly wandering through the rooms of my huge sprawling house. They see me. I see them. We exchange glances.

"Your husband's looking for ya'," they say.

"Don't have a husband," I answer.

"He says he is. He's lookin' for ya'."

They disappear down a long corridor that is lined with rich, green palms. I enter through a door to my left and am in my giant garden room. Jade and olive palms, ferns, false aralias, bromeliads, flowering maples, dieffenbachia, schefflera in pots and baskets bask in filtered light in corners, by chairs, interspersed between tables. They have been strategically placed, but intended to look random and set to look inviting. I see her there hump shouldered still, sitting with her back turned toward me, avoiding me, or ignoring me, or just unaware. She is still holding the pearl and diamond earring in her hand. "Where's the other one?" she says angrily to a man with no face. I stare, wondering about her, about him. Do they feel? Is she upset about her tiny breasts, about who she is, about what she has become? And what does he feel about having no face, no eyes, and no voice? My anger is gone. I just look, and pass numbly by, ambling back into the corridor.

"Your husband's lookin' for ya'," a voice says.

"Don't have a husband," I say again, but suddenly he is there, taking my hand, leading me away into a chapel, a chapel in my big house.

"You're so beautiful," I hear him say. "I want t' make love t' ya."

I look for his eyes then, waiting for them to disappear with his grin but the face is blank, a sheet of taut skin over a boney facial structure. Is deceit hidden there? Is sick pleasure lying underneath? The face has no mouth with which to speak and no eyes to see, yet the words I have heard flutter in the air like delicate butterflies, flitting amid a row of boxed up memories.

The dream was typical in its absurdity and left Sheila confused and shaking. She wrote it in her diary remembering every detail adding annotations in the margins. She went back and read over what she had written in the days that followed, trying desperately to sort out her written ramblings, but to no avail. She then begrudgingly carried the dreams into her consciousness, her wonderings dominating lunches with friends or meetings at work. She took Lainy to Sharon's or Sara's at times and could not remember a thing about the drive, being too immersed in the colorful movie that played in her head. Days later another dream would dominate her sleep. Each became more bewildering until she was so distressed she was constantly fighting nausea.

I am in my big old house again. There's the ocean. I can see it. I am on a balcony looking down on a big area that's like a living room and parking lot combined. There are people milling around. I watch them and wonder what they are doing in this house, which is mine. I begin to search my house and find hallways with bedrooms and bathrooms and more rooms than I ever imagined. Why had I not seen these rooms before? I am intrigued by what I am finding.

"Hey, did ya' know I have another bedroom an' bathroom here?" I am shouting to anyone who will listen, but my cries are falling on deaf ears. I wonder why no one shares in my excitement.

Sheila told one person about her dreams. She told her mother, and as she always had done, Sara listened, not judging, not explaining; she simply listened. But when Sheila began to cry one afternoon after telling about another dream, she offered a suggestion.

He's cooking dinner in the kitchen of my big house. I am late. I've been away somewhere. I find him there in my kitchen, and it feels really strange for him to be there because we're already apart. He left a while back with that pearl and diamond earring in hand, but now he's in my kitchen cooking as though he has the foggiest notion what to do. I don't want him there. He's there, he says, because the children are coming to dinner too.

"We have no children," I say.

He looks at me incredulously, "'Course we do. We got plenty, all runnin' round outside."

"I don't want ya' here," I say.

"But I love ya', sugah. You're beautiful. I want t' make love t' ya'," *he says. I can't see his eyes and there is a bloody smear where his mouth should be.*

"Don't ya' know how I feel?" *I stare at him coldly.*

"Here's some pictures of our fam'ly," *he says, shoving them at me. They are wrapped in some kind of plastic. They look tacky and I don't recognize anyone.*

"Why'd you wrap 'em in plastic?"

"They'll last."

"Mom, Sharon's kids are in the hallway lightin' matches." *I hear a voice yelling.*

"Mom, the commode's overflowin'. Shit ever'where. Mom, help me clean up the shit," *a teenager is shrieking. Maybe it's Lainy. I can't see for sure.*

What's happening in my big house?

Why is he here?

Why are Sharon's kids trying to burn my house down?

Why do I have to clean up the shit?

"Then I woke up, Ma. I woke up askin' all those questions," she told her mother.

"Reckon ya' might want t' talk t' a counselor, Sheila? Ya've got t' know a few folks, maybe someone ya' work with, someone who can help ya' figure out what's goin' on up there in that pretty little head a' yers?"

"I've thought 'bout that, Mother. I have. But t' tell ya' the truth, I'm a little bit embarrassed. Don't want t' have someone I know thinkin' I'm crazy!"

"Yer not crazy, Sheila Masie Jenkins. Yer jist sortin' things out. Ya've had s' many things happen in the last few years an' what with James's passin', maybe ya' jist need t' talk t' someone who's smarter 'an me. Not that I mind listenin'. I'm always here fer ya'."

"I know ya' are, Ma, but there's somethin' else that's been botherin' me."

"What?" Sara stared intently, betraying her worry.

"I've been thinkin' 'bout my daddy."

Sara could feel her body drawing up inside and she seemed to stop breathing for seconds and then she said, "Why, Sheila, in all these years, ya've never said a thing 'bout wantin' t' know him. Have ya' been wonderin' 'bout him fer a long time?"

"No, Ma. I never really thought much 'bout him at all, but when James passed, well, I thought 'bout Lainy an' how she'd never know him, not that that's a bad thing. He was pretty much of an ass!" A tiny smile crept to her lips. "But, it got me thinkin', wonderin' where my own birth daddy is, what he does, if he's got kids. Ya' know . . ." Her words drifted into silence and she looked at her mother whose face had paled.

"Ya' know, I don't think 'bout him, haven't fer a good long time now, 'specially since Ray's in my life an' has taken on such a big part a' providin' fer us over the years. I reckoned Ray was kind a' like a Daddy t' ya' an' thought maybe ya' felt the same way." Sara was defensive. An unexpected irritation moved over her. She knew her voice had begun to quiver and she fought to keep unwanted tears from welling in her eyes. She had never really expected this moment to come. Sheila's natural father had drifted into and out of her life so quickly and their affair, as sweet and tender as it was at the time, now was only a fleeting vision in her memory. Yet as distant and detached as she was from that time so many years ago, the reality of it suddenly gripped her and she burst into sobs that made her shoulders shudder in heavy silent shrugs.

Sheila was beside herself with guilt and shame. She realized at once that she had ripped open a wound her mother had hidden for many years. "Oh, God, Ma. I'm s' sorry. I didn't mean t' hurt ya' an' make ya' cry." She was grasping at her mother, trying to pat her, to hug her, to comfort her, but Sara would have none of it.

"No," she said. "No. I don't want ya' t' touch me right now. I jist have t' sit with this fer a minute or two. Jist let me sit with it." Her words came in stutters as she spoke between her cries.

Sheila sat stunned. She had had no idea that the mention of her father would have created such a scene, and she was undone herself. Was she selfish for wanting to know more? Was it wrong? Her mind fluctuated between being ashamed and being righteous. "I do have a right t' know, don't I?" she thought. "How can my own mother keep this from me?" Her egocentric craving to understand more was prevailing in her own personal conflicting struggle.

"Ma," she tried again. "I don't want t' hurt ya' an' I'd never want t' hurt Ray. I love ya', ya' know, more than tongue can tell, an' I love Ray too. He's the best. It's just that somethin's missin' all of a sudden. An' I'm wonderin' if maybe findin' out more 'bout my heritage, 'bout my real daddy will help me, with my dreams, with my life. God, Ma, ya' know as well as I do that I haven't been real lucky with the relationships in my life. They've either been shitty or they haven't happened at all. I know I'm soundin' real selfish, but I want t' know who my birth father is, if I can, if he's even 'round anywhere."

She sat silent then and waited. She waited for many minutes, for Sara had pulled away and had wrapped her arms protectively around herself. The crying had stopped, but her face was flushed and moist, and her visage took on the look of a mask, rigid, unmoving, and stolid. When finally she spoke her voice was emotionless and so quiet Sheila had to lean in to hear what was said.

"Liam," she said. "His name is Liam. William. William Morrison. I reckon he's fifty somethin' by now, or older, an' he lived, like I told ya' years ago, up in Indiana. Don't know where, but think it was 'round South Bend. I don't know nothin' more, Sheila, jist that ya' look like him, same eyes, same smile. If ya' find him, ya'll know."

"I need t' know, Ma," Sheila answered her. "Never in a million years did I want t' hurt your feelin's or make ya' think I don't love ya' more 'an any girl could love her mother. Please don't be mad at me, Ma."

"I'm not mad at ya', honey. Maybe I'm jist mad at myself. Maybe I should a' been more honest with ya', with him. Ya' know, he don't know ya' exist, s' I reckon if ya' do find him he'll be a little more 'an surprised." She smiled a tiny smile then and reached for Sheila's face. She touched it gently, patting her cheeks and pulling her close. She began combing her hair with her fingers then, a gesture that had forever been a signal of a bond that would not be broken.

❦

With a fervor that gave new meaning to her life, Sheila launched into her pursuit to find her father. She had taken the time to talk to Ray first, with her mother by her side, to explain. She had been nervous that he might be offended, insulted, or even angry, but he was none of those things.

"Honey, I can understand yer wantin' t' know," he had said the moment she had explained.

"I reckon ya' know how I feel 'bout ya' an' how I feel 'bout yer mother. I couldn't love two people more, but I'm a purty big boy now," he laughed. "I may seem t' be Mr. Milk Toast sometimes 'cause I can be real easy goin', but what ya' need t' understand in no uncert'in terms is that I got a purty good head on my shoulders an' I know who I am. I'll stand up fer myself in front a' anybody. I ain't the least bit threatened by yer wantin' t' know yer daddy. Fact is I think maybe it's 'bout time. The ol' boy's liable t' be shocked, but he'll git over it. A daughter like you'd make anybody proud."

He paused for a moment and then continued, "I know yer mother's mama would tell us all that pride's a sinful thing, but I'll be darned if I'm not goin' t' enjoy a little bit of it. I'm s' proud a' my little family here, I couldn't ask fer another thing."

"Thank ya' for understandin', Ray," Sheila said throwing her arms around him and squeezing him tightly. "Ya've made me s' happy. An' I love ya' too. Ya' know that don't ya'?"

"I do, honey. I do."

Sara watched the interaction between the two in awe. Ray was the most compassionate person she'd ever known and just being around him made her feel as though she was a better person because of it. Did one person's goodness rub off on another? Maybe not, but watching the way Ray dealt with life from up close made it seem that way and at this very moment, she felt good about herself. She felt happier and more satisfied than she had ever felt in her life. Beyond that observation, however, she had some niggling qualms about the possibility of laying eyes on Liam

Morrison again. Maybe she wouldn't have to; maybe Sheila would be satisfied just seeing him herself, if indeed she even found him.

Sheila had little to go on as she began the search for her father. She knew his name now and the area he had come from, but other than that she had little else. He mother had shown her the birth certificate. Where the father's name was supposed to be the word UNKNOWN had been typed in capital letters. Knowing the hospital where she was born was meaningless, for her father had not been there. She knew his name, his branch of the service, and his rank. He had been a private first class in the United States Army. Private First Class William Morrison. It was something.

Sheila looked in phone directories and called cities in Indiana asking the Information operators if they had a listing for William Morrison, or Liam Morrison. Morrisons, it seemed, were a dime a dozen, but William Morrison was an illusive name for some reason. "Maybe it's because I want t' find it s' badly," Sheila admonished herself, as though by wanting something so desperately she was creating her own bad luck. She started her search by calling cities in the North, phoning Gary, Elkhart, and South Bend. She even drove one week all the way to Indianapolis, thinking the capitol might hold some answers, but the state buildings were closed for the weekend and the phone directory offered nothing. Disappointed but determined, she moved on to Terra Haute, Evansville, New Albany, and multiple hamlets in between, finally crossing the wide gray Ohio River back into Louisville, Kentucky. She had Lainy Raye with her for company and the little girl chatted ceaselessly, drawing Sheila's attention to gleaming cars that drove too fast, to a broad yellow school bus loaded with children whose heads bobbed up and down like puppets held by strings, to more than one long line of cows lumbering down muddy paths toward dirty open barns to be milked. She pointed to beautiful shiny black and chestnut thoroughbred horses trotting like princes across immaculate meadows, and to fat wooly sheep who stood with black nostrils between the slats of fences that lined the roadways, their lazy black eyes like glassy jumbo marbles, gazing forward, and their ears alertly projected towards the highway noises.

Lainy had learned her colors that summer and proudly and happily described the scenery that flew past. "There's a red barn, green grass, blue sky, a black horsey, a brown moo cow, a red, orange, and yellow tree," she'd report. It was the autumn again and the countryside from Tennessee, through Kentucky, and into Indiana was awash with such vivid colors that Sheila would have to stop from time to time just to absorb the beauty. She and Lainy collected leaves of every color gently placing them in a paper bag for safe keeping. Later they would press them into the pages of a photo album and revisit them from time to time until they eventually crumbled into tissue-like ash. Gathering autumn leaves had become a seasonal tradition for them, just like rolling snowballs into snowmen in the winter, picking yellow daffodils in the spring, and chasing fire flies on warm summer evenings. Sara would often join them laughing joyfully and say, "I jist love buildin' memories, don't ya' too, Lainy Raye?" Lainy would answer by hugging her grandma's knees and burying her head into Sara's abdomen to smother her giggles.

On this fall day, however, when Sheila drove across the bridge over the wide Ohio River into Louisville, she was tired, and more than a little disappointed. Lainy had fallen asleep in the back seat of her car, her angelic face pressed against her favorite pink pillow and Sheila knew she could not continue without some sleep herself. She found a decent motel at the edge of town and checked in for the night. Once inside she called her mother and Ray, assuring them she was fine. She'd be home in a day or two. "I'm thinkin' 'bout drivin' over t' Lexington t' see Elaine an' Steve, if they have time t' see me. I know they're s' busy," she told them. "An' I haven't told Elaine a thing 'bout what I've been tryin' t' do. I bet she might have some ideas 'bout locatin' somebody."

"I think that's a real good idea, honey," Sara said, "but ya'll be careful drivin' now an' give kisses t' Lainy Raye from Grandma."

With the pleasant but obligatory conversation to her mother completed, Sheila called Elaine.

"Hell, yes," Elaine gushed into the phone. "Ya'll come on over. Steve'll be workin' but I'm only on duty in the mornin'. For some lucky reason I'm off the rest a' the day an' Steve'll be home for supper. So ya'll come. I'll meet ya' at the house. Can ya' find it, ya' think?"

"I'll find ya'. I'll be there sometime in the early afternoon. Got a whole passel 'a things t' tell ya'."

Elaine and Steve lived together in an old established row house that had been renovated to look spectacular inside. Three intricately laid white stone steps led up to a front door that was painted a deep burgundy a complement to the reddish brick structure that was trimmed in rich forest green. The hardwood floors inside had been refinished and shone beautifully in the light that filtered through shuttered windows. Elsewhere thick beautiful carpets with complex shapes and lines woven into them were placed precisely in front of plush white divans and under a wide coffee table on which stacks of heavy books had been placed purposefully to draw interest and conversation. Behind the living room was a dining room dominated by a large cherry table with sleek modern chairs to match and a hutch filled with fragile china and knick knacks on one wall. Behind that lay an avant-garde kitchen and a small bathroom both refinished to modern perfection. Up the carpeted staircase were two large inviting bedrooms and a study crowded with rows of books and magazines, some neatly stacked on book shelves and some thrown haphazardly around the floor and on a small leather settee. While the beauty of the place was impeccable, it offered a warm, inviting ambiance. Sheila was at home the moment she walked through the front door and Lainy was too, happily talking to her two favorite dolls as she sat perched on a high stool at the kitchen bar, munching dry Cheerios from a plastic cup.

Elaine and Sheila's friendship was so deep and reliable that even though they had not seen each other for some time, they were immediately immersed in glib conversation that was as natural as taking in air. Elaine talked about her internship, her studies, and about Steve. They would be married in the summer, without a doubt, back in Tennessee at the insistence of Elaine's parents. The Crabtrees were as proud as peacocks about their daughter and wanted all of Nashville to know it. Sheila would be the matron of honor, and Joan, Sharon, and Melanie would be the other attendants. "On the outside, it seems like a repeat a' your weddin'," Elaine said, "only with a nicer groom, sorry t' say!"

"You're right 'bout that," Sheila said, believing it to be true but also bristling a bit at the rather cruel judgment about James who could not have defended himself even if he wanted.

"For goodness sake, Sheila, I've been talkin' my head off," Elaine said after half an hour of prattling conversation. "What in the hell are ya' doin' in Kentucky?"

"That's what I wanted t' tell ya' 'bout," Sheila answered. "Lainy an' I've been up travelin' 'round Indiana, 'cause, well, 'cause I'm lookin' for my daddy, my real father."

"Sheila, you're not."

"I am. Feel like it's time. What with James's dyin' an' knowin' Lainy'd never know him, I figured I ought t' find out 'bout my own father. Don't have much t' go on, just a name an' his rank in the Army years ago. An' my mother says he was from somewhere 'round South Bend, Indiana. So, I took Lainy with me an' we've been lookin' for any records we can find. No luck though."

"And what's Ray an' your mother sayin' 'bout this?"

"They think it's the right thing t' do. Oh, my mother was upset at the beginnin'. Think I dredged up some memories for her, but she came 'round. An' Ray? Well, ya' know how he is. He's so nice, so acceptin'. Why he'd do whatever I asked t' help out, only I didn't ask for help, just some understandin' an' he was right there with that!"

"What's his name, your daddy?" Elaine asked awkwardly.

"William Morrison. Ma said she called him Liam, but I haven't found a William or Liam Morrison anywhere. Do ya' think this is a wild goose chase?"

"Maybe. Maybe it is, but I think it's worth it. Could give ya' some answers as t' your heritage an' t' your daddy's family's where'bouts." Elaine was quiet for a second, thinking, and then she blurted, "Morrison. Ya' know Sheila, there's a nurse at the med center named Morrison. Think her first name's Maggie. Real sweet. Kind a' plump. Little round face an' big ol' dimples ya' could sink a ship in! Reminds me a' Joan a little bit. Think she's married too, but no kids. Don't know what her husband's name is. Want me t' ask? Wouldn't that be somethin', Sheila, if she knew your father? Could be related in some way."

Elaine's mind was in full action already. Sheila could almost see the whirlwind stirring behind her blue eyes.

"Why sure, why not ask? I guess it couldn't hurt anything."

In seconds Elaine had her phone in hand dialing a number from memory. She had called the medical center and was quickly in an animated conversation with someone on the other end of the line. "Angie, it's Elaine Crabtree here. Wonderin' if ya' could help me out with a little somethin'."

Maggie would be working, Elaine found out, over night. She was the head night nurse and would be off at 6:00 a.m. in the morning. Elaine planned to meet her at her station at the end of her work shift. From there, who knew what would come next? Elaine loved the intrigue and Sheila found herself caught up in the plan. What did she have to lose?

Elaine was not a cook. In fact, she hated to cook, but with company at hand, she did her best. Fortunately, Sheila jumped in to help her and the two created a spaghetti and meat ball concoction that had Steve asking for more, and had Lainy Raye's little face and neck covered in red sauce. Sucking up slippery strips of spaghetti was more fun than even her dolls, and when Steve dropped his pretenses and joined her, she slapped her hands together happily. Elaine watched for moments appalled at her future husband's behavior, and then gave in to the merriment. This silly respite seemed a welcome break for him for in his profession seriousness and sometimes sadness were often the norm. Sheila took the whole scene in stride. She was use to messes and was adept at cleaning them up. In no time at all, the kitchen had been cleaned, Lainy had given in to a gentle sleep, and Steve was sipping brandy by a crackling fire in the living room with Elaine by his side. Sheila joined them briefly before slipping up to bed exhausted and this night to another dream.

I am in my big house. And in my big house is a bathroom, a public bathroom with marble walls, wide white porcelain sinks, and bronze fixtures that are spotted with water, soap scum, and who knows what else. It smells of feces, urine, and Pine Sol. I want to hold my breath while I am in this room. Plenty of people are coming and going through the door that swings on great tarnished hinges. I too enter my bathroom, my public bathroom. I notice the folks who pass into and through the room, and I also notice a small baby, lying quietly and unattended on a large leather couch. I take little notice though, like everyone else, and leave it there babbling nonsense into the empty space around it.

Later, I am back. The baby is still there, lying naked on the brown leather couch. Its little legs are chubby and are thrust into the air; tiny hands grasp at the legs and feet creating a miniature "O". The infant's shiny brown eyes move with me when I walk toward it. It looks at me; I look back. No one notices me; no one notices the baby. Just I do. I reach for it, carefully holding it to my chest. It clings to me, petite fingers grasping a wide wisp of my long, brown hair. I'm sure at that moment that the baby is mine. I'll take care of it. After all I have found it in my big house unattended. That is the last time it will be left alone, abandoned.

I am enlightened suddenly as I carry my baby out of the public bathroom that is in my big house. I am clear that I will care for this baby. I must, for the baby is me. Together we will explore the rest of the big house that is ours.

Sheila awoke in the darkness of the strange bedroom and clutched the pillow to her beating heart. "This dream. . ." she whispered to herself. "I've been waitin' for an answer an' I'm done now. I don't need t' dream craziness any more. I'm done. I'm goin' in the right direction. I know I am. I'm doin' the right things now an' I'm all right. Ever'thing's all right." And then she slept for dreamless hours until morning.

Chapter Twenty-Five

Before Sheila and Lainy Raye were even awake, their hosts were gone, Steven to the hospital and then to his office with Elaine following closely behind. She was on a different mission this day however, for curiosity was leading her unabashedly towards the meeting with Maggie Morrison, who at this moment, was at the end of her shift and was looking forward to the short ride home and much needed rest. Little did she know that the new day would result in an encounter that would alter her life in ways she could never have imagined.

Maggie was at the nurse's station adding details to her notes and giving instructions to the day nurses who where taking over that morning. Elaine saw her studying her paperwork, but interrupted bluntly asking, "May I talk t' ya' for a second, Maggie, when you're done there?"

"Sure Dr. Crabtree. Is there a problem?"

"No, no problem. I just want t' ask ya' somethin', for a friend, actually, not s' much for me. Let's go over int' the waitin' area for a second. Do ya' mind?"

Once settled in the small seating area, Elaine began. "I have t' ask ya' this outright an' I hope I don't sound unfeelin' by doin' it. I know ya've been married for a long, long time now, but I've never asked ya' what your husband's name is? Would it be William by any chance?"

"Liam. It's Liam, short for William. Why? Why are ya' askin'?"

"Well, I think I have a story t' share with ya' that may be a surprise, an' maybe even a shock."

Elaine elaborated then on the information that would change lives forever. Maggie was a silent listener, taking in all of Elaine's animated words without moving. She was stunned but not surprised. She had met Liam Morrison thirty years before at the Veteran's Administration Facility in Lexington. He had been there as a patient at the time, having lost use of his legs in an explosive vehicle accident that had flipped his jeep into a muddy bog on the northern shore of Belgium. He had spent several years undergoing operation after operation and more physical therapy than he could ever have imagined until finally under his own power he was able to manipulate his wheel chair and take charge of his life again. Maggie had been the sweet and adoring nurse who never left his side from the moment he had been placed in her care. She had fallen instantly in love with him and in a few short months after coming to grips with the disability that would last a lifetime, complete with the anger and depression that accompanied it, he reciprocated. They were married by a chaplain in front of a scruffy group of servicemen who had been wounded and were slowly healing under the careful eyes of the dedicated nurses and doctors at the hospital. When they had completed their vows, the men and medical staff had burst into applause and hip hip hoorays that disrupted the entire ward for nearly an hour.

They had left the hospital that day happier than they could have imagined and after consummating the marriage in the privacy of their little apartment nearby, they began their married lives together. Liam had sought and been given the position of social director for the facility. With experience to back him up, he became a regular cheerleader of sorts for the men who were sent there for treatment. In the thirty years he had been there, he had never lost his enthusiasm and was known for his brilliant smile and dark sparkling eyes that flickered with gold, eyes that spoke volumes when he was happy or sad, enthused or agitated. Whatever his emotion, the eyes spoke first.

"Well, I guess I need t' talk t' Liam," Maggie finally spoke. "He's not likely t' know a thing 'bout what ya've been tellin' me. Oh, I know he knew some girls early on before me. What young soldier didn't back then? He was s' handsome, an' still is in my mind, but I'd be willin' t' bet my bottom dollar he doesn't know 'bout this. An' I don't rightly know how he'll take it. He's always been a man t' follow the straight an' narrow. Never would hurt a fly. Wears his heart on his sleeve, he does. I'm afraid he'd be heart broken t' know he'd abandoned a child."

"But he wouldn't a' known."

"Don't matter. He's liable t' be real aggravated if what you're tellin' me's true. Then again, I could be wrong. Wonders never cease, do they, Dr. Crabtree?"

"You're right 'bout that," Elaine answered. "Ya' never know what's goin' t' lie 'round the corner. An' I'm real sorry t' have t' deliver this kind a' news. I know it's kind a' shockin'."

"Well, it certainly is, but if we're goin' t' have this meetin' I'd like t' see it happen sooner than later. Rather not have t' dwell on it, selfish as that might sound. Can the girl come over t' our place this afternoon?"

"I'll arrange it. Oh, an' there's another thing. She has a daughter. She's four, an' as cute as a button."

"Lord, help me!" Maggie said, "Bring 'em over 'round two o'clock. I'll make sure Liam's there, an' I'll warn him 'bout what t' expect. Like I said, he's goin' t' react t' this girl one way or another, but I believe he's apt t' fall t' pieces if he believes it's true."

※

Elaine was able to convince Steve to accompany them to Maggie and Liam's home that afternoon. The couple now lived in a lovely old clapboard home on a tree-lined street in Lexington near the university. A wide veranda extended the width of the house and four ancient wooden rocking chairs had been placed there stationed like young gunners overseeing the grassy yard. A shallow ramp led from the driveway to the porch and the banister that ran along the side of the house had been worn smooth with use. The broad stairs that led to the front door were warped and peeling giving the appearance of disregarded neglect. When Sheila stepped onto them for the first time, she was shaking visibly and they creaked beneath her feet. Steve compassionately and gently took her arm to steady her and patted her back at the same time. Lainy skipped up behind them, holding Elaine's fingers with one hand and her floppy yellow-haired doll with the other. Her innocent lack of awareness was a blessing once again.

Maggie opened the door slowly and looked first at Elaine and Lainy who had scooted in front of her mother dragging Elaine with her and was looking up at the woman with curious big brown eyes. Maggie was taken aback by them and when she looked up into Sheila's face behind her she was stunned. It was her husband's face. The young woman before her was a female version of her husband. She had no doubts. In her mind no further evidence was needed. Liam Morrison had a daughter, and a granddaughter for that matter, of that she was sure. Her emotions imploded then, and she caught her breath and held it not wanting to cry out loud. Her heart pulsed wildly and for a moment she was faint for she knew from that moment on her life would change. She had had Liam to herself for thirty years and in a moment the structure and stability of life as she knew it was turned upside down. She didn't need Liam to see. She saw.

Without a word Maggie gestured for the foursome to enter the dim entryway of the house and then directed them to follow her into the living room that was alive with sunshine blistering through the windows that filled the western wall of the house. The group stood awkwardly in a loose circle until Maggie motioned for them to sit. She was still searching for her voice.

"I'll get Liam now," she finally said flatly, but before she could leave the room, a wheel chair could be heard rumbling softly down the hallway. In seconds it had arched its way around the corner sinking into the soft carpet where it stopped dead like the silence surrounding them.

Sheila, who still clung to Steve's arm, broke the quiet, her clear, calm voice surprising even her. "Mr. Morrison. My name's Sheila, Sheila Jenkins, an' I think maybe, an', well, I'm hopin' maybe that you're my father." She forced a smile then and a dazzling smile it was. Her brown eyes sparkled in the light and the golden flecks were lost on no one, save Lainy who had been drawn to the man in the chair as though he were a giant, for he was tall. Even seated he was tall and his face was serious and stern. Not allowing a response, Sheila continued. "My mother is Sara Mae Jenkins, or was. She's married now, but for years she wasn't. It was only my mother an' me livin' together for a long time down in Tennessee. She told me 'bout my daddy when I was old enough t' know, but I never knew a name 'til a couple months back. With circumstances bein' what they've been back home, I decided I wanted t' find my father. Been lookin' for William, Liam Morrison ever since. Did ya' know Sara Mae Jenkins, Mr. Morrison?"

The man in the wheel chair stared at her while she spoke, and then in a ragged voice answered, "I did know Sara Jenkins, so many years ago, I'd almost forgotten, but I recall her. She was a real sweet an' pretty thing back then. An' as for Liam Morrison, well, I think maybe ya've found him, young lady." And then the grim look was broken and he smiled too, as he looking intently into the face that mirrored his.

"I don't know what t' say," he said then. "Honey, Maggie. Are ya' here?" He turned his head looking for his mate and found her hand reaching toward his, as it had for thirty years. She had held his hand through crisis after crisis: when he had first entered the hospital years before, a broken man with a mangled body, in the aftermath of operations that left him ventilated and afraid he'd never breathe on his own again, and in painful physical therapy sessions where his legs were raised and bent in search for a reaction, a response that would indicate feeling, that would show even a remote nerve response. She had been there when phantom legs had made him cry and when he had been told he would never walk again. She had been there, and he knew in his heart that she always would be, even now, in the face of this new awakening.

"What do we do now?" he asked. "How do ya' pick up a life from here?" And he began to cry, great drops that slid down his cheeks and dropped onto his fuzzy sweater.

In moments Sheila was at his knees crying too. Lainy stood by her mother patting her back sweetly while she also tapped the giant's unfeeling knees. Not one person in the room was dry-eyed, including Steven Matthews, who had dealt with illness and injury and even death that did not emote the feelings he had now. For this was a discovery, a treasure, a miraculous event that pulled on his passions as he had experienced only once before, when he had found Elaine, the incredible woman who had agreed to marry him. She was gazing at the scene before them, sobbing so deeply that he could do nothing else but cradle her in his arms and watch.

When the time came, Steve spoke to Sheila and Liam professionally. "Right now, 'bout the only way t' determine relationship for sure, is with a blood test. Don't feel lookin' further int' DNA is feasible right now, not in this case. Too costly an' we're not equipped t' go that direction. In years down the road I hope we will, but for now, we can compare blood types. It's simple enough. Ya' willin' t' do that? It'll give ya' a little more peace a' mind."

Maggie spoke then. "I reckon they should do it, but t' tell ya' the truth, it won't change a thing. If these two aren't related, I'll be watchin' hogs fly."

The rest of the afternoon was spent making up for lost time. Sheila told Liam about her childhood, her education, about her daughter's birth, her divorce, and about James's death. She talked about her mother, about Ray, about her job as a social worker, about her friends, about her house, about Tennessee. She talked and talked and the ease with which she spoke bordered on being eerie it was so natural. Liam talked too. He told Sheila about his job at the VA hospital and about how important it was for him to help other people just like she was doing every day. Their professions held an uncanny similarity as well and it did not go unnoticed by them. Maggie listened and chimed in from time to time making sure Liam kept the story straight. By evening, Lainy had climbed into Liam's lap insisting that he help her get her baby doll to sleep, but soon had fallen asleep herself in the arms of the grandfather she had never known before that day.

Shelia's next step would be to tell her mother and Ray which she did that night from the comfort of Elaine's house. Armed with a glass of brandy and with her friends beside her, she made the call.

"Mother, I found him. I found Liam."

Silence was the answer.

"He's nice, Ma. He's married an' works at the Veteran's Administration facility in Lexington, real near Elaine. His wife is Maggie an' she's a nurse. Real sweet too. An', Ma, he's confined t' a wheel chair. He can't walk, hasn't for years. Accident in the Army. He's good though, Ma. Happy an' workin' an' helpin' out other folks at the VA hospital. Ya'd be real proud a' him, I think. He likes Lainy Raye too."

"Good grief, Sheila," Sara said. "Kain't get a word in edgewise!"

"Sorry Ma. It's kind a' amazin' isn't it? Steve arranged blood tests for us, t' help make sure, an' we actually match. We're both A negative, but more 'an that, Ma, ya' were right. We look alike. Ever'body thinks so."

"Well, I'm glad fer ya', honey. I truly am. It's like a dream come true, isn't it? An' it looks like ya've filled in a big empty place. I'm s' happy fer ya' I could cry myself. Ray'll be glad too. He's been real worried."

"No need, Ma. I'm good. Had a dream . . ."

"No, not another one." Sara was instantly concerned.

"No, this was good. This one was 'bout me. I think I finally figured it out. Ya' know how I was always dreamin' bout houses an' wanderin' 'round 'em, findin' new places t' explore or needin' t' clean up messes here an' there, messes that other folks made. Well, this last dream was 'bout me pickin' up a baby an' carryin' it from a nasty ol' bathroom. Somehow I figured the baby was mine but when I walked out a' the door, I realized the baby wasn't just mine.

It was more. It was me. When I was walkin' out a' that bathroom with that baby, with me, in my arms, I knew. I knew I was goin' in the right direction. An' the house, Ma, that's me too, I believe. In all these dreams, it's like I've been explorin' myself, tryin' t' find where t' go. By walkin' down hallways an' int' big ol' rooms I've been tryin' t' figure out where I've been an' where I want t' go. Maybe it sounds crazy but it somehow makes sense t' me. An' I'm excited by what's goin' t' come next."

Sara had listened, liking what she heard. A spark and excitement was present in Sheila's voice. The dreams were bizarre, no doubt about that, but the end result was encouraging to her. For the first time in many months, her daughter sounded happy and confident. It made her smile.

"I kain't wait t' see ya', honey," Sara said. "Ray an' I've missed ya'."

"I'll be home in two days," Sheila told her. "Be there before ya' know it."

When Sheila finally saw her mother and Ray again she ran to them and literally threw herself into their arms. Lainy Raye had to scamper as fast as her little legs would carry her to catch up. Sheila's words came to her faster than she could spit them out as she relived the first moments with her father. Sara listened quietly and finally leaned back in her cozy recliner and laughed.

"Sheila, slow down. Good grief."

"Well, you're goin' t' get t' meet Liam again, Mother, this summer. Maggie's goin' t' drive 'em down for Steve an' Elaine's weddin'. You an' Ray are goin' t' love 'em both."

Chapter Twenty-Six

When Liam Morrison saw his daughter's mother for the first time in over thirty years that next September he grasped her hand in both of his and held it tightly, looking up at her face that was remarkably unchanged. She was older, of course, with soft lines beneath her dark eyes and deeper ones under her cheeks beside her mouth. She had thickened a bit around the hips and stomach and her hair had partially grayed, but it still held much of the rich dark color he remembered so well. It fell softly beyond her shoulders and lay above her breasts in silky waves. And when she smiled, his heart gave a tiny flutter, for he remembered her sweetness. The memory of how she had given herself to him so quietly and tenderly came back to him for an instant and he felt his neck tingle slightly under his collar, but he was quick to recover from the momentary lapse, saying, "Ya' look wonderful, Sara Mae. I still would a' recognized ya'. I'd like ya' t' meet my wife, Maggie. She's been by my side for thirty years now an' I don't know what I'd do without her." It was important for Liam to ease any discomfort for his wife, for she had been an incredible partner and companion for whom he held the deepest respect and an incomparable love.

"I'm s' happy t' meet ya'," Sara said genuinely and then turned to Ray who stood behind her. "An' this is my husband, Ray. He's been the love a' my life fer too many years t' count now."

Sara too recognized the potential for Ray's uneasiness with the reunion that just months ago none of them could have imagined happening, but with his usual aplomb, Ray made them all feel as though this auspicious meeting would be a highlight in their lives.

"We've been lookin' forward t' this moment fer so long an' we couldn't be happier fer our Sheila here, 'cause she's bubblin' over, as ya' can see! She's taken the good with the bad over the last few years, but I reckon this is the bee's bonnet. We're s' happy ya' could make it down here t' Tennessee t' see us, an' on such a great occasion what with Elaine an' Steve gettin' married. It's goin' t' be a fine time fer ever'body."

Sheila looked at Ray as though he were a saint. "I've made us supper," she said, an edge of nervousness in her voice. "Come on, sit ever'body. Hopefully ya' can catch up while I get things ready."

"Can we help ya', honey?" Sara asked.

"No, ya'll just get t' know each other. Supper'll be on in a jiffy."

"Don't know if ya' know this yet, Liam, but ya'll are in fer a treat! Sheila here's the best darn cook in Tennessee," Ray bragged.

"Well, I didn't know that, but I'm sure ready t' find out! Smells delicious," Liam replied grinning alluringly.

Ray's ability to break the ice and make everyone feel comfortable was a calming gift and a blessing to Sara, for it felt as though she had been holding her breath for the last twenty minutes. Liam looked the same and of course different. She knew his smile as well as she knew the back of her hand because she saw it every day in Sheila, and his eyes were Sheila's eyes, sparkling now with the same energy and passion their daughter revealed no matter what her frame of mind. And he looked tall. Even in his wheel chair he sat tall and proud, the atrophied legs betraying him only to the degree he would allow which was next to nothing. It was apparent to anyone watching that his disability was not who he was. He was as strong and vigorous as a fighter and his attitude and enthusiasm were clear and infectious. She knew why she had fallen for him so many years before, and as she watched Maggie watch him affectionately, she was smitten with a nagging envy that irritated her. "What in God's Earth are ya' thinkin', Sara Mae Jenkins?" she thought to herself, mentally squashing the feeling forcefully.

She talked then, sometimes directing her eyes to Liam and often at Maggie. She engaged Ray as well and soon the foursome was chatting as though they had known each other forever. Lainy Raye was passed around from one person to the next and she absorbed the attention like a sponge, finally falling into an exhausted heap on the divan with her doll enveloped in her arms, her head supported by her well-traveled pink pillow.

Supper was, as Ray had predicted a feast for them all and by the time it was over they found they had been seated around the table for hours, consuming more than any of them should have, sidetracked by stories of years gone by, and speculation about what the future held for them all. They laughed until they cried, and cried until they fell into self-conscious giggles.

Sheila was beside herself with joy as she joined them at the table, but when she caught her mother's eyes, she saw an inimitable look of melancholy. In the midst of this unusual and unsought-after gathering, Sara couldn't help but envision what could have been. She had not asked to be reminded of what unmistakably had occurred so long ago and the realization that nothing could bring that distant past back again sat heavy on her heart.

※

Two days later on the last day of summer when the September heat was at its steamy hottest, Elaine and Steve were married. Sara's home was the staging sight again for this wedding as it had been for Sheila's.

On this day, however, in an atypical mood for her, Sara was angry and anxious. She had not slept well since the meeting with Liam and Maggie, and Ray had commented that her nighttime gibberish had begun again. She was tired, and felt old.

"Why it's hotter 'an Hades 'round here t'day," she complained. "I reckon I sure know why my mama hated this awful heat. Why she'd be s' hateful on days like this, she'd be fit t' be tied. I'd have t' hide down by Turtle Creek 'til sundown an' when I'd go home she'd be mad as a hen in a wolf's den 'cause she couldn't find me all day an' Katie bar the door if I came home dirty. She wouldn't know whether she was comin' or goin' on days like this. Folks jist had t' stay out a' her way."

"Well, calm yourself down, Ma," Sheila said. "We have t' make Elaine's day perfect. The weddin's not 'til dusk anyway, so it'll cool down by then."

"I know it. I know it," Sara said. "It's jist that the heat's brought back some memories a' my mama that kind a' set me on my ear. An' what with meetin' Liam an' Maggie at yer place, an' bein' throwed back int' those times, my equilibrium's jist upset. I'll git over it. Give me a minute or two. Where is ever'one anyway?"

"Ever'one's goin' t' be here any minute," Sheila said and fortunately as if on cue, the door bell rang.

Sharon, Elaine, Joan, Melanie, Charlotte, Maggie, and Elaine's mother, Mary, filed into the living room anxious to find relief from the heat.

"Good grief, Elaine," Joan said, "This is the hottest September day on record. I think we're all goin' t' melt." Her face was beet red.

"An' a big mess that'll make if it happens. Be two tons a' grease 'round here," Sharon said sarcastically while giving Joan's fat cheek a gentle pinch.

"Good heavens, Sharon. Don't ya' ever let up?" Joan snapped.

"Girls, do ya' have t' start this now?" Melanie asked before she could stop herself. She knew instantly that Sharon would spit her venom at her too but her comment unfortunately could not be retracted.

"Well, Miss Goody-Two-Shoes, first off, I'm not a girl. I'm a woman, an' second who gave ya' the say-so t' try an' keep us all up t' snuff? Time t' get off your high horse, Miss Melanie! God almighty, some people never change," Sharon blurted, gleaning as she did a hostile stare from Charlotte who had never liked Sharon's rough and callous character and was more than protective of her companion.

"I wonder who hurt her as a little girl?" she had wondered and voiced to Melanie on other occasions when Sharon's barbs jabbed a little too cruelly or too close for comfort.

Elaine stopped the bickering in its tracks. "Cut the shit girls. I know it's hotter 'n hell. I know you're all uncomfortable as shit, but this is my weddin' day, an' I don't give a damn how ya' feel. This is my day, an' I aim t' keep it happy or ya'll can take a bloomin' hike. Ya'll understand?

'Cause Steve an' I would a' had no problem elopin'. I'm here 'cause a' my mother. This is a real important day for my mother too. Right, Mary?"

Sheila hated it when Elaine referred to her mother by her first name, but she did it often. It seemed disrespectful to her, but Elaine insisted it was done with affection. "I love my mother," she had said to Sheila once, "but Mary's her name an' I respect that too. Think it's kind a' pretty anyway. I just like t' say it."

Mary nodded to Elaine without saying a word. It was no secret that Mary Crabtree operated a little off line from center sometimes. She wasn't stupid, but at times it seemed her responses and reactions were slower than others. She was a watcher, and a listener, and spoke seldom. "Havin' a conversation with Mary Crabtree's like pullin' teeth," Sara had told Sheila when the wedding plans were being made. "Hope she can keep up with all the jabberin' that's likely t' be done at Elaine's primpin' party." Sara had coined that term for Sheila's get-together with her attendants before her wedding.

"She'll be fine," Sheila had assured her. "I know she can be slow as molasses sometimes, but she's real sweet. She knows what's goin' on an' she wants this day t' be just right too."

Sheila smartly stepped in then with a cue that refreshments were ready. She and Sara, along with Lainy Raye's eager hands, had created a lovely luncheon complete with watercress and crème cheese sandwiches with the crusts delicately sliced away, wedges of red and green tomatoes, a spinach and sour cream dip, and a plate heaping with raw vegetables and fruits: snapped green beans, crisp carrots, green and purple grapes, and thinly sliced cucumbers. To the side, resting sweetly on white doilies were delicate white meringue shells loaded with chocolate covered strawberries and whipped cream. Lainy Raye couldn't take her eyes off of them.

Fortunately food was the salve needed to calm nerves and reconcile snipped feelings. As part of the luncheon, Sara served chilled champagne in tall fluted glasses. It didn't take long for the women to lose the edge that had accompanied them inside after enduring the oppressive heat outside. Although the house was warm, they were protected from the intense rays of the sun and if they moved slowly they could manage. With the windows just slightly ajar, a delicate breeze wafted through the living room, causing the thin lacey curtains to flutter gracefully in front of them. Elaine found a place on the long flowered divan and sat with a champagne glass in one hand and a tiny pink rose pilfered from the dining table bouquet in the other.

"Why, Elaine, I do believe ya' look just like Mr. Fitzgerald's Daisy," Joan offered, "Why you're a lovely vision there."

"Why, I thank ya' my dear," Elaine answered with the deepest Southern drawl she could manage. "But I reckon' I never thought too highly a' Mr. Fitzgerald's Daisy. Thought she was a real bitch, t' tell ya' the truth." And then she laughed heartily and one did not have to look twice to see that she was radiantly happy.

As the afternoon wore on, the anticipation increased again and soon the women in the wedding party were darting here and there, slipping on frilly undergarments, arranging their hair, gobbing on make-up, and talking incessantly. The wedding would take place at the Mission Baptist Church, the same setting of Sharon's wedding years before. However, this time the guest list was much shorter, Elaine and Steve insisting that only their closest friends or colleagues and family members attend. If the number of well-wishers topped one hundred they would be surprised. Sheila, Sara, and Mary had worked together to select the decorations with long-distance input from Elaine who had been too busy at the hospital to attend to details. Sheila and the mothers were more than delighted to make the decisions. Although Mary was a quiet mouse-like woman on the outside, she had impeccable taste that was evident when the final decisions were made. "Mary, ya've done it again," Elaine said to her mother when she was apprised of the result of their efforts. "Ya've been there for me my whole life, through thick 'n thin. Thank ya', from my heart. What ya've selected is beautiful."

What was most beautiful that day was Elaine herself. "Brides are always beautiful, I reckon," Mary said when Elaine stepped from the bedroom dressed elegantly in an absolutely plain strapless satin wedding gown that touched the floor in flawless symmetry. "But, I'm biased, I guess 'cause I ain't never seen prettier." She looked at her daughter tearfully, dabbing her eyes with a crumpled Kleenex. As was usual for Elaine, she wore only light make-up, enough to outline her blue eyes and accent her full lips and cheeks. A diamond necklace that had belonged to Steve's grandmother glittered at her neckline drawing attention to her thin neck and exquisite face that blushed pink like the rosebud she had held in her hand earlier that day. Her blond hair fell naturally over her shoulders and down her back in thick waves and curls. Atop her head she wore a tiny tiara with a soft veil cascading from it. She needed no other adornment. She was stunning in her simplicity.

The attendants' dresses were equally simple in style and draped to the floor in deep forest green satin. Lainy Raye was the flower girl who bounded into the room aglow in a pale green and white dress tied with a forest green sash. She wore a tiny tiara, a replica of the bride's, and carried a basket that would soon be filled with pink rose petals that she would drop on the aisle of the church when the time came.

Maggie looked at the little girl, her newly acquired granddaughter and said, "And you're as pretty as a picture!

My goodness, all a' ya'll look s' fine. Don't they Sara? Don't they look fine?"

"They do. Ya'll are jist candy t' the eye," Sara answered wondering why Maggie's comment had been directed to her. "The limousine's goin' t' be arrivin' any minute now though, s' I reckon we'd better make sure we're all ready."

She left the room then and found her bedroom through tears that appeared out of nowhere. At her dressing table she looked sadly at her reflection. She was growing older now. She saw it. She saw her mama in her face and remembered thinking how old she'd grown right before her very eyes. "Did Sheila think that about her too?" she wondered. "Is that why I'm feelin' s' strange t'day? I feel like I could fight a feather," she thought. "Why here I am again, cryin' at the drop of a hat!"

At that moment a gentle knock pulled her from her reverie. "Come in," she said, looking in the mirror to see who was there. It was Maggie, plump pretty Maggie.

"Sara, I wanted t' have a word. Just a word with ya', 'cause I can see that the last days have been hard on ya', an' they've been hard on me too."

Sara could not speak.

"Ya' don't have t' say anything. It's okay. I just wanted ya' t' know that I'm sorry ya' never had a chance t' tell Liam 'bout his baby. It's prob'ly weighed on ya' for all these years an' I know how hard it is for ya' t' see him now, 'specially in his condition, an' with me in tow, but I love him, Sara. Have my whole adult life. An' we've been happy together. Never expected such a reunion t' happen, but it has, an', well, now I guess we have t' just hold it in our hands an' own it."

"It's been harder 'an I thought, Maggie," Sara said honestly. "I know ya' love Liam an' he loves ya' too. It's real clear. I loved him once, a long, long time ago, an' out a' that time came Sheila who's more special t' me than anythin', her an' little Lainy Raye. An' Ray a' course. I love him too. Wouldn't want t' hurt him fer the world. Next t' Sheila, he's the best thing ever happened t' me. I jist didn't expect all this emotion t' rear up inside an' it's been kickin' my guts real bad fer a spell."

"I'm sorry, Sara," was all Maggie could manage to say.

"I don't want yer husband, Maggie. I got a real good man in my life, an' I hope this'll be the beginnin' t' a friendship a' sorts. Reckon we can make that happen?"

"I want it worse than anything," Maggie answered. "I want t' be your friend. I'm s' happy t' be Sheila's step-mom, an' a Grandma t' little Lainy Raye, but I know, I know for certain, I'll never take your place, an' I'm not askin' for that. Only want t' be friends, if we can do that."

"We can. We can do that, Maggie. I want it too."

They had been talking through the refection in the mirror for all those moments, and then Sara turned and stood. She walked to Maggie and leaning a bit to meet her height, she hugged her. The hug was returned tightly and genuinely.

"I don't want t' cry now," Sara said.

"Don't cry, Sara. This is a good thing that's happened. It's good."

"Ma! Maggie! Come on! Limousine's here," Sheila hollered.

The two women walked out to the others clutching hands and holding back their tears.

The Mission Baptist Church that evening was awash in filtered light from a relentless sun that had heated the September day so abysmally. Yet now, as the orange sun slipped behind the horizon, the day had cooled to warm, and in the softness of the evening friends and family of the bride and groom slowly walked up the wide stone steps into the foyer of the church. They smiled, they nodded, and they wrote their names in the great white open book that invited their signatures and that welcomed the essence of their presence. A spray of roses and lilies stood behind the book, the sweet smells radiating through the entranceway in the moist heat that lingered there. Steve and his groomsmen where fidgeting in the anteroom of the church waiting for directions to enter. The limousine was on its way, filled with the women who clearly were lost in their own daydreams, for they were silent now, but they touched each other, one gloved hand reaching for the next until they were a circle of friends united in their purpose and joined together in a camaraderie that was more cohesive than any of them could have articulated.

At the church they were greeted by the ushers and by Jake Crabtree, Elaine's father, who gasped audibly when his daughter exited the limousine. In all his life, he had never seen such a beautiful being and the love he felt for her radiated from his face. He did not have to say a word for she felt it in his touch as he pulled her gloved had through his arm and led her up the steps of the church.

The final guests were assisted to their seats, the mothers of the bride and groom escorted expertly to the front rows and then the music began. The crowd rose and eyes turned to watch the entrance of Elaine's life-long friends. Sharon was first, looking from side to side and smiling widely as though she were a contestant in a beauty pageant; she was followed by Joan who ambled behind, her dimpled smile alive with warmth and joy; and then Melanie walked in, slim and statuesque. She offered a shy smile, her head tilted slightly to one side. Sheila was next, exquisite herself in the forest green satin gown that accented her figure and complemented her dark brown hair and eyes with their golden flecks. She was autumn herself, so beautiful every eye followed her until she reached her place beside the altar. Lainy Raye followed, grinning from ear to ear, fairly skipping down the aisle and almost forgetting to throw her rose petals. She remembered in time though, and found her place kneeling at her mother's feet. She was so cute she drew murmurs and giggles from the audience as Sheila watched as only a mother could, tears slipping onto her cheeks.

The music ramped then, and the foyer doors were flung wide open. Jake Crabtree, proud and tall, escorted Elaine to Steve who could not take his eyes from hers.

"We are gathered here t'day in the sight a' God an' angels an' the presence a' friends an' loved ones, t' celebrate one a' life's greatest moments, t' give recognition t' the worth an' beauty a' love an' t' add our best wishes an' blessin's t' the words that shall unite Steven an' Elaine in holy matrimony." The minister's voice virtually sang the words.

Elaine and Steve left the church that day as man and wife, but they were also friends and at the country club reception that carried on well into the night, they not only acknowledged their own union but that of their extended family. It was a party to remember. The prime rib supper was perfect, the champagne and wine flowed freely, and when Elaine tossed her bouquet of tightly gathered pink rose buds, it fell firmly into Sheila's outstretched hands. Elaine had danced with every man at the function until she fell into her husband's arms exhausted. Lainy Raye lay asleep in Ray's arms, a bundle of satin and lace, her tiara clutched in her hands. Liam had wheeled his chair next to them and held one of her feet, now bare of shoes, in his big hand. Maggie and Sara stood behind them watching the three remaining couples on the once shiny wooden dance floor that was now scuffed and dirty. Sharon had her arms completely around Billy's neck and the two swayed together, barely moving like supple birches in a spring breeze. Despite the caustic nature that had dominated her past, Sharon had mellowed within her marriage and she and Billy were as much in love as they had ever been. Sharon's head was nestled into his neck and his eyes above her were closed, his lips moving to the words of the tune that carried them. Sheila was dancing closely to one of Steve's colleagues, a young doctor whose height matched hers exactly, but whose broad shoulders dwarfed her. He had played college football and his physique could not be masked even under his dark charcoal tuxedo. From time to time Sheila would speak to him, smiling demurely, and Sara could not help but wonder if this might be the next man in her life.

"Look at that," Maggie whispered into her ear.

"I'm noticin'. Don't ya' worry!" Sara smiled.

Joan and Dwayne held their hands together all four intertwined, atop a table nearby, their bodies bent toward each other clearly at ease and comfortable just to be observing the scene play out before them. When the music finally ended they said their good-byes to the wedding party, and dragging Melanie and Charlotte behind them, stepped out into the still warm night for the short ride home. It was a signal to the rest that this extraordinary day, a chapter in itself, had come to a close. Yet everyone present instinctively understood that their connections were bound forever. There would be more to come.

At the end of the day as Sara held Ray's hand tightly and leaned into him at the doorway of their home, one phrase spoken by the minister resonated in her mind. She didn't remember it exactly, but the gist of it remained: *Every individual is granted a single and unique life, yet we must learn to live together. Love is a gift given by family and friends and by being loved and accepting it, we learn to love as well.* It was a sentiment which she was certain Mama would have adored hearing, and would have repeated often, conceivably without fully understanding or practicing it. The recognition of that reality made its cut.

Yet beyond the words and her memories of her mama, Sara knew for a fact, from years of experience, that by giving love with no strings attached, it would come back sooner or later and sometimes in unexpected or surprising ways that could be hard to grasp. She had felt the magic of it more times than she could count, and in the latest installment, Maggie Morrison had given her friendship and affection sincerely. What Maggie had offered openly, Sara had willingly returned. It was the mirror image.

About the author . . .

Judith DeChesere-Boyle was born in Elizabethtown, Kentucky and with the exception of living for three years both in England and Texas, was raised there. She first attended the University of Kentucky, and then moved to California, graduating from College of Marin with an AA degree in English with a Creative Writing emphasis and San

Francisco State University with a BA degree in English. She attended Sonoma State University, earning two teaching credentials and an MA in Education. She taught English at the secondary level, retiring early enough to pursue her love of writing more seriously. She has raised two wonderful sons and now lives in Sonoma County, California with her husband, Rick. Besides writing, she reads avidly, gardens, adores her three grandchildren, sails her Ericson 35 sloop, and walks her German Shepherd and Chocolate Lab/Britney three miles a day. She also dotes on her a one-eyed cat and enjoys tending the family's pond full of koi.

Made in the USA
San Bernardino, CA
23 December 2013